A SISTER'S SACRIFICE

ANNEMARIE BREAR

Copyright © 2025 by AnneMarie Brear

All rights reserved.

Cover Images: Christop Zimmermann BookBrush

No part of this book may be reproduced in any form or by any electronic or mechanical means, including information storage and retrieval systems, without written permission from the author, except for the use of brief quotations in a book review.

The story, all names, characters, and incidents portrayed in this production are fictitious. No identification with actual persons (living or deceased).

CHAPTER 1

West Yorkshire, England
Spring 1914

IN THE MORNING room of Hawthorn Manor, parlourmaid Olivia Brodie wiped a damp cloth over the sill of the tall sash window. The early rays of sunshine brightened the room, highlighting the lemon-coloured silk wallpaper and brought out the sparkling myriads of colours from the pieces of elegant crystal displayed in the glass cabinets.

Olivia paused in her cleaning, savouring the quietness in the room, then impulsively pushed up the window and listened to the dawn birdsong resonating across the manor's parkland. The scent of early roses drifted from the garden bed skirting the wall and she could see dew drops on the petals. The rising sun shone from a clear blue and cloudless sky. It'd be another warm April day.

'Why is that window open?' a stern voice spoke from behind.

Olivia spun to face the housekeeper, Mrs Hewlett. 'Forgive

me, Mrs Hewlett. I thought the mistress would enjoy the scent of the roses coming into the room.'

'Perhaps, but I doubt she'd *enjoy* the flies that came with it.' Mrs Hewlett marched across to the window and pulled it closed, locking it for good measure. 'This room has two vases of cut flowers. I'm certain that is perfume enough. Are you finished in here?'

'Yes, I am.' Olivia gathered up her cleaning tools, placing the beeswax, polishing cloths, brushes and dusters into her box. It was unlike Mrs Hewlett to be snappish, especially not to Olivia, who'd been at the manor since she was twelve years old, over ten years now. 'Is everything all right, Mrs Hewlett?'

'Of course it is,' the older woman said dismissively. Her starched black uniform rustled and the keys at her waist jingled as she adjusted the print curtains hanging beside the window.

Olivia wasn't too sure about that. The last few weeks she'd noticed Mrs Hewlett and Mr Skinner, the butler, had been whispering in corners, or were often huddled in Mr Skinner's office with serious expressions. She thought it strange that when James, the first footman, had resigned a month ago to go work for another family in Leeds, he'd not been replaced. Also, the spring dinner party the Broadbents hosted every year had been cancelled last month. The reason given that Mrs Broadbent was not well enough, which again didn't ring true to Olivia. The mistress never seemed ill to her. Even in her seventies, Mrs Seraphina Broadbent ruled Hawthorn Manor with a rule of iron, more so than her husband, Anthony.

Mrs Hewlett, her black hair pulled back severely into a bun at her nape, pensively stared out of the window. 'It's your half day off, isn't it?'

'Yes, Mrs Hewlett.' Olivia braced for the news she was needed to stay at the manor.

'Your father's birthday?' The housekeeper kept looking out of the window. 'You mentioned it yesterday at breakfast.'

'Yes.' Olivia silently prayed she could still go and see him.

'We have visitors this evening.'

Olivia frowned. She'd not been told.

'I've only just found out myself,' Mrs Hewlett said, as though reading Olivia's mind. 'Reverend Middleton, his wife, and Captain Middleton and a friend of his, Mr Parkinson.'

'Captain Middleton?' Olivia's eyes widened at the thought of the Broadbents' grandson coming to the manor. 'He's not been here for years.'

'Three years. He's recently returned from serving in India.'

'I didn't see him when he last visited. It was the same time my mam had died. I was home with my father and brothers. By the time I returned to the manor, Captain Middleton had gone again. I barely remember the time before that. He'd been serving in South Africa.' But she knew his handsome face from dusting his portrait.

'Captain Middleton fought in the Boer War. He'd joined the army at such a young age… Broke his grandmama's heart. He's her favourite.' Mrs Hewlett shook herself slightly. 'Enough of all that. You'd best get on with the rest of your work. You've finished in the dining room?'

'Yes, it's all set for breakfast for Mr Broadbent. Molly helped me get the cleaning done.' She spoke of the maid-of-all-work, a girl of twelve. The youngest staff member in the house.

Nodding, the housekeeper headed for the door. 'I noticed that the candles in the drawing room need replacing and the lamps need taking down to the cellar for cleaning and refilling of oil. That, and your cleaning, should see you through until one o'clock when you can go to visit your father.'

'Thank you, Mrs Hewlett.'

'Be back for six to help with setting the dining table this evening. Mr Skinner will attend the table, as always, but without James, you'll be needed to go between the dining room and kitchen.'

'I'll be back in plenty of time.'

Olivia hurried to the front of the house and into the spacious drawing room decorated in light blue and white. Occasional chairs and lush blue velvet sofas dotted the room, taking advantage of either the warmth of the fireplace or the light from the windows. She polished the ornamental tables, small round ones made of rosewood, and the larger square card table with its inlay of ivory in the centre.

Using the feather duster, she carefully dusted the wall paintings, including Captain Middleton's portrait. She paused to study it once more. A handsome young man of twenty-one in an army officer's scarlet dress uniform. He stood beside a potted palm, his hat under his arm. The artist had his dark brown hair glinting slightly and had given the captain a warm, friendly expression, as though the captain was about to smile. At least, that was what Olivia imagined.

She cleaned the gold-gilded mirror above the fireplace, being tall enough at five feet seven to reach the top of it standing on tiptoes.

Her height, taller than the average of most of the women she knew, was usually a cause of annoyance for Olivia, but not when she needed to reach things above her. She didn't like to be inches taller than all the girls. It made her stand out, that and her pale blonde hair and light blue eyes. Father said it was her Scottish blood that had originally come from the Nordic countries when the Vikings invaded.

Her thoughts on her father's tales of ancestry were interrupted when Molly, the maid-of-all-work, sidled into the drawing room.

'Mrs Hewlett has sent me up here to ask if you've got the lamps ready to go down?' Molly whispered nervously, not liking to be in the main rooms after breakfast in case Mrs Broadbent found her. The young girl was terrified of the mistress, despite the fact the girl had never even spoken to Mrs Broadbent in the three months she'd been working at the manor, for her work of cleaning the fireplaces and resetting them was all done before the mistress was awake. The rest of the time the girl worked below stairs in the kitchen, scullery, or wherever else she was needed.

Olivia gave her the brass lamp from the mantlepiece. 'Take this one and...' She lifted the painted glass lamp from one of the round tables near a sofa. 'And this one.'

'The candles?' Molly grabbed the lamps, inching backwards, ready to flee.

'I'll bring the candles when I'm done in here.'

'The library lamps?' Molly glanced over her shoulder.

'Send Ray to come and get them from me.'

'Ray?' The girl's eyes nearly popped from her head. '*He* can't come up here.'

Olivia sighed. Ray, the hall boy, like Molly, was not allowed in the main rooms, once the master and mistress were out of their bedrooms, but sometimes, if Olivia needed a hand to move something heavy and Mr Skinner was busy elsewhere, she'd sneak Ray upstairs to help her now that James had left. 'Fine. I'll bring them down.'

Molly scurried off like a scolded cat and Olivia turned her attention to taking the candle stubs out of the silver candelabras.

'Olivia,' a whisper came from the doorway.

She turned to smile at Flora, the chambermaid who also doubled as Mrs Broadbent's lady's maid since her former lady's maid, Miss Mullings, resigned last year to marry.

'Do you need my help?' Olivia asked, placing the candle stubs in her apron pocket. She was conscious of the time ticking by and she needed to still give the library a good going over.

Flora held a basket of cleaning goods. 'No, I'm fine. I know it's your half day off. I'll get Molly to help me prepare the extra bedrooms we need for tonight.'

'Good luck with that. The girl is frightened to step beyond the baize door.'

'She'll not last. She's like a mouse, squeaking at the slightest thing.' Flora grinned. 'Not that it'll matter if the rumours are true.'

'Rumours?' Olivia lowered her voice. 'What rumours?'

Flora stepped closer, her words barely above a whisper. 'Money problems. I heard the master and mistress arguing about it again last night while I was putting away the mistress's jewellery in the dressing room. The master came in and started talking about the bank loans and how his grandsons were in for a shock. The mistress must have motioned to him that I was in the other room and Mr Broadbent shut up until I left the room.'

'How serious is it?' Olivia murmured.

'I'm sure we'll find out soon enough.' Flora glanced at the door as Mr Skinner walked past. 'I'm off!' She hurried out of the room.

Olivia finished her cleaning, and the chores required of her by quarter to one, and then raced up the back stairs to the attic rooms where the female staff slept. She washed her face and removed her print morning uniform and coarse hessian apron used for the dirty work and changed into her own clothes. She chose her best dress in honour of her father's birthday. The cream cotton dress was patterned in tiny pink flowers and after brushing her hair she plaited it and let the plait hang down her back, its end nearly reaching her bottom. Her straw boater hat and boots completed her outfit. From a drawer, she took out the rectangular box that held the pocketknife she'd saved up her wages to buy for her father's present.

Returning downstairs, she entered the staff dining room, a room off the kitchen. The nine indoor staff were eating their midday meal. The outdoor staff, the groom, head gardener and the under gardener ate in the gardeners' staffroom. For a moment Olivia remembered her first day at the manor coming into this room as a young girl to be a maid-of-all-work like Molly. Back then, the house had been full of people. The Broadbents had three daughters and a ward living here at that time. All three daughters had died since: one in childbirth, Captain Middleton's mother; one from fever: and the youngest in a carriage accident. The ward had married and moved to America, never to be seen again.

Ten years ago, the indoor staff had numbered twenty and nine worked outside. It'd been a frightening and exciting place to be for a village girl. By going into service at the *big house,* she'd followed in her mam's footsteps.

'You're late, lass,' Mrs Digby, the cook, said to Olivia, bringing her back to the present. 'Grab a slice of bread and some cheese and take it with you.'

Mr Skinner stood, signalling the end of the meal. Everyone rose together, whether they had finished eating or not. Mrs Hewlett followed Mr Skinner out of the room. Molly and Fanny, the scullery maid, gathered all the used plates, while Ivy, the kitchen maid, took away the cups and saucers. Ray collected the scraps to feed the chickens housed behind the stables.

Flora came to Olivia. 'You look nice. Wish your father a happy birthday from me.'

'I will.' She smiled her thanks.

'Lass, there's a small basket of food for your father and brothers,' Mrs Digby added. 'It's on the counter in the scullery.'

'That's kind, Mrs Digby. I'll not forget to bring back the basket.' Olivia collected the hamper and headed out of the back door and up the stone steps to the cobbled yard.

Outside, the warmth of the day hit her after the coolness of being inside. She waved to Clarrie, the laundry maid, who was hanging out white sheets on a line strung between two poles near the path that lead to the stables.

'Olivia!'

She turned at the shout, knowing it was Arnold, the under gardener. She waited for him to sprint across the lawn, his smile wide and warm.

'My, you're a sight and no mistake,' he said appreciatively. His black hair flopped over his face, and he pushed it back with his hand. 'Heading off to your father's?'

'Yes, it's his birthday,' she reminded him, having told him that information yesterday in the yard.

'I can walk some of the way with you.'

'There's no need.' She held him off. 'You must have jobs to do. Where's your hat?'

'Atop of a scarecrow in the middle of the lettuce patch.' He grinned. 'I put it there while I washed my face in the water bucket, then I saw you walking down the path.'

'You'd best get back to work before Mr Dennison sees you.' She took another step, wanting to be on her way.

'I can walk with you,' Arnold repeated, but there was a slight hesitation in his voice as he glanced back over his shoulder. 'We don't seem to spend much time together anymore.'

'Arnold, I've got to go. Father is expecting me.' She gave him a tight smile, feeling embarrassed.

'Right, aye. Enjoy your afternoon off.' He nodded and turned away.

Olivia hurried on, gripping the basket, going over his words. Arnold had kissed her at the May Day celebrations and since then seemed to think they were courting. At first, Olivia enjoyed his attentions, their secret walks in the lanes when they had a spare hour to themselves, which was rare. A few times they had met in the yard in the evening, sitting on crates, chatting. Sometimes they'd been joined by other members of staff like Flora. Only, Olivia never thought of Arnold as anything but a friend. She wanted nothing more from him and had told him so, but her words had fallen on deaf ears. She wasn't ready for marriage. She didn't want to give up her position at the manor to be a wife, not yet, anyway, and not to Arnold.

Once away from the house and gardens, Olivia cut across the

fields towards the little hamlet she called home and near the village of Little Woolton, which was no more than one narrow road with houses and shops on either side. A mile on either side of Little Woolton, a mere speck on the map, were the larger villages of Woolley to the east and Bretton to the west. Seven miles north was the large town of Wakefield; a place Olivia had only visited once when she was a small child. She'd been in awe of the noise and the roads thronged with horse-drawn vehicles and so many buildings.

She much preferred the quiet of the countryside, and once she became a maid at the big house, she'd not had the time nor the reason to visit the town again. She spent her half days and her once a month full day off visiting her father and brothers. Since her mam's death three years ago, Olivia had felt it was her duty to spend her time off cooking and cleaning for her family as her mam had done.

The whistle of a train made her jump. She watched the train rattle along the Barnsley Line before it disappeared into the Woolley Edge Tunnel and the sound of nature resumed.

In the distance, collieries dominated the horizon, but on either side of the lane where she walked were farms and she knew each family who owned them as she knew each and every person who lived in the cottages lining the road through her hamlet.

She waved to Mr Cleaver, an elderly retired miner, who had lost a leg in a mine roof collapse several years ago. He sat each day at his front window. In the warmer months, like now, the window was open so he could chat to whoever walked past, and in winter it would be closed, but he'd wave or beckon someone inside for a cup of tea.

'Now then, lass,' he said to Olivia from his chair, a pipe hanging out of his mouth. 'Good to see you. Afternoon off, have we?'

'Yes, Mr Cleaver.'

'I thought so, it being a Wednesday. Though last week it was Thursday you had off.'

'Last week I had to swap my afternoon as Mrs Broadbent had a ladies' afternoon tea event on Wednesday with the church charity from Woolley, and she needed me to help Mr Skinner serve.'

'How is everyone up at the big house?'

'All well.'

'Have they replaced James, the footman?'

Olivia smiled. Mr Cleaver knew all the gossip. 'No, not yet.'

'Your Lachie has been calling on me lately.'

'That's nice.' Her youngest brother, Lachlan, aged fourteen and named after her father's father, a Scot she'd never known, worked alongside her father and her other brother, Stuart, in the family blacksmith forge. Stu was closer in age to her, being twenty. Between Stu and Lachie had been three babies born and lost, each one breaking her mam's heart.

Mr Cleaver sucked on his pipe. 'Your dad fixed the hinges on my back door and young Lachie has come each day since to give me a hand about the place. He's brought in coal and left buckets of it by the fire for me and done odd jobs I'm not able to do. He swept the ceiling for cobwebs. He's a good lad, your Lachie.'

'He is.' She smiled. 'I'd best be off, Mr Cleaver.'

'Aye, lass. See you next week.'

She walked on until she reached the last cottage on the left before the wide-open fields spread out again. Open double gates that she had never seen closed drew clients down the short drive beside the cottage to the blacksmith outbuilding behind. Between the back of the cottage and the outbuilding was a cobbled yard, where her father tied up horses that came to be shod.

Banging rang out from the large outbuilding, a sound she'd heard all her life, the ringing of hammer on iron.

She stepped inside the doorway. The high ceiling made the room seem even larger, but the domed canopy and chimney suspended over the forge dominated the space. Two anvils sat upon wooden blocks and enormous bellows were hung in an iron frame to feed the forge fire air. Bricked bays held the piles of coal needed for the fire. A variety of tools hung on the walls between square windows that let in plenty of light.

Her father, Fergus Brodie, stood by a vice secured to one of the work benches and was twisting a red-hot iron rod into a curl. 'Here's my beautiful lass,' he said with a welcoming smile, without pausing in his work. A tall lean man, he was the strongest person Olivia had ever known. He didn't look at it. However, swinging heavy hammers for most of his life had given him powerful strength in his arms and back.

'Happy birthday, Father.' She reached over and kissed his sweaty cheek. 'Shall I put the kettle on?'

'Aye, lass. I'm nearly done with this and can take a break.'

She crossed the small yard and entered the cottage. As always, she faltered a little on entering the kitchen, fully expecting to see her mam cooking over the range. Her mam's death still cut deeply. The cottage still held her things, for Father refused to throw anything away that belonged to his beloved wife, Rebecca.

With the hot water on the range to boil, Olivia checked the cupboards to check the food situation. Neither her father nor brothers were good cooks and got by on slices of bread, cheese and ham and whatever Mrs Bean next door gave them or the tasty food Mrs Digby put in the basket each week.

This week, Olivia took out of the basket half of a meat and potato pie that the staff had eaten last night, a currant cake, a parcel of wrapped bacon, six eggs and a small loaf of bread.

Olivia put the food in the larder and mashed the teapot. On a plate, she placed two slices of currant cake for her father. She never ate when she was home, seeing that she was fed well enough at the manor without taking the food off her father's table.

'Where's our Stu and Lachie?' she asked, carrying a tray out to the wooden table and chairs in the yard. Eating outside in nice weather saved the men from wearing their filthy clothes inside to mucky the house. A rule her mam had set out as soon as she married. In the warmer months, Fergus and his sons also washed and bathed out in the yard.

'They'll be back soon,' Father said, sitting down and drying his hands on a towel after washing them in a pail. 'Stu has taken a horse back to Low Moor Farm as we heard old Mr Renshaw is ill and couldn't come and get his horse, and Lachie has gone to Crigglestone Pit to drop off some door hinges.'

Olivia poured out the tea and passed a cup to him, then handed him his present.

'Nay, lass. You shouldn't have bought me something.'

'I wanted to. It's not every day you reach fifty years.' She grinned, watching him open it.

'My, that's a worthy gift.' Father admired the knife. 'Good craftmanship. Thank you, blessed girl.' He put the knife away in its box.

They sat chatting for a bit about the village people and her brothers, but Olivia noticed her father wasn't his usual cheery self. His worried look stilled her hands as she lifted her teacup. 'Is everything all right, Father?'

'Aye, lass…' He took a bite of cake. 'Has our Stu mentioned to you about going away?'

She stared at him. 'Going away? Where?'

'Anywhere but here it seems.' Father sighed. 'You know Les Overton, Stu's mate?'

'Yes.'

'Well, Les and his brother have left for America to work in the coal mines in Kentucky. They asked Stu to go with them. I said he couldn't. Stu's not spoken to me in three days.'

'Stu isn't a miner.' Olivia wasn't surprised her brother wanted to leave. He'd spoken to her in confidence of wanting to explore the world, a novel thing for a country boy of limited education to say.

'Anyone can learn to be a miner. Working in a mine wasn't the reason he wanted to go. He wants to see the world.' Father grunted. He took off his flat cap and scratched his head. Olivia noticed that his former blond hair that held a touch of ginger in it was becoming whiter with each passing week she visited.

'You shouldn't have bought that atlas years ago and encouraged us to study it,' she teased, trying to lighten his mood.

'I didn't want my children to be ignorant. My father, your grandfather, was a believer in education, even though he taught himself to read. He used to say education opens the mind.'

'Then you can't be mad at Stu for wanting to explore outside this hamlet,' she said quietly. 'If I was a man, I'd be travelling as well.'

Olivia turned her head as Lachie came down the side of the cottage whistling. The boy was always whistling. At fourteen, he was tall like their father, with the pale blond hair and light blue eyes they all sported.

'Livvy!' He grinned and ran to her as though he was still a lad in short pants.

She laughed as he barrelled into her. 'Steady on!'

'What did you bring in your basket today?' he asked excitedly. 'That plum pudding last week was the best.'

'No plum pudding, but there's currant cake. Pie for later. Go and get another cup for some tea.'

'Did you make the delivery without any problems?' Father asked his retreating back.

'Aye, Father. All good,' Lachie shouted over his shoulder.

Olivia spotted the broken bicycle leaning against the wall. 'Who does that belong to?'

'Me,' Lachie said, coming back outside, carrying a cup in one hand and a slice of cake in the other. 'I found it in a ditch, completely broken into pieces. Father's helping me to fix it. Then I'll have my own bicycle.'

'He's working on it more than me. He and Stu.'

'Stu is really good at bicycles,' Lachie said with a mouthful of cake. 'He wants Father to become a bicycle repair shop.'

Father snorted. 'You don't see many people riding them around here. We're too out of the way. There are plenty of those repair places in Wakefield.'

'We get a lot of cyclists on these lanes,' Lachie argued. 'And when they break down, there's no one to fix them.'

'He has a point,' Olivia said, sensing this was an argument her father and brothers had often.

'Between automobiles and bicycles, I'll soon be out of business.' Father drank his tea sullenly.

'There'll always be horses, Father,' Olivia soothed. Her father lamented the coming of the motor car. His bread-and-butter business was shoeing horses.

As if fate was making a point, the quietness of the countryside was shattered by the coughing and spluttering of an engine.

Father frowned. 'Who is that?'

A couple of horses in a nearby field behind the forge ran off, tails arched, heads thrown back. A break in the hedge showed a motor car jerking along with smoke coming from the front.

'They need help!' Lachie jerked up from the table, nearly upsetting the teacups.

'You foolish boy,' Father fumed, but he also stood and stared at the automobile inching to a stop.

Lachie ran up the short drive to the lane. 'Stu!'

'Stu?' Father marched forward.

Lachie reached the motor car first as its occupants, including their brother Stu, climbed out.

Stopping halfway up the short drive, Olivia stared at one of the men, who was smiling at something Stu said. She knew that man. He wore a dove-grey-coloured slimline suit with a black fedora hat and shiny black shoes. When he turned his head to assist the woman out of the motor car, Olivia gasped. The gentleman's warm gaze on the woman as she stepped clear of the door made her heart skip.

Captain Spencer Middleton.

She stared at the Broadbents' grandson, her chest tight with awareness. She'd dusted his portrait many times. Today he wasn't in uniform, but she recognised that handsome face anywhere.

Father, Lachie and Stu all gathered around the engine, lifting the side bonnet and peering inside. Captain Middleton and his gentleman friend did the same, but the woman stood back, looking around until she spotted Olivia.

'Oh, divine, another female.' The woman, wearing a long linen skirt and jacket the colour of butter, headed for Olivia.

The servant in her made Olivia nod her head to the woman and smile even as she studied the lady's features. Black curled hair under a brimless hat, dark eyes, a sharp nose, flawless skin and a small, red-painted mouth gave the woman a unique appearance, foreign, mysterious. 'Good day to you.'

'Do you live here?' The lady waved her hand towards the cottage.

'This is my family's home.'

The lady leaned in closer, lowering her voice. 'I must visit the lavatory. Do you have one? I am so desperate, I am happy to use a pot in a back room somewhere.'

'We have an outhouse lavatory. Please, follow me.' Olivia led the woman behind the forge to the narrow upright structure that housed the lav. She'd not used it herself since arriving and usually gave it a good scrub, but there hadn't been time, and she hoped the males in her family hadn't left it in a state.

Waiting outside for the woman to relieve herself, Olivia wondered who the woman was and what was her relationship to the captain.

'I feel so much better now.' The lady emerged, adjusting her clothes. 'That will teach me to drink tea when travelling.' She walked past Olivia and headed back around the forge. The men were pushing the automobile off the road and down the drive.

Olivia waited near the table and wondered if she should offer Captain Middleton and his friends some refreshments. She could make a fresh pot of tea. She took a step towards the cottage as the men surrounded the engine, discussing possible problems.

She glanced at Captain Middleton just as he noticed her. He straightened, his eyes narrowing as he stared at her. She faltered, heart skipping. It was suddenly difficult to breathe. She couldn't stop staring at his attractive face.

The lady nudged the captain, drawing his attention to her, and Olivia hurried into the cottage. She rested her hands on the Welsh dresser, dragging air into her lungs as though she'd been running. She didn't understand what had just happened. Her senses had been heightened and dulled at the same time. Nothing had existed at that moment but looking at him, absorbing his presence.

At the sink, she splashed her face with cold water, snorting at herself. What a foolish girl she was, reacting to Captain Middleton like that. She'd seen him before, albeit not for many years, probably at least six years ago when she'd been an under-parlourmaid. Not that she'd ever spoken to the man. Back then, she'd made herself invisible to any member of the family. So why was she behaving like a foolish child at the sight of him? Was it because she'd studied his likeness too often when she dusted and polished the drawing room where his portrait hung?

'Liv!' Lachie shouted, coming into the kitchen.

'Stop yelling,' she demanded sternly. 'You're not a little boy needing to shout all the time.'

'Father asks for you to come outside.'

'Why?'

'The Crossley is out of action.'

'The Crossley?'

'Aye, the motor car. We need to figure out what's wrong with it. Stu has a book about the engines, which includes the ones the Crossley Brothers use in their models. Stu reckons if we identify the problem, we can write to the Crosby Factory in Manchester and then—'

'I don't care about the blessed motor car.' She stopped him, having been bored enough over the last year as her brothers became more interested in the automobile industry.

'Anyway, the newcomers are visiting the big house. Father said you'd show them a shortcut across the fields as they need to walk there now.'

Olivia groaned inwardly at being their guide. 'I've still got a couple of hours before I'm due back to the manor. Surely, Captain Middleton knows the way?'

'You know him?'

'He's the Broadbents' grandson.'

Lachie shrugged. 'Father said to fetch you.'

Olivia squared her shoulders, annoyed that she'd have her precious hours of freedom cut and marched outside.

CHAPTER 2

Captain Spencer Middleton listened to Stu Brodie speak of certain parts of the engine. The motor car wasn't his. He'd much rather have a horse, but it belonged to his friend, Orville 'Parky' Parkinson. Parky had collected him from his father's home in York before stopping to indulge Valerie, Parky's sister, who impulsively wanted to join them on the trip.

From York to Wakefield, the car had behaved admirably. But they had stopped overnight in Wakefield to meet up with friends, Bernard and his wife Gloria, and the next morning the motor car had belched and stuttered from the moment the engine started.

Luckily, about a mile back, they had found young Brodie waking beside the road and he'd offered to show them the way to his father's forge, with the idea that he could fix whatever the problem was. Stu had introduced them to his father and brother and mentioned his sister worked at the manor, his grandparents' manor.

Suddenly, movement from the cottage doorway had his head turning. He watched as the young woman came out of the cottage. He studied her, wondering if his first startling glance of her earlier had been untrue. That she wasn't as stunning as he thought she was.

His gut clenched at the sight of her. She was real enough, and so was his body's response to her. How in God's name did such a beauty exist out here in the middle of the countryside? Her father said she worked at the manor. He couldn't believe it. No maid of his acquaintance had ever looked as regal as this girl did. She had the beauty of a noble born lady. He couldn't drag his gaze away. She was tall for a woman, slender, with such a tiny waist and her hair, such paleness... She wore no hat, and the sun turned the light blonde plait to near silver.

'Captain Middleton, my daughter, Olivia Brodie.' Mr Brodie broke into Spencer's absorption of the girl.

He savoured the name. *Olivia.* She even had a beautiful name, not a common name like Mary or Jane or Ann or Bessie. *Olivia.* He smiled at her, wanting very much for her to smile back at him. She didn't.

Good manners came to the fore, and he bowed his head. 'Pleased to make your acquaintance, Miss Brodie.'

'Olivia will take you a shorter way back to the manor, sir. It'll save you time. Taking the roads would be a longer route,' Brodie continued.

Spencer didn't care how long it would take, but he noticed Olivia, and yes, he would think of her as Olivia, that her eyes narrowed slightly at the mention of her father's proposal. 'Would you be kind enough to show my friends and myself to Hawthorn Manor?'

'I assumed you would know the way, sir,' she said, her gaze locked with his. 'You have stayed many times before.'

'Not for some years have I ridden the countryside around here, Miss Brodie, not since I was a boy. I could, of course, take the roads.'

'Olivia?' Her father raised an eyebrow.

'No need, of course I can take you, sir,' she murmured.

'There is no rush. Should you be busy doing something else?' He didn't want her annoyed with him.

'Goodness!' Valerie snapped. 'Can we make a decision? This heat is insufferable. Though how you expect me to walk miles in these shoes, Spencer, I don't know.'

'Perhaps you should stay here,' he suggested. 'My grandparents don't own a motor car, I'm afraid. However, I can have a carriage sent back for you once I reach the manor.'

'Would you?' Valerie simpered with a coy grin that didn't fool him in the slightest. 'Aren't you the best?' She turned to Brodie. 'Mr Brodie, would that be too much trouble for you, if I were to stay here?'

Brodie inclined his head. 'You're very welcome, miss. You could sit in the cottage out of the sun.'

'I'll stay as well,' Parky added. 'No point us both going.' He looked at Stu. 'Perhaps you can show me the book you have on engines?'

Spencer watched Olivia's shoulders slump. It had been taken out of her hands. As a servant she was used to doing as she was bid. Yet, he didn't like how that made him feel. Normally, he wouldn't have given it another thought. He'd grown up in York with servants doing his bidding. He didn't abuse his power, but the staff were there for a service. Only, Olivia, standing in her father's home, wearing a pretty dress, looked less like a servant than he'd ever seen. He didn't want her to feel obligated or even worse, used.

'Daughter,' Brodie spoke. 'I'm sure Mr and Mrs Broadbent would be pleased that you helped their grandson.'

'Yes, Father. I'll just fetch the basket.'

When she returned, now wearing her hat, Spencer felt ridiculously pleased that it would be just him and her on the walk. He waited by the gate as she kissed her father and brothers goodbye, telling them she'd see them next week.

'I appreciate it that you cut short your visit home to take me to the manor,' he said as they walked through the village. 'I don't know my way through the countryside beyond the manor. No doubt I could have found my way, eventually.'

She remained silent, walking at a good pace.

'Do you enjoy working at the manor?' he asked, before realising that might be a difficult question for her. If she didn't like it, she'd not tell him, a member of the family.

'I do, sir.'

'But not enough to want to cut short your time away from it?' he joked, wanting to see her smile.

She kept her face straight. 'Mrs Hewlett will be pleased I've returned well in time to help Mr Skinner to set the table for your dinner, sir.'

'Hewlett and Skinner are still both at the manor?' he mused. 'I've not been back for years.'

'They are, sir.' She kept walking, giving him nothing.

He watched her out of the corner of his eye. She held herself straight, shoulders back, her blue-eyed gaze ahead. Christ, she was spectacular. His blood raced, and he experienced that familiar tension in his groin. It'd been a few months since he last bedded a woman, a woman in London when he first arrived back in England, a woman known for her services to gentlemen. Somehow this was different. He didn't understand why it was different only that he wanted Olivia to look at him, smile, talk to him. Yes, bedding her would be a pleasure, but amazingly, he wanted more than that, and that puzzled him.

Acknowledging that need surprised him. He was a career soldier. Women had their uses, but he never thought beyond that basic bodily need. Until now. Until meeting this young woman with the pale hair. He wanted her to talk to him, tell him things, smile and laugh with him.

His mind raced. What was he thinking? He couldn't understand his darting thoughts. Perhaps this extended leave he'd taken had turned him soft? For the first time, his brain had too much time to think about other things outside of the army. If so, the sooner he returned to active duty the better.

He took a deep breath and strove for something to talk about as they cut through an opening in a tall hedge and into a field. 'See? I would never have thought to go through this hedge.'

'It's only known to locals,' she explained. 'Farmer Miller allows us to cut across his fields, knowing we won't disturb his newborn lambs.'

Encouraged she wasn't completely irritated by him, he continued to talk. 'I believe my grandparents are well?'

'Very well, sir.'

'Have you worked at Hawthorn Manor for long?'

'Ten years, sir. I started when I was twelve.'

'What work do you do at the manor?'

'I am the parlourmaid, sir. I care for all the downstairs rooms. I also help Mr Skinner serve in the dining room when needed, especially now James has left.'

He was inordinately happy that he would see her about the house. She wouldn't be stuck down in the kitchen or in the laundry. 'James?'

'First footman, sir.'

'Right, yes.' He vaguely remembered him from his last visit, but for the life of him he couldn't remember Olivia, and he would have done if he'd seen her, he was sure of that. 'When I was staying at the manor three years ago, I don't remember seeing you there.'

'No, sir. My mam had died at the same time you visited. I went home to help my father organise the funeral and so on.'

'Ah. I'm sorry to hear that.'

'Lachie was only eleven and took Mam's passing very hard. We all did, but he is the baby of the family.'

'Did your father not want you to stay at home and care for him?'

She shook her head. 'No, sir. Father is very practical. He knew I had a good position at the manor and that I actually enjoy my work. Father, Stu and Lachie soon learned how to manage the cottage as well as the forge. I do what I can on my days off.'

'Like today?'

'Today was a half day.'

'A half day? I apologise. I didn't realise.' He felt terrible to have shortened her time away from the hard work she did.

'You weren't to know. It's fine. My full day off is on Sunday. It'll come around quickly.' She stopped by a wooden stile that climbed over a stone wall between two fields.

Spencer offered his hand, and she paused for a second before slipping her hand into his. Contact with each other was like an electric charge. Spencer gazed at her and she at him. It thrilled him that she sensed the attraction as well as he did.

On the other side of the wall, they walked through fields of new grass. Sheep grazed, lifting their heads to watch them balefully as they passed. Lambs kicked and frolicked about their mothers.

Spencer took off his jacket and slung it over his shoulder.

'May I ask why you aren't in uniform, sir?'

'I'm on extended leave, and I'm allowed to wear civilian clothes if I choose. My grandmother prefers me in a good suit, so I wear suits for her when visiting. She says my uniform reminds her too much of the risks I face in my role.'

Olivia grinned. 'Mrs Broadbent has her ways.' Then she slapped a hand over her mouth. 'I meant no disrespect, sir.'

'None taken, Olivia. I know my grandmother's ways very well.' He laughed, glancing up at the clear sky. 'It's as warm as any day in India, or Africa for that matter.'

'Really? India. Africa…' She smiled, her first proper smile at him. 'I've read about such places.'

'You enjoy reading?'

'Very much. My father used to read us stories in front of the fire when we were little.'

Spencer was surprised at that. Brodie, dirty and sweaty, didn't look like a man who read, but perhaps he was being unkind. He didn't know the man.

Soon they were on Broadbent land. Hawthorn Manor's roof and chimneys could be seen between the tops of the trees. When he was a child, he and his brother and sister used to come and stay with his grandparents. They were happy times. His grandparents loved them dearly and spoilt them. He spent many summer climbing trees, swimming in the lake, eating delicious food and receiving his grandmama's kisses at bedtime. Something he never got at his father's home where they were raised by nannies. At thirty-three years of age, he still missed those idyllic times.

'Would you wish for me to go to the stables and ask the groom to prepare the carriage and go and fetch your friends, sir?' Olivia broke into his thoughts.

'I'll come with you.'

She frowned but gave no reply, turning direction for the back of the manor and the stone stable block at the edge of the field.

'It's a shame my grandparents don't own an automobile,' he mused. 'It'd be much quicker than getting the carriage out.'

'Do you think they might buy one?' she asked, then blushed. 'Sorry, sir. I spoke out of turn, that's none of my business.'

He smiled, wanting to put her at ease, but liking that she'd warmed to him enough to speak freely. 'It's a fair question, and no, I don't think they will. My grandparents are slow at accepting change.'

'Aye, they don't even have electric lights!' She snorted, before looking at him horrified. 'Again, I didn't mean any disrespect, sir. Lord, I need to learn to keep my mouth shut.'

'You don't have to worry, Olivia. I'll not mention our chat and

I'm sure electricity would be most convenient for all the staff and a lot less work.'

'Yes, sir, it would be. I spend the morning replacing candles and taking the lamps down to be filled with oil. The mistress only uses the gas lights in certain rooms and even then, it's only when guests are visiting.'

'My sister, Anthea, lives in Paris. Her whole apartment is fitted with electric, gas and running hot water upstairs in the bathroom, including a flushing lavatory. Her chef has so many electric gadgets. It's amazing to watch him demonstrate the newest invention for the kitchen.'

Her eyes, such an unusual light blue, gazed at him. 'I remember your grandparents coming back from visiting your sister last year and Mrs Broadbent said that the apartment was like living in an exhibition of curiosities.'

Spencer laughed with abandon. 'Trust Grandmama to say such a thing, but she's not wrong.'

At the arch leading into the stable courtyard, Spencer stopped when Olivia did. One of the grooms spotted them and walked towards them, dashing Spencer's hopes for any further conversation. 'Thank you, Miss Brodie.'

'You're welcome, sir.' She hurried off along another path and disappeared between two outbuildings.

'Captain Middleton, welcome, sir,' the approaching groom said.

'Jones, isn't it?' Spencer said, remembering his grandpapa's head groom.

'It is, sir.'

'The motor car I was travelling in has broken down in the hamlet near Little Woolton. My friends are there, at Brodie's, the blacksmith. Can you take the carriage and collect them, please?'

'Aye, sir. I'll do it now.'

Walking along the path, he went around the side of the manor and to the front door, which was opened instantly by Mr Skinner.

'Welcome, sir.' Skinner bowed, his expression one of confusion.

'I had to walk here, Skinner. It's damn warm.' He told the butler the breakdown story.

'Goodness, Captain, please come into the drawing room and I'll fetch you a cool drink,' Skinner said. 'Your grandparents are waiting for you.'

Despite the heat outside, inside was cooler and Spencer donned his jacket to appear tidy as he crossed the hall into the drawing room.

'Spencer!' Grandmama jerked to her feet and hugged him. 'Oh, look at you. You are as tanned as a peasant in the fields.'

He kissed her cheek. 'India is hot, Grandmama.'

'Spencer, dear boy.' Grandpapa shook his hand and Spencer noticed how much his grandpapa had aged, they both had, since he'd been in India. His dear grandpapa was stooped-backed and without much hair now, whereas his grandmama had become stout, wrinkled and her knees creaked as she regained her chair.

'Come and sit down,' Grandmama beckoned. 'Your brother will be here shortly.'

'And it'll be good to see him.' He loved his brother, Ralph, dearly, just as much as he did his sister, Anthea. 'I've not come alone, Gran.'

Her face altered slightly when he called her gran. She didn't like it when he called her that, saying it was common, but she indulged him because he was her favourite and he knew it. She looked at the open doorway. 'Your letter mentioned that Parky was coming with you?'

'Yes, Parky, but also his sister, Miss Valerie Parkinson decided to join us. I hope you don't mind?'

She waved her hand airily. 'Not at all. We have met Valerie, haven't we?'

'Yes.'

'Not for some years though.' Grandmama frowned in thought. 'I must inform Skinner about the extra person staying.'

'I told him as I came in.'

'And I thought we'd have you all to ourselves?' Grandmama pouted, and he took the opportunity to explain their current absence and that the carriage had been sent for them.

'How long will you stay?'

'Until Monday.' He bore the guilt just by saying it.

'Monday?' Grandmama exclaimed, looking at grandpapa. 'Why such a short stay? We've not seen you for so long!'

'Forgive me, but I must be at my barracks by Monday and back on duty. On my way to England, I stopped at Paris to see Anthea and her family, and then I spent some days with my father before coming here. I don't have much time left of my leave at all.'

Grandmama shifted in her chair. 'We received a letter from Anthea only yesterday, she told us you'd been for a visit. Pray tell me, how is your father?'

Skinner walked in, carrying a tray of tea things, including sandwiches and cake and a crystal jug of lemon cordial. He poured out three cups without barely making a noise and left the room.

'Spencer?' Grandmama urged him to answer her question.

'Father is well.'

'He never visits,' Grandmama complained. 'Is he still courting that dreadful woman?'

'No.'

'Good.'

'Grandmama, my mother died twenty-eight years ago. Father deserves to remarry should he wish. He's been mourning our mother for a long time.'

'He has our blessing to remarry, naturally he does, but not

that Steepleton woman. She's nothing more than a servant, his servant! It's a stain on my daughter's memory.'

'Mrs Steepleton is a decent woman,' he argued. His father falling in love with his housekeeper had rocked the family, especially his grandparents. Spencer didn't mind so much, for he had long left home to join the army and rarely visited his old home in York.

'Shall we not discuss the matter?' Grandpapa stated. 'The courtship has finished, has it not?' He looked at Spencer.

'Apparently. Father said Mrs Steepleton was tired of the gossip it caused. She's serving her notice and will leave York altogether in a few weeks.'

'It's about time she came to her senses. Imagine a housekeeper marrying her master. It's unthinkable.' Grandmama ate some cake.

He thought of Olivia, a maid in this very house, and knew for a fact that he wanted to get to know her better. It seems the apple didn't fall far from the tree, and he was more like his father than he realised. 'The world is changing, Gran. The old ways are dying out.'

'Yes, because of those disgraceful suffragettes. You cannot open a newspaper without reading some headline about them. Emily Davison jumping in front of the King's horse last year is a martyr to the cause and now those women are doing untold damage. A bomb exploded in a theatre in South Yarmouth. Can you consider such a thing?'

'There's no evidence so far it was done by the suffragettes,' his grandpapa stated.

'Of course, it was!' Grandmama sniffed with disdain. 'They are an embarrassment to our sex, that's what they are.'

'Not many would agree with you,' Spencer said. 'I certainly don't. Emily Davison died for her cause like a soldier. How can anybody dismiss that? These are educated women, fighting for what they believe in. We should admire them, not censure them.'

'Gracious me!' Grandmama clutched at the pearls she wore. 'Have you become a rebel? It's all those wild places where you've been stationed. That's what has done it. Beyond England's shores the world is savage and unrestrained from decent behaviour.'

Spencer laughed. He couldn't help it. His grandmama was a wonderful woman, but she belonged to the previous century ruled by Queen Victoria, where social boundaries kept the gentry away from the rest of the lower population. Spencer had been mixing with all classes for years and didn't restrict himself to his own class. Again, Olivia came to mind, and he was impatient to see her again.

Movement had them turning to smile at Ralph, who entered the room with his small plump wife Mildred. Spencer stood and embraced him warmly. His brother had matured, grown a thick moustache and now wore spectacles. Where had his young brother gone? Three years in India had changed his family without him witnessing it.

'It's good to see you, Spence.' Ralph grinned. His brother's grin showed him that the old Ralph was still there, under the white collar and severe black suit he wore.

'And you, Ralphie.' Spencer turned to Mildred. He'd only met her once before, on his last visit to the manor when Ralph and Mildred were married, and Ralph was given the nearby parish for his livelihood courtesy of grandpapa's contacts.

Skinner walked in and behind him Parky and Valerie.

Spencer stood to introduce Parky and Valerie to Mildred, they both knew Ralph and his grandparents but not Mildred. Once greetings were over, chatter filled the air.

'Shall we sit out on the terrace and take refreshments? It's a lovely afternoon in the shade.' Grandmama stood and gave a nod to Skinner. 'Take Miss Parkinson up to the green bedroom. I'm certain she'll want to refresh herself.'

'Certainly, madam.' Skinner bowed and led Valerie out of the room.

'Yes, dear, take everyone out for refreshments,' Grandpapa said. 'I'd like a word with Spencer and Ralph. Excuse us everyone.'

'Now, Anthony?' Grandmama raised an eyebrow at him, showing her displeasure.

'We shan't be long, dear.'

Spencer watched his grandparents exchange a look and instinct put him on alert. This was highly unusual.

He followed his brother and grandpapa out and along the corridor to the east side of the house and the large oak-panelled study.

'What's this about?' Ralph whispered to him.

Spencer shrugged. He wished he knew. He didn't like surprises.

'Sit down, my boys.' Grandpapa sat behind the oak desk, inlaid with burgundy leather on the top. 'I shall get straight to it. As you know, both of you and Anthea are my sole heirs.'

'Are you ill, Grandpapa?' Spencer asked, unable to help himself.

'What? No. Unless you call old age an illness.' Grandpapa gave a ghost of a smile. 'As it stands currently in my will, Spencer is to inherit this manor and the lands that go with it. Ralph is to have the four terraced houses in Horbury, and Anthea an annuity.'

'And we are very grateful, Grandpapa,' Ralph said.

Grandpapa put up his hand. 'All that has to change.'

Spencer's gut dropped. 'Change?'

Suddenly, Grandpapa looked very old. 'It wounds me deeply to tell you that it's all gone.'

'Gone?' Ralph repeated, his expression one of confusion.

'Bad investments.' Grandpapa sighed heavily. 'I have lost it all, my boys.'

'Everything?' Spencer whispered in astonishment. 'This house?'

'All of it. My debts have been piling up for years. I kept investing to recoup my losses until the bank refused me another loan. Last week I had a meeting in Wakefield with my bank manager, one of many. I even travelled to London to speak with the banks I deal with there. My solicitor has been helping me to try and sort out the mess, but the end result was the same with them all...'

'You are bankrupt?' Spencer could barely say the words from shock.

'I am. The banks have foreclosed on me. This house is already up for sale.' Grandpapa shook his head sadly at Spencer. 'I'm sorry. I know this was to be all yours.'

Ralph gasped, his face pale.

'Luckily your grandmama had some jewellery which, unbeknown to anyone, we have sold, and we have the cash to buy a small apartment in Paris. We shall leave England.'

Spencer jerked to his feet, astounded by the revelation. His heart raced. Gone! All of it gone? 'Why did you not tell us before it became so ruinous?'

'I was trying to spare you from the ordeal.'

'We could have *helped* you.'

'How?' Grandpapa raised his hands. 'Ralph is a vicar, beholden to his patron for his parish, his living, and you are an army officer.'

'Our father may have been able to help,' he stated. His father, Stanford Middleton was a wealthy man having made his fortune in coalmines and more recently in gasworks.

'Stanford is a good man, but I would not allow myself to go and beg to him to bail me out of my own mistakes.'

'So, you'd rather leave all this, your home which has been in the family for centuries, and go and live in Paris?' Spencer snapped in frustration at the old man's stubbornness. 'Our father may have been able to save the manor at least.'

'There was no other option. Nothing could be saved. The

debts are too high. Your grandmama doesn't wish to stay in England with the stigma of bankruptcy attached to our name.'

'But to move at your age...' Spencer couldn't take it in. Hawthorn Manor to be sold. It was the one place he had truly been happy in.

'At least you'll be close to Anthea,' Ralph murmured.

'Exactly, and that pleases your grandmama. It is the only thing that she can cling to in this disaster. I have failed her and this family.' Grandpapa rose from the chair. 'We shall talk some more tomorrow. For now, while we have guests, we shall pretend everything is normal.'

'When will you let the staff know?' Spencer asked.

'As soon as we have a buyer. There is already some interest.'

The news rocked Spencer to the core. He'd always known the manor would be his one day, but it had been a far-off event, something for him to address when he retired from the army. Losing the manor was a blow for certain, but for his grandparents to be bankrupt, it devastated him.

In the hall he looked around with fresh eyes, seeing the people who had visited in the past, he heard the piano playing at parties, the laughter. He saw the childish games he played with his brother and sister, sliding down the banister without being caught, of the day he walked in through the front door dressed in his officer's uniform for the first time. The day he kissed his grandmama goodbye when he was deployed for Southern Africa to fight the Boers.

'Spencer.' Grandmama slipped her arm through his. Her eyes held a sheen of tears in them as did his.

'I cannot believe it.' He puffed out a long breath.

'No... But we must think of it as a new beginning in our lives...'

He gripped her hand where it lay on his arm. 'I wish I could have helped.'

'No one could. Your grandpapa didn't tell anyone in time but fought the battle alone for years and paid the price.'

'Paris is what you want?'

She nodded. 'I will be near Anthea and the children. That is the only thing that is keeping me from crumbling.'

He suddenly embraced her tightly. 'You are very brave, Grandmama.'

'That or foolish, I'm not sure which one.' She pulled back and tapped his cheek. 'Let us smile and return to the others.'

He desperately wanted time alone to think, but he knew she needed him with her and so he took her arm and pasted on a weak smile, for her.

CHAPTER 3

Adjusting her white cap, Olivia made sure no tendrils of her hair had escaped her plait which she'd rolled and pinned at the nape of her neck beneath the cap. In her bedroom mirror, she checked her starched white cuffs were straight and that her pristine white apron held no stains as she tied it over her black serge dress, smoothing out the lace on the straps that crossed over her shoulders and tied at the back.

With a last look in the mirror and pleased that the mistress, Mrs Hewlett nor Mr Skinner would find no fault, she left her bedroom. The attic corridor was quiet, and she had a few minutes of panic. She'd be assisting Mr Skinner with the evening meal, a task she'd done many times before but never while being attracted to a member of the family.

The heat rose to her cheeks again as she replayed the walk back to the manor with Spencer Middleton. She remembered everything, his green hazel eyes with long eyelashes, the way he walked, his relaxed chatter, his disarming smile. He'd treated her like an equal, engaging her in conversation, a rare thing indeed. With each step she'd become more aware of him. When he helped her over the stile, when their fingers touched, she wondered if the jolt she'd experienced was one-sided, but the look he gave her told her it wasn't. She knew he felt it and that unnerved her even more. Just thinking of him made her chest tighten. How was she going to cope being in the dining room while he was there?

Forcing her legs to work, she hurried down the three flights of stairs to the kitchen in the basement. The hectic organisation of the kitchen took her mind away from her walk with the captain and to the pressing concern of Mr Skinner's orders. She rushed up and down the back stairs from the kitchen to the pantry next to the dining room. The pantry was Mr Skinner's domain, a place where the silverware was cleaned and locked into glass-fronted cabinets, where the family's best crystal and delicate porcelain dinner services were kept, and it also contained a long bench where the food was placed on warmers in readiness to be taken into the dining room.

'Olivia, you have served at the table before. You know what to do,' Mrs Hewlett said, giving Olivia a critical eye over her uniform. 'We've not had a dinner party this large since James left, so Mr Skinner will look to you for efficiency in understanding and pre-empting all his orders. Understood?'

'Yes, Mrs Hewlett.' She usually wasn't nervous, but knowing Captain Middleton would be at the table made her mouth go dry. She pulled on her white gloves and took a deep breath.

Mrs Hewlett nodded as Mr Skinner joined them from the dining room. 'I'll be staying in the pantry to be on hand should you need it, Mr Skinner. Ray and Flora will go between here and the kitchen with the courses.'

'Thank you, Mrs Hewlett. It isn't ideal to have a hall boy and the chambermaid acting as footmen, but we must do what we can to make this evening run smoothly. We are fortunate that the menu is an easy one tonight and only four courses.' Mr Skinner pushed out his chest, resplendent in his formal black suit and white gloves. 'Are we ready, Olivia?'

'Yes, Mr Skinner,' she replied, desperate to do well this evening.

'Ready as we'll ever be, Mr Skinner.' Mrs Hewlett gave a grim smile as Ray and Molly brought up the first course of consommé.

On purpose, Olivia kept her gaze lowered, concentrating on serving each course with deft hands, and clearing away quickly and unobtrusively. She ignored the way her stomach flipped whenever she leaned close to place the captain's food before him. She saw out of the corner of her eye that he smiled and said thank you each time she did it. The smell of the sandalwood soap he used lingered in her nose. It took every effort not to stare at him.

'You're doing excellently,' Mr Skinner murmured to her in the pantry as he checked the dessert course of fruit tart and cream. 'One more to go.'

She nodded happily, pleased that he had found no fault in her service. She followed him around the table as the butler placed the plates of fruit tart down and she gave each person their own small jug of cream until all seven seated had dessert in front of them.

While Mr Skinner topped up glasses of wine, Olivia, her duty in the dining room completed, finally glanced over her shoulder at the captain as she went out. He looked up from pouring cream on his fruit tart and their eyes locked. His wry smile made her smile back, she couldn't help it. He continued to stare at her and she at him until a cough drew her back to the room. She checked to see if the other diners had witnessed the exchange, but no one saw them. Stupidly joyful, she slipped out of the room.

'You'll be needed in the parlour to serve the ladies their port or Madeira,' Mrs Hewlett told Olivia. 'But first go down and have a drink for a minute or two while the family finish their dessert. I'll help Mr Skinner should he need anyone.'

'Thank you, Mrs Hewlett.' Olivia sprinted downstairs where Mrs Digby poured her a refreshing cup of tea.

'Sit yourself down. You've been on your feet for hours.'

'I can't, Mrs Digby. The ladies will be in the parlour shortly.' Olivia sipped her tea, and it revived her flagging body. It'd been a long day.

'We need another footman,' Mrs Digby announced. 'We can cope when it's an ordinary day with the master and mistress, but not when there are guests staying.'

'Has Mr Skinner had any enquires?' she asked.

'He's been told to not advertise the position just yet,' Mrs Digby whispered. 'What does that mean I ask you?' The older woman raised her eyebrows in question.

'Well, as you say, we can cope without a footman when no guests are staying.' Olivia placed her teacup and saucer in the sink and with a look in the mirror to make sure she was still presentable, she dashed upstairs to be in the parlour waiting for the ladies to enter.

Mrs Broadbent led Mrs Mildred Middleton and Miss Parkinson into the room. 'Ah, Olivia. A port for me.' She turned to her guests. 'Mildred? Valerie?'

Olivia poured out their preferred drinks. She also presented the ladies with a tray of nuts and dried fruit in crystal bowls, which the three of them waved away. Standing beside the drink's trolley, Olivia kept a watch on the glasses, ready to offer a top-up the moment any glass was less than half full. The ladies talked of current national affairs, mainly the suffragettes and their hunger strikes while in prison, before turning their focus to fashion, at Valerie's prompting.

'Simple classic lines are the thing now,' Valerie said airily. 'Wide lapels.'

'Classic lines are my staple.' Mildred nodded. 'As a vicar's wife, my clothes must be respectable.' She plucked at the silk brown dress she wore. 'Sometimes I would enjoy wearing something pink or yellow.'

'I do not see why you cannot wear whatever you like.' Mrs Broadbent tutted. 'You are a vicar's wife not a nun.'

'Speaking of pink, your parlourmaid here wore a lovely simple dress today.' Valerie glanced at Olivia. 'A cream cotton dress with little pink flowers on it. Very sweet, innocent.'

Olivia froze, heat flaming her cheeks. Why had Miss Parkinson singled her out? That wasn't the done thing.

'How nice it must be for you to be out of uniform.' Mildred smiled kindly.

'She was a delicate flower amongst the blackness of her father's blacksmith forge.' Valerie smirked.

Mrs Broadbent frowned. 'I would like to think all my staff appeared presentable while away from the manor. They are representing this family.'

Olivia kept her gaze on the swirl-patterned rug beneath her feet, embarrassed to be spoken about in front of the mistress.

'You must have saved up your wages to purchase such a dress?' Valerie persisted.

Reluctantly, Olivia looked at her. 'The bolt of material was a present from my father for my birthday. I sewed the dress myself, miss, from a pattern, with Flora's help.'

'*You* made it?' Miss Parkinson's nostrils flared with a false laugh. 'What a skill. You are wasted as a parlourmaid.' She didn't say it as a compliment, her stare hard and dismissing.

Olivia lowered her eyes once more. Miss Parkinson's sarcastic tone made her feel unworthy.

'The working class have many skills,' Mildred said. 'Some of the women I meet are dreadfully clever at all sorts of things.'

'We consider the working class as stupid at our peril,' Mrs Broadbent muttered as the door opened and the men joined them.

Mr Skinner took over from Olivia, whose feet were aching. She kept her head down and left the parlour, wishing that in another life, she could have stayed and talked to the captain just as the rude Valerie Parkinson was doing.

The following morning, Olivia was in the library. Once a month, the books were taken off the oak shelves, which reached from floor to ceiling and the shelves dusted and the books inspected for book mites. Olivia had been performing the task for years and knew every book in the library. From the centuries old Bible that she handled very carefully, to the modern novels of American Edith Wharton, Arthur Conan Doyle and Edgar Wallace.

The master had a love of books that she admired. He had seen her once, some years ago, caressing a book cover with a smile and he'd asked her if she liked to read. When she said yes, he told her she must borrow any book she wanted, but with strict instructions to care for it and return it undamaged. His generosity indulged her passion and once a fortnight she would select a book to read when she was in bed, although frustratingly she often was so tired that she only read a few pages before she fell asleep, hence it took her a fortnight to finish a book.

Olivia stood halfway up the ladder, replacing the books on the shelf she'd just wiped down with a cloth when the door opened. She half expected to see the master walk in. It was a habit he had of coming into the library after breakfast. Sometimes it was to replace a book he'd finished reading, or to select a place for a new book that had arrived in the morning's post. Depending on the old man's mood, he would chat with her about certain titles, or other times he'd simply nod and go about his business, leaving the room as quietly as he entered.

She placed the last book on the shelf and turned her head with a smile, which quickly dropped as she stared at the captain.

'Good morning,' he greeted her, his eyes warm.

'Good morning, sir.' She scuttled down the ladder and gathered her cleaning equipment.

'Do not stop on my part.'

'I can't clean while you're in the room, sir.' She grabbed her box and headed for the door.

'What were you doing up the ladder?'

She paused a few feet from him. 'Replacing the books I'd taken down to clean the shelf, sir.'

'This is my grandpapa's favourite room.' The captain glanced around. 'As a child and young man, I never understood the fascination of books. I'd much rather be outside playing, or riding, fishing, anything but being indoors and reading. My brother, Ralphie, was the reader. Anthea and I would tease him about it.' He picked up a delicate Wedgwood Jasperware trinket box and put it down again. 'Do you like reading, Olivia?'

She shivered at the sensual way he said her name. She couldn't take her eyes off him. 'I do, sir.'

'It wasn't until I was serving in Africa, marooned out in the desert that I first willingly opened a novel. Grandpapa had sent me a box of books that he thought I might enjoy. Amidst the heat and the flies, I started reading for pleasure. Those books saved my sanity out there and I finally understood their appeal.' He grinned as he gazed at her, as though self-conscious for his faults.

Her heart flipped against her ribs. Just like when they walked across the fields, he was talking to her as though she was a normal person in his company, not a servant, not someone beneath him, and she adored him for it.

'What is your favourite book?' he asked.

She couldn't think of one, she could only stare at him and think that he was the handsomest man she'd ever seen. Her senses were sharpened by his presence. She heard the tones of his voice, saw the green flecks in his eyes, smelt his soap, and she was wishing with everything she had that she could touch him, taste his lips on hers…

'Ah, there you are!' Valerie Parkinson stood in the doorway, her cat-like eyes piercing them both. 'We are having a picnic, Spence. Ralph can't come, some tedious parish duty apparently, but Mildred will join us.' She turned to Olivia. 'You are to serve us.'

'Very good, miss.' Olivia fled the room, her heart racing at her wild thoughts of the captain.

Once past the baize door that divided the formal rooms to the servants' area, she took a deep breath to steady herself. She had to get a grip! What was wrong with her, acting like some man-mad fool? She'd never been this irrational over any fellow before. She banged her head slightly on the wall. She had to control herself. Falling for the captain would be one of the most stupid things she could ever do.

'Stop being an idiot,' she whispered to herself.

Taking a calming breath, she descended the back steps to the kitchen.

'Olivia.' Mrs Hewlett came out of her office along the corridor. 'The family are to have a picnic along the River Dearne. You will go with them and serve luncheon.'

'Not Mr Skinner?'

'No, this is simply sandwiches and tea for six. You can manage. Go up and change.'

'Yes, Mrs Hewlett.'

She put away her box and then hurried up the stairs to her bedroom in the attics to change into her black uniform. She didn't want to go on the picnic. Standing in the sun wearing black wasn't pleasant, and she didn't want to be in Miss Parkinson's presence more than she had to be. A wicked little voice in her head told her she'd also be spending the afternoon watching the captain.

The Broadbents, Mildred and Mr Parkinson rode in the carriage with Olivia sitting up with the driver. Behind the carriage, the captain drove the gig with Miss Parkinson beside him.

Twenty minutes after leaving the manor, the party was choosing a spot by the river. The day was warm but not unpleasantly so and under the shade of a huge chestnut tree, it was decided to place the picnic rug. Mrs Digby had packed several baskets with food and drink, but before Olivia could serve, she had to set up the two folding tables and six chairs.

'Let me help you.' Captain Middleton took the table from her. 'Parky, give us a hand,' he called to his friend.

'Thank you, sir.' She blushed, her thoughts of earlier returning to make her feel clumsy and out of breath. She had to get a hold of herself.

'I'm sure the servant can manage, Spencer.' Miss Parkinson stood by the rug. 'We could go for a walk.'

'We don't call our staff, servants, Valerie. They have names.' Captain Middleton secured the table legs.

'How am I supposed to remember a maid's name?'

'We can go for a walk later,' the captain told her.

Mildred handed Olivia a basket with a strained smile. 'What can I do to help?'

'Nothing, Mrs Middleton. Thank you. I can manage.' Olivia had never been addressed as a servant before, and it took the wind out of her. Her occupation was listed as a servant, certainly, but she'd never been called one to her face. The Broadbents always referred to them collectively as the staff, or individually by name. Perhaps if she worked in a larger establishment, she might not have been offended as much, but working in a small manor out in the countryside, she'd been protected by the quiet social life of the Broadbents.

A little perturbed by the other woman's superior manner, Olivia chose to ignore her. Her father said there was always a wasp at a picnic.

She took out the white tablecloth and laid it over the food table while the captain and Mr Parkinson arranged the chairs around one of the tables near the rug.

From the baskets, she took out plates and cups and saucers.

The stone hot water flask was used to make tea in a silver teapot. She had another bottle for milk. After unwrapping the array of sandwiches, egg and cress, ham and pickle, beef and mustard, she placed them on silver trays. Next, Olivia carefully arranged slices of sponge cake, lemon curd puffs and wafers. On the final tray she placed fruit scones with accompanying bowls of whipped cream and jam. In a silver bowl she added apples, figs, pears and apricots.

'Olivia.' Mrs Broadbent came over to her. 'This is a picnic. We shall serve ourselves. Just be on hand should we need you.'

'Thank you, madam.' She bobbed her knees to the mistress and began setting out the glasses for anyone wanting a cold drink of raspberry cordial and bottles of ale for the men.

'Come and sit down, Spence,' Valerie called from the rug. 'Mildred and I want to discuss something with you.'

'Am I not included?' Parky sulked.

'Absolutely, you are.' Valerie shuffled along on the rug to make room for the captain and her brother.

Olivia watched them as she worked. Their laughter filled the air, causing Mr and Mrs Broadbent to smile indulgently at them from the chairs.

'We must remember this day, Anthony,' the mistress said to her husband.

'We will, my dear,' he replied softly.

Olivia thought it a sweet moment. She was very grateful to work for such a nice family.

For a time, she was occupied with keeping the flies from the food and helping the members of the party to select sandwiches and cake onto their plates. She made tea for the ladies and opened bottles of ale for the captain and Mr Parkinson.

'Seraphina and I shall go for a walk down by the river,' the master announced to the others once he and his wife had finished eating.

Olivia collected the empty plates and packed them away.

Captain Middleton came up to the table with his empty plate. 'It is a fine spread, Olivia. Mrs Digby has done herself proud.'

'Indeed, sir.' She smiled, hands behind her back. She hoped he'd stay and chat with her for a while.

'Do you often get the chance to have a picnic?' he asked, not in any hurry to rejoin the others.

'Sometimes, in the summer, on my days off. We used to do it more often when my mam was alive, but not much since she died.'

'You must miss her a great deal.'

'I do, sir, very much.'

For a long moment they simply stared at each other, absorbing the other's details like studying a painting.

Laughter from the rug broke their absorption of each other.

The captain seemed to recover his senses first. 'Are there any more beef sandwiches?'

'Um…' Flustered, she searched through the baskets and found the last paper-wrapped parcel of sandwiches. 'There is, sir.'

'Fabulous.' He watched her place them on his plate. 'It's a beautiful day, don't you agree?'

'I do, sir.' She glanced up at him. A mistake as once more she experienced the jolt of attraction between them.

'It's probably one of the loveliest days of my life,' he murmured, his green hazel eyes not leaving her face.

'I hope you have many more, sir,' she whispered, wanting nothing more than to take his hand and walk with him down by the river as his grandparents were doing. She had to stop these mad thoughts.

'Leave something for the rest of us, Spence!' Miss Parkinson sidled up beside him and slipped her arm through his. She offered her teacup to Olivia, her expression cold. 'More tea.'

Olivia picked up the teapot and poured, only at the same time Valerie moved her hand, and tea missed the cup and splashed all over the captain's plate of sandwiches and across the white tablecloth. Miss Parkinson dropped the teacup and saucer with a scream.

'You clumsy dolt!' Miss Parkinson yelled. 'You have scalded me!'

Mr Parkinson and Mildred hurried up to them.

'Are you hurt?' The captain grabbed his friend's hand to check. 'No, you're fine. The tea missed you.'

'Stupid girl!' The other woman's face turned ugly as she scowled at Olivia. 'I could have been disfigured because of you.'

'Now, Valerie. Calm down,' Captain Middleton soothed. 'It was an accident, and no harm was done.'

'Calm down? She should be sacked!'

'Come and sit down, sister.' Mr Parkinson drew her away over to one of the chairs.

'Spencer, will you check my hand again?' Miss Parkinson asked tearfully.

He went over to kneel beside her and Olivia turned away to clear away the mess, her hands shaking at the ordeal.

'Are you all right?' Mildred asked gently.

'I'm fine, Mrs Middleton. I don't know why it happened. Miss Parkinson moved the teacup away as I poured.'

Mildred glanced across at Miss Parkinson, who was smiling sweetly at the captain. 'No doubt Miss Parkinson wasn't paying attention.' She looked at Olivia carefully as though ready to say something more but then gave her a tight smile and turned away.

Olivia kept her head down and mopped up the spill with a cloth. The incident had ruined the afternoon.

CHAPTER 4

Reading the telegram that had just arrived for him, Spencer sighed, folded the piece of paper and put it in his pocket.

'Bad news?' Parky asked from where he sat opposite eating his breakfast.

'We're being deployed to Ireland next week.' The breakfast he'd just eaten sat heavy in his stomach.

'Squash those damned rebels and all that?' Parky snorted.

'Something like that…' He sipped his coffee as his grandpapa and Valerie walked into the dining room, and he said good morning to them.

'What shall we do today?' Valerie asked, selecting a slice of toast from the rack on the middle of the table.

'Without my motor car, not a lot,' grumbled Parky.

'What a bore.' Valerie pouted, scraping butter across her toast.

Grandpapa opened his morning post as Mr Skinner poured him a cup of coffee. One letter held his attention for some time.

Spencer wondered if it was more bad news.

'Perhaps tonight we could go to the theatre in Wakefield?'

Valerie suggested. 'If we could borrow the carriage?' She fluttered her eyelashes at Spencer sweetly.

'Grandpapa?' Spencer asked.

'Er… pardon?' Grandpapa lowered his letter.

'Do you need the carriage tonight?'

'No, not at all.' Grandpapa returned to his letter, frowning heavily.

'Well, let us look in the newspapers and see what's showing.' Valerie snapped her fingers at her brother so he would pass her the newspaper he'd been reading earlier.

'You two go.' Spencer wiped his mouth with the napkin. 'I'm not in the mood for a show.'

He left the room, ignoring Valerie's protests, and headed across the hall into the library hoping to find Olivia in there. She wasn't. He'd barely seen her since the picnic the day before and after the tea incident she'd not looked his way.

'Hey, old chap,' Parky addressed him, coming into the room.

'Yes?'

'Is there something wrong?'

'Wrong?'

'Since we've arrived, actually since the meeting with your grandfather on the day we arrived, you've not been yourself. I know you very well, my friend. You've not been able to keep anything from me since we were eleven years old and had beds beside each other in our dorm.'

Spencer walked to the window. 'There is news. Tragic news, really.'

Parky joined him and they stared out at the parkland. One gardener was digging over a garden bed and another was on his knees weeding the edges.

It hit him suddenly that this would be the last time he watched such a scene or stand at this window. Soon, he'd be gone, and the manor would also be gone by the time he returned to England. He suffered the blow keenly.

'Spence?' Parky glanced at him. 'I'm worried now.'

'It's all lost,' he murmured. 'Grandpapa is bankrupt. Everything has to be sold.'

'Everything?' Parky's voice rose in surprise.

'Keep quiet.' He coughed away his emotion. 'No one knows. Not yet. You can't tell anyone.'

'I'll not tell a soul,' Parky promised. 'Does this mean you'll not inherit this manor?'

'That's exactly what it means.'

'What a shock. A disaster.' Parky patted his back. 'I know how much you adore this place.'

'This house is more of a home than any other, really. My father's house in York holds a sadness that I've never wanted to return to either as a child on school holidays or even now as an adult when on leave from the army.'

'I know.' Parky nodded. 'I think you joined the army to get away from the unhappiness in that house, from your father's grief.'

'And now my grandparents are leaving, going to live in Paris. All this will be sold, and I am devastated.' Emotion swelled in his chest. How was he to say goodbye to this lovely place?

'I can't believe it.' Parky shook his head.

'Neither can I!' Valerie spoke from the doorway.

Spencer and Parky whipped around.

'Valerie!' Parky snapped angrily.

She walked in, clearly unconcerned that she had overheard a private conversation. 'This is very shocking!'

'It's none of your business.' Parky glared at her.

'We are Spencer's friends. Naturally, it's our business.' She raised her eyebrows at Spencer. 'You are penniless?'

'Valerie!' Parky warned.

'Oh, shut up, Orville.' She scowled at him. 'Do you know what this means? Spencer is no longer an eligible bachelor within our circle. That is news.' She stared at Spencer. 'Will you have any inheritance from your father?'

He stiffened at her rudeness. 'Why do you wish to know?'

'All the single women in our circle will want to know. You may have the looks of Adonis, but without wealth what woman in her right mind will take you?'

Her words slapped him, making him reel.

She softened her stance slightly. 'I don't mean to wound you, darling, but we have to be realistic here. I, and many other women, would marry you in a heartbeat normally, but...'

'But now I am simply a soldier without a manor, I'm not worthy?' Anger gave his voice a low and harsh sound.

'Don't be upset. It's the way of our world, isn't it?' She shrugged.

'Is it just?' he mocked.

'It's an insufferable dilemma for us ladies. Looks or wealth? Sadly, you'll not have the pick of ladies now,' she warned.

'Perhaps I shall see this as a lucky escape then?' he said, with a curl of his lip.

'I'm only speaking plainly, Spence. Giving you some truths.'

'They are *your* truths, Valerie. However, I can see this development might be a good thing for me. I would hate to marry someone who simply wants this manor, my money.'

She made a gurgling sound. 'Don't be ridiculous. You're the one everyone wants, but they also want to live in style.'

'And not on a soldier's pay?' he said sarcastically. 'Thank you for clearing that up for me.' He had seen her true colours and didn't like the hue. He turned to Parky. 'I ask you again not to repeat this information about my grandparents' situation until the manor is sold. The staff are yet to be informed.'

'You have my word.' Parky nodded. He turned to his sister. 'And Valerie's. Isn't that so, sister?'

She tossed her head. 'I'll not tell anyone.'

A slight knock on the door heralded Mr Skinner. 'Excuse me,

Captain, but Mr Parkinson's motor car has been returned from the blacksmiths.'

'Brilliant!' Parky dashed forward.

Valerie gave Spencer a long look. 'I think it's time my brother and I make our farewells. You obviously have serious matters to contend with and don't need visitors.'

'As you wish.' Spencer inclined his head. He couldn't wait to see the back of her.

Mr Skinner still stood by the door. 'Sir, your grandfather would like to see you in his study.'

'Very good, Skinner.' Spencer strode down the hall to his grandpapa's study and knocked on the closed door.

'Enter.'

'You wanted to see me, Grandpapa?'

Grandpapa was placing papers into a case on his desk. 'Indeed. Close the door.'

Closing the door, Spencer waited for him to speak.

'Things are moving fast, dear boy.' Grandpapa poked an arthritic finger to a letter on his desk. 'There is a confirmed interest in the manor. A few days ago, a Mr Peck asked my solicitor for all the details.'

'Someone wants to buy it already?'

'Peck is an American it seems. He and his English wife want to visit the place in a few days.'

'That happened fast.' Too fast for Spencer to cope with. He'd only been given the awful news just days ago.

'They want a quick settlement, Spence, if they like it. They want us out in mere weeks.' Grandpapa looked grey. 'I can see no reason to hold them off. The sooner it sells the sooner the debts are paid and the noose around my neck is loosened.'

'I still can't take it all in, Grandpapa.'

'Indeed. It's a bitter pill to swallow for us all and it's all my fault.'

Spencer couldn't argue with that or say something soothing

because he felt shattered. 'I leave for Ireland soon, I wish I wasn't, but I'll try and get back to see you both before we depart.'

'It would please your grandmama if you could, but I know it's difficult.' Grandpapa put more papers into the case. 'Again, I want to say how sorry I am. I wish I had done things differently. I have dishonoured the family. Ruined your inheritance and embarrassed my beloved wife. It's a terrible crime, Spencer, to lose one's self-respect. Take heed of my mistakes.'

The door opened and his grandmama walked in. 'There you both are. The Parkinsons are leaving.' She glanced at Spencer. 'Did you know?'

'I did.'

'And is your heart broken?'

'Not at all, Gran.'

'Thank the Lord for small mercies.' She closed her eyes briefly. 'I know a fortune hunter when I see one, and Valerie Parkinson is certainly that!'

'When there is no fortune, there is no hunt,' he replied with a grin.

'They know?' Grandmama raised an eyebrow.

'They've been sworn to secrecy.'

She let out a long breath. 'Well, what does it matter if our friends find out? They will know soon enough.'

Grandpapa closed the case. 'Not before the staff, Seraphina. They must know first. A couple are coming to inspect the house with the intentions to purchase it.'

'So soon?' Gran's eyes widened. 'I thought we'd have months.'

'I'm afraid not.'

She turned to Spencer. 'Will you be able to stay longer?'

'No, I'm sorry. I received a telegram this morning. We are bound for Ireland.'

Her expression fell. 'Damn those Irish rebels.'

He knew she was angry about her situation more than the

Irish. 'If I can make it back before we depart, I will try, even for just an hour.'

Gran kissed his cheek. 'Thank you.' She turned back to her husband. 'I should start writing references for the staff I suppose.'

Grandpapa nodded. 'I think that would be a good use of your time, my dear.'

'Ralph and Mildred are coming for dinner,' Gran said, going to the door. 'They want to spend as much time with us and Spencer as they can before we are no longer here.'

Seeing her unhappiness, Spencer wished there was something he could do to prevent all of this from happening. It hurt that he couldn't.

* * *

'Your brother is in the yard, Olivia,' Molly told her as she came into the staff dining room.

'Which one?' she asked, wondering why either of them would come to the manor.

'The one who drove Mr Parkinson's motor car,' Ray said in awe. 'I saw him coming up the drive in it.'

Olivia hurried outside to the yard where she found Stu sitting on a pile of crates having a cup of tea with Arnold. 'Stu?'

'Now then, sis.' Stu grinned.

'You drove Mr Parkinson's motor car here?' She couldn't imagine it.

'Aye. I fixed it. So, I thought to return it.'

'You drove it without his permission!'

'Aye. No harm was done.'

'Are you mad? What if you'd crashed it? You couldn't afford to fix or replace something like that.' She was livid with him. He was always the risk-taker in the family, the one to find everything a joke.

'Ahh, you're worrying over nothing. It's done now.' Stu threw the dregs of his tea onto the cobbles.

'You should be proud of him, Liv,' Arnold said. 'Not everyone can drive a motor car.'

'*He* couldn't either until today!' she snapped, hating when Arnold called her Liv. Only her family called her that.

'I've been driving the car about, testing the repairs, for two days.'

'You had no right.'

'Don't give me a tongue lashing. You're not my mam.' Stu stood and placed the teacup on the crates. 'I'll head off. Good to see you, Arnold.'

Olivia took a step. 'I'll walk a bit with you as it's our morning teatime.'

He glared at her. 'Not if you're going to have a go at me again.'

'I won't.' She stepped alongside of him, pleased when Arnold didn't offer to join them.

'You know that fella is mad for you?' Stu said, jerking his thumb back towards the gardener.

'I don't care about Arnold.'

Stu grinned. 'He just told me he wants to marry you. I told him to ask our father's permission first.'

'You never did!' She slapped his arm in horror.

Stu laughed. 'You deserve it.'

'I'm not ready to marry yet.'

'Nor me. I plan to see a bit of the world before then.'

'Father told me about you wanting to go to America.'

'I want to go anywhere that gets me away from here.' He shrugged.

'It's not so bad, is it?' She didn't understand his driving hunger to escape their home. They lived in a beautiful part of the country.

'Working on Mr Parkinson's motor car was the best thing I've done, Liv. I've hardly slept, wanting to learn as much as I could about how the engine worked. I worked by lamplight because it fascinated me so much. I drew sketches of the engine pieces before I took it apart. I want to work with engines, Liv.' His passion was evident in his voice and manner. 'Being a blacksmith isn't for me.'

'Then talk to Father about opening a repair shop for bicycles and motor cars.'

'We're not close enough to town. The odd breakdown wouldn't sustain a business. Besides Father won't listen to me.'

She stared at him. He sounded so mature. When had her brother grown up?

Stu stopped where the path veered towards the stables. In front of them was a wooden fence and beyond that the open fields, which he'd cross. It was the way Olivia had taken the captain.

Suddenly Stu hugged her tightly. 'Look after yourself, Liv.'

Taken aback at the rare show of affection, she gave him a strange look as he pulled away. 'Stu? Is everything all right?'

'Aye, it will be, sis.' He grinned and climbed over the fence. He gave her a wave without looking back and sauntered across the field.

She watched him for a moment but conscious of the time, turned and hurried back to the house.

'Olivia.' Mrs Hewlett summoned her as soon as she walked into the kitchen. 'Come with me.'

She followed the housekeeper up to the floor above and into the small morning room, her mistress's domain.

Mrs Hewlett shut the door. 'Mrs Broadbent is wanting a list of all the items in this room, and in every room.' She passed Olivia a piece of paper and a pencil. 'Can you manage the task?'

'Of course, Mrs Hewlett.'

'I shall be taking stock of everything in the drawing room and Mr Skinner is doing the same in the dining room. We shall have to work together in the library for the sheer number of books is daunting.'

'I was to finish cleaning the library shelves this afternoon.'

'Don't worry about that now.' Mrs Hewlett studied the room. 'Write everything down with as much detail as you can.'

'It's a strange request.' Olivia knew she could say something like that to the housekeeper when they were alone.

'We are to do as ordered, Olivia,' the older woman replied. 'But yes, I do not understand the need for it.'

Olivia started with the walls. Writing down each painting, the artist's name and a short description of the scene. There were five paintings in total. She then wrote down the large pieces of furniture.

'This is where you are hiding.' Captain Middleton came into the room with a smile.

Olivia straightened from where she'd been bending over a central table writing. Hiding? She hadn't been hiding. It thrilled her though that he'd been looking for her. 'Did you need me, sir?'

His eyes widened sensually. 'Yes, I need you, Olivia,' he murmured very quietly, but she heard him.

Her cheeks grew hot. She quickly bobbed her knees and headed for the door as she'd been taught to do.

'Oh, no. I didn't mean to disrupt you.' The captain put out his hand to stop her going. 'I understand that my grandmama has decided to make an inventory of everything in the house?'

'Yes, sir.'

'I thought I would help.'

'Help?' She couldn't have been more surprised if he'd asked her to waltz around the room.

With his hands behind his back, he studied a painting. 'How much have you done?'

'The paintings and the pieces of furniture, sir.'

'My grandmama has a lot of ornaments.' He paused in front of a waist-high, glass-fronted cabinet full of figurines and ornaments.

Olivia didn't know what to do. 'Mrs Hewlett or Mr Skinner wouldn't want you helping me, Captain, as kind as you are to offer.'

'I don't take orders from the butler or housekeeper, Olivia, only my grandmama or my superior officers.' He grinned.

She smiled, unable not to. At that moment she didn't care what the others would think. The captain wanted to help her and that's all that mattered.

'Tell me where you are up to,' he said, stepping close to her to peer at the paper on the table.

The fine hairs rose at the back of her neck at his nearness. 'Er... I'm...' She couldn't think clearly.

His gaze found hers. Their shoulders were nearly touching, and she ached for him to reach for her. 'Shall we start with that cabinet over there?' he asked.

Nodding because speaking seemed impossible, she followed him to the corner where a tall cabinet held several books, a carved wooden box, an elaborate silver candlestick and some miniature portraits.

The captain called out each item, and she wrote it down. They moved onto the cabinet filled with figurines.

He knelt and opened one door with a groan. 'Why would anyone need so many figurines? I'll start on the top shelf.' He glanced over his shoulder. 'Ready?'

'Ready?' She had pencil poised.

'One ugly porcelain woman with strange orange hair and a demented dog by her side.'

Olivia stared at him.

He burst out laughing.

Her eyes widened, and the laughter bubbled up. She fought it and covered a hand over her mouth as she giggled.

'Next. One hideous purple vase with flowers on it which seem to be dying.' He grimaced. 'Why paint such sad-looking flowers?'

She bit her lip to stop the grin forming as she wrote a more simplified description.

'Here we have a figurine of a bird that appears to be either blind or its winking.' He held it up to the light. 'Something isn't right about that bird.'

'Maybe because it's been staring at that tiger for years,' Olivia joked, suddenly knowing instinctively that she could relax with him and be herself.

He lifted up a striped tiger baring its teeth. 'Yes, you're right! Poor bird.' He chuckled.

The captain kept up a light-hearted commentary about everything in the room, making her laugh. He joked about his grandmama's collection of ornaments, inviting her opinion. They chatted comfortably at ease with one another until finally they were done.

Reluctantly, she put down the pencil, wishing the room was a massive saloon crammed with ornaments and furnishings so they could stay in each other's company for longer.

'That was an enjoyable way to spend a couple of hours.' Captain Middleton adjusted the position of a lamp. 'Who knew writing an inventory could be so amusing?'

'You made it amusing. I wouldn't have enjoyed it at all without you in here.' It was difficult for her not to place her hand on his arm. It seemed a natural thing to do.

'I will think of this afternoon when I'm in Ireland chasing revolutionaries,' he said softly, moving closer to her.

'And I will think of it every time I enter this room.' She knew she shouldn't have said those words. She was only a parlourmaid and he her master's grandson. However, she was so comfortable with him, deeply drawn to him and in her mind their roles blurred. They were just two people who liked each other's company. More than that, their gazes locked every time they looked at each other. She wanted him to touch her, to wrench her into his arms, and she hoped he felt the same. The tension between them was like something physical, an invisible cord that pulled the other towards them.

The door opened and Mrs Hewlett stopped mid-stride on seeing the captain. 'Forgive me, sir. I didn't know you were in here.'

'That's quite all right, Mrs Hewlett, I was just leaving.' He walked out without another look at Olivia.

'Have you finished?' Mrs Hewlett took the paper from her.

'Yes, all done.'

'Good work. Mr Skinner is about to serve afternoon tea to the family. He doesn't need you as it's just the master, mistress and the captain. Go down to the kitchen and grab a quick cup of tea yourself.' Mrs Hewlett paused. 'Why was the captain in here?'

Not wanting to lie, she told her the truth. 'He was helping me.'

'Why?' Mrs Hewlett's eyebrows rose in question. 'Was the task too difficult for you?'

'No, not at all.'

'Then why would Captain Middleton feel the need to spend his precious leave hours in here counting his grandmother's porcelain?'

Olivia blushed. 'You'd have to ask him, Mrs Hewlett.'

'Is there something going on that I should know about?'

'No, nothing at all. I promise you.' It wasn't a lie. Neither of them had touched the other, or said anything inappropriate, but only because they both had been exercising control. Every innocent look and word told something different to what was meant.

'Captain Middleton has never struck me as the type of gentleman to play false with the female staff, nor would I expect it from you either.' Mrs Hewlett's brow puckered. 'Be careful, Olivia. Hearts are easily broken. The captain is a fine-looking man, no one can dispute that, but there's more to life than falling for a nice gentleman. Don't do something you may later regret. Go downstairs now.'

Olivia took her time going down the back staircase, wanting to ponder on the time she spent with the captain, to recall his laughter, his funny comments, his gorgeous smile. Not once did he make her feel like a servant, like someone beneath him, but she couldn't ignore Mrs Hewlett's warnings. Her heart was in danger, of that she was in no doubt, and it staggered her how swiftly it had happened.

The sound of something shattering brought her thoughts back to the present. Mrs Digby shouting at Molly for being a clumsy dolt echoed up the staircase.

Sighing, she returned to the sights and sounds of the staff areas and her daydreams of the captain were locked away to be brought out later when she was alone.

CHAPTER 5

The voices of the last hymn slowly drifted away, and the organ grew silent. From the back of the church, Olivia couldn't see the Broadbents or the captain, but she had a clear view of the vicar on the raised pulpit. Mr Middleton kept his sermons short, thankfully, and she didn't mind him as their vicar. He spoke well, clearly showing his interest on the topic he was speaking about to his parishioners. He was so much better than the previous vicar, Mr Rixby, who was old and frail and mumbled. He'd sent a lot of people to sleep during his sermons.

When they were free to leave, Olivia said goodbye to the staff and headed down the village road towards her own hamlet a mile or so away. She had the full day ahead to spend with her father and brothers. She planned to make them a meal and clean the cottage.

Crossing a small bridge over a brook, she was glad the overnight rain had stopped, and the sun shone from a cloudless sky. So many times, she'd made this walk in all weathers, arriving at the forge either drenched or freezing when it snowed. She wore her best dress again, the cream and pink cotton, the dress Valerie Parkinson had mentioned. She was happy that woman had left the manor. Still, even without the judging Miss Parkinson, there was a tension at the manor that Olivia had never experienced before. She didn't like it.

Leaving the road, she slipped through a gap in the hedge, to take a shortcut across a field when she heard her name called. The captain was running down the road towards her. Was there a problem? Was she needed? She quickly went to him. 'Is everything all right, sir?'

'Yes, quite all right.' He wore the same grey suit he'd worn the day he arrived. 'I thought to take a walk… I saw you and thought I should give my thanks to your father and brother for fixing Parky's motor car.' He bent through the gap in the hedge and started walking.

'You don't need to, sir. I'm sure you've better things to do.' She had no alternative but to fall in beside him, not that she wanted to walk away. Any time spent with him was a godsend.

'Today is my last day of freedom. Tomorrow, I leave for my barracks and I'm back under army laws and restrictions. It suits me very well to have a walk in the country.' He beamed at her with eyebrows raised. 'If you don't mind?'

'Not at all, sir.' She was both surprised and happy he was walking with her, but also slightly nervous. He shouldn't be seen with her, people would talk.

'Do you have plans for the future, Olivia?'

She glanced at him. 'No, sir.'

What an odd thing for him to ask. She was his grandparents' parlourmaid. She worked in a good house with good people. She had no intention of leaving.

'Would you not like to see new places, meet new people?'

'I'm from the working class, sir. It's not so easy for me to do that.'

'Forgive me, I hope you don't think I'm being insensitive. It wasn't my intention.' He had the grace to look embarrassed.

To save him from his discomfort, she smiled. 'If I had the

choice, I would travel. Stu, my brother, has a great need to leave here. I don't, but I'd like to visit London or Paris. I've heard the mistress speak of both those places and they sound wonderful.'

'But you'd return here, to Yorkshire?'

'I would, yes. My family is here.'

'Those cities, London and Paris, can be delightful.' He nodded thoughtfully. 'But there are beautiful and ugly parts to any place.'

'I've seen pictures in one of your grandfather's books of the Eiffel Tower and London Bridge and Buckingham Palace. You have seen them I suspect?' She chuckled, knowing full well he would have done.

'Yes. My sister, Anthea, lives in an apartment that has a view of the Eiffel Tower. London is an exciting city, full of shops, interesting people from all walks of life, the underground trains, the boats on the Thames, restaurants, theatres and just... life, I suppose, all passing by.'

Olivia tried to imagine how incredible that would be to see. 'Very different to this quiet part of the countryside.'

He smiled at her. 'This countryside has its own beauty.'

She blushed, but before she could reply, they entered the village, and she groaned on seeing Mr Cleaver's window open. He was talking to one of the miners he used to work with, and she hoped they could pass without him calling them over. They were two houses away from his window when the other man walked away, and Mr Cleaver waved to them.

'Oh no...' she whispered.

The captain's expression became questioning as he saw the old man in the window. 'What is it?'

'Mr Cleaver. Word will be all over the village that we were walking together. He's an old gossip.'

'Leave him to me,' he reassured her kindly.

'Olivia, lass.' Mr Cleaver waved her closer, his look of interest not at all hidden. 'Good to see you.'

'And you, Mr Cleaver.' Her footsteps faltered. She desperately wanted to keep walking, but manners instilled in her from a young age made her pause. 'This is Captain Middleton.'

'Ah, the Broadbents' grandson. Yes, I've seen you go by over the years. Pleased to meet you, sir.'

The two men shook hands.

'What brings you to our little hamlet, sir?' Mr Cleaver's eyes were laughing as he glanced at Olivia, insinuating that it was Olivia.

'I've asked Olivia to allow me to pay a visit to her father and brother to pass on my personal thanks on behalf of my friend, Mr Parkinson. His motor car stopped working and Stu was kind enough to repair it.'

'I heard that Stu worked all hours on that engine.' Mr Cleaver rubbed his whiskery chin. 'It's a skill to fix engines.'

'Indeed, it is. My friend has returned home and asked me if I would call at the blacksmith's for him before I leave tomorrow.'

'You're leaving us so soon, sir?' Mr Cleaver asked.

'I'm away to Ireland shortly. Duty calls.'

'Put those rebels in their place, sir.'

The captain smiled tightly. 'Well, we should be going. I have a lot to do today. A pleasure to meet you, Mr Cleaver.'

'And you, sir. Good luck across the water.'

Olivia quickened her step away from the window before Mr Cleaver could prevent her. 'Thank you, sir.'

'No need to thank me.'

'There's every need. Mr Cleaver will be telling all and sundry that he spoke to you and embellish every sentence with each telling. He'll have us conducting a sordid dalliance before nightfall.'

'I wouldn't mind that so much, and it wouldn't be sordid,' he murmured.

She didn't have time to react to his murmured words as Lachie came running up the drive to them. 'You've not brought a food basket!'

'No, I came straight from church.' Her mind was spinning with what she'd heard the captain say, or what she *thought* she heard him say. His voice had been low and with Lachie's yelling had she misheard the captain? Nevertheless, she was flustered as she embraced her father and he shook hands with the captain, inviting him to sit outside.

Fleeing to the kitchen to make the tea, Olivia's hands shook slightly as she heated the kettle and set out the teacups. Through the small window she saw the captain take a seat at the wooden table, her father and brothers taking the other chairs. They were talking and smiling, and she admired the captain even more for being able to put her family at ease. He had no false pretensions and as a solider she expected he could chat with any type of person, no matter what their rank.

Taking the tea tray outside, she felt a little uncomfortable serving it to the captain without the finery of the manor's tea service. 'I apologise, sir, we have no cake to serve and it's only milk, no lemon or cream, but we have sugar.'

'It's fine, Olivia, please do not worry yourself. Sometimes, in the battlefield, I was lucky to have sugarless black tea that was lukewarm!' He gave her a warm smile that melted her insides.

'Your mam's roses need tending to, Daughter. There are many buds forming.' Father nodded to the row of roses growing by the fence, her mam's favourite flower. 'You should take a bunch back to the manor and put them in your room. You've not done that since last summer.'

'I've been adding manure to them,' Lachie announced, giving Olivia his chair and sitting on a wooden stool. 'Like Mam used to do.'

'And it stank to high heaven,' Stu snorted.

'I'll take some back to put in my bedroom,' Olivia agreed, gazing at the colourful blooms. 'The pink ones especially fill my room with a wonderful scent that reminds me of Mam.'

'Father, tell the captain about that time old Lightning ate Mam's roses,' Lachie encouraged.

'Captain Middleton doesn't want to hear that,' Father said.

'I certainly would.' The captain crossed one leg over the other and relaxed in the chair.

'Well, my wife, she was not only beautiful, Captain, but had a temper.' Father smiled fondly. 'I used to shoe a horse called Lightning. It was a bad-tempered beast, sixteen hands and a weighed a tonne. Huge thing it was.'

'It frightened all of us children,' Stu added.

'It frightened me!' Father took a sip of tea. 'Anyway, one day I had him here, trying to summon the nerve to shoe the creature for it used to bite and kick like a wild thing. One time it tried to bite Lachie when he was little more than a baby. The farmer who owned it hated it, for it once kicked at him and broke his leg, but he kept it because it could pull the plough through the heaviest of soils. Anyway, on this particular day, we had a terrible time of holding Lightning still. He was prancing about, kicking and biting and trying to get to the roses. Lightning loved eating the roses, my wife's most prized possessions, and he started nibbling them and we were trying to hold him back, cursing at him, trying not to get injured. Then my wife walks down the drive, sees the horse eating those roses.' Father pointed to the row of plants by the fence. 'She drops her basket of shopping and runs at the horse.'

Father shook his head with a grin. 'Now this horse was an angry beast. He bared its teeth at her, ready to bite, its mouth full of petals. My wife, who was a small woman, strides up to Lightning and slaps its face, and tells it, *no!* Like he was a naughty child.' Father chuckled. 'To this day I don't know who was more shocked, me, the farmer, or the horse.'

Captain Middleton laughed. 'That's fabulous!'

'Lightning never went near the roses again.'

'Your wife sounds like she was a wonderful woman, Mr Brodie.' The captain sipped his tea.

'She was, Captain.' Father's eyes grew dreamy. 'We have to keep her roses going, caring for them, in her honour.'

Olivia grieved the loss of her mam sharply and gazed at the roses.

'May I have more tea, please?' the captain asked.

She turned quickly and grabbed the teapot. 'Of course, sir.'

'In South Africa, I was billeted for a time at a farm. They had a rooster. We called it *The Devil*, for it used to attack us at every opportunity.' Captain Middleton shook his head, remembering. 'It was so clever it would hide in barns or behind carts, that kind of thing, and suddenly from nowhere it'd come charging at us, ready to strike. It drew blood on many of our legs that bird.'

'Roosters can be mean birds,' Father said.

'We'd rather face the Boers than *The Devil*.' Captain Middleton smiled his thanks for the refilled teacup.

'What is South Africa like?' Stu asked.

Olivia listened to the captain speak of another world she could hardly imagine; the heat, the desert, the wild animals and the people. He had such a lovely voice. While he talked and Lachie and Stu asked questions, she could freely watch him, something she could never do at the manor. She studied his handsome face, noting the green-gold hazel eyes, the long dark lashes, the fine lines at the corner of his eyes that crinkled when he smiled. The way his lips curved, his brown hair shining in the sun as though newly washed. The way his fingers played with his hat that rested on his bent knee and how his suit stretched across his shoulders. She wanted to run her hands over his shoulders and down his back.

'Olivia?' Father leant forward to bring her gaze to him.

'Yes?' She blinked, having no idea what Father had asked.

'We thought to go for a walk down by the river?'

'A walk?' she repeated.

'All of us. The captain has agreed to come with us. Lachie and Stu are going to fish.'

'Right...' She stood, a little confused for her father hadn't suggested they walk by the river since their mam had died. It had been a Sunday ritual that the family all go to the river in the summer. Something that had stopped happening three years ago and never been suggested since.

Excited, Lachie ran to grab the fishing rods, while Stu and her father found their hats and Olivia packed away the tea things.

'Are you displeased that I was invited to join you?' Captain Middleton asked her as they strolled along a dirt track through the fields towards the river.

'No, not at all, sir.'

'You can tell me the truth. I have invaded your precious time with your family, *again.*'

'Honestly, sir, it's fine. I'm just surprised that we're doing this.' She told him the story of how this walk used to be a family treat.

'Perhaps your father is wanting to shed some of the weight of grief and embrace the things that used to make you all happy?' he suggested. 'I could, however, leave you to enjoy the day with your family.'

'No, sir. I'm glad you're here.' She revealed what she felt and again the line between them blurred.

He was silent for a long time.

Olivia wondered if she'd spoken out of turn.

They stopped on top of a grassy bank. Further up, Lachie and Stu, each carrying a rod, looked for spots to fish under the shade of tall trees. Her father sat down on the bank, knees bent, his gaze distant.

Mixed emotions cursed through Olivia. She wanted to comfort her father, but he seemed in his own world. She wanted to join her brothers in their fun, for it wasn't often she had fun. More importantly, she simply wanted to stand beside the captain and watch the lazy flow of the water.

'For the first time since joining the army, I wish I wasn't leaving England,' he suddenly said, looking at her.

'Why?' She gazed at him.

'Can you not guess?'

Did he mean her? No, he couldn't possibly mean her. She was a servant in his family's manor.

'Olivia, the world is changing, changing fast. What wasn't once acceptable is now becoming more tolerant.'

Frowning, she wasn't sure what he was talking about.

'The class divide is growing narrower. The suffragette movement is showing the country that woman are much more than what us men consider them to be. The time will come when the laws will alter, allowing women of all classes to not only have the vote but to have control of their lives.' He stopped talking and sighed as if unsure how to continue. 'I admire you, Olivia. A lot.'

Heat flooded her cheeks. She wanted to answer him, tell him her heart's wishes but how could she?

'Do you like me?'

'Of course,' she blurted out.

'I'm just a soldier, Olivia.'

She raised her eyebrows at him. 'You're more than that. You're an officer and a gentleman.'

'My father has made his wealth. His father before him was in trade. I'm not nobility, Olivia, and I can marry whoever I please, even a maid.'

Shocked, she stared at him. 'No, you couldn't. Your family wouldn't have it.'

'I will do what pleases me.'

'Society wouldn't have it.'

'Then I'd take my wife somewhere where we were both accepted.' His intense stare sucked the breath from her lungs.

'Do you understand what I'm saying, Olivia?'

Did she? Was it even possible? She needed him to speak more clearly, to make her understand exactly what he meant.

'Liv! Come fish with us!' Lachie shouted.

'Will you shut your gob, Lachie,' Stu warned him. 'You'll scare the fish away and we'll catch nowt.'

Olivia dragged her gaze away from the captain and to her brothers and back again.

'Ponder on what I've said, please.' He briefly touched her hand, knowing her father watched.

What exactly was he saying that she needed to think about? He talked in riddles, but his tone, his eyes, his manner told her something else entirely. Her heart answered him in kind, but her head told her to be careful.

'I've shocked you.' He nodded, more to himself. 'I didn't handle that well.'

'Captain...'

'I shall head back.' Captain Middleton abruptly stepped down the bank to her father and shook his hand. He waved goodbye to the boys and then climbed back up to Olivia. 'Good day, Olivia.'

Shocked by his sudden departure, she nodded. 'Good day, sir.'

She refused to watch him walk away and instead walked down to sit beside her father.

'You all right, darling girl?'

'Why wouldn't I be?' She plucked a blade of grass and pulled it apart.

'Because I've seen the way you look at that soldier and I've seen the way he looks at you.' Father gripped her hand. 'I know that look, lass. It's the same one your mam and me shared for years.'

She didn't know what to say. There was an attraction between her and the captain, she couldn't deny it.

'Just be cautious, Liv,' Father said softly. 'Thankfully, I sense Captain Middleton is a man of honour and wouldn't act unlike a gentleman towards you.'

'It's fine, Father. He is the Broadbents' grandson, I'm their maid. Tomorrow, he leaves to join his regiment and I'll be dusting the furniture. That says it all.'

Father put his arm around her shoulders. 'My sweet girl. I hope one day you find the love like what your mam and me shared. It's rare, I know, but don't settle for anything less, understand?'

She kissed his cheek. 'I won't.'

'I got one!' Lachie yelled, his rod bending in the water.

'Will that boy ever learn to be quiet?' Father laughed. 'Come on, let's see what he's caught. Hopefully it's bigger than my little finger.'

Scrambling up after him, Olivia shook away thoughts of Spencer Middleton and ran down the bank. The sun was shining, and she was with her family. What more could she ask for?

CHAPTER 6

Olivia cleared away the breakfast plates from the table in the dining room after Mr Skinner gave her the order that the master and the captain had finished and left the room. Mr Skinner had served them while Olivia brought up the food into the pantry. She'd not seen the captain and kept herself busy, knowing with a sinking heart that the captain was leaving today. The thought depressed her. The weather matched her mood as overnight rain clouds appeared and heavy downpours had occurred all morning.

She stacked the plates on a tray, scraping the food waste into a bowl. Foolishly, she lingered holding the captain's knife and fork, knowing his hands had held them. When would she see him again? Not for years probably. Sleep had been difficult last night as she pondered over in her head their conversation by the river. Was he offering her something? If so, what exactly?

'Olivia.' He came into the room quietly, his voice low, barely heard over the rain hitting the windows. Closing the door behind him, he crossed to her. He was dressed in his khaki army uniform, transforming him from the Broadbents' grandson wearing light summer suits, into an officer of the British Army.

In his portrait, that she had dusted so many times and studied, he was a lean young man wearing a bright scarlet tunic dress uniform and about to face his first adventure in South Africa. Now, he appeared the same, yet different. He wore a different uniform, was older, stronger, superior, and yet when he smiled at her she saw the same warmth in his eyes that was in the portrait of his younger self.

'Captain, good morning.' She bobbed her knees unable to stop staring at him. Her heart hammered in her chest. She wished she was free to speak openly to him.

'I'm leaving now, but I hope to be back for a visit before we sail for Ireland, even if it's just for an hour or so, whatever I can manage.'

'I hope you can, sir.'

'However, now, I just wanted to say thank you for yesterday. I enjoyed spending time with your family, with you.'

She clasped her hands together to prevent them from reaching out for him. Her body ached for his touch. 'I enjoyed it also, sir.'

'You did?'

She nodded, letting her eyes tell him how much.

He took a step towards her, his green-hazel eyes intent. 'What I said yesterday, I meant it. There is so much more I want to say but I have no time. I will try and make it back soon. Next week, if I can. Perhaps we can talk some more then? If that's what you want also?'

'I do, very much. I look forward to your return, Captain,' she whispered. She wanted nothing more than for him to come back to the manor and look tenderly at her again as he was doing at that moment.

His fingers softly touched her cheek. His head lowered and fleetingly he kissed her.

Olivia leaned into him, wanting so much more. That slight caress on her lips wasn't enough, nowhere near enough.

'When I return...' he whispered against her lips. 'I'll kiss you again.'

'Yes...'

Voices on the other side of the door drew them apart.

'Spencer! There you are.' Mrs Broadbent came into the room. 'The carriage is out the front. You'll miss your train if you don't hurry.'

'I'm coming, Gran.' He gave Olivia one last lingering glance and strode out of the room.

Olivia turned away, picking up the tray she couldn't see properly because of the misty tears blurring her vision. She silently prayed he'd return soon. His deployment to Ireland could last years and she hated the idea of having to wait that long to see him again.

For two days after the captain departed, Olivia couldn't summon a smile or any enthusiasm for anything. The rain showers continued, giving the countryside a damp smell and keeping people inside. She often went to her room straight after her duties were finished in the evening and read a book, instead of sitting in the staff dining room playing cards or chatting with Flora and the others. She didn't want company, she wanted to replay every moment of being with the captain.

On the third morning, she duly worked at her duties, noticing that the master and mistress had visitors. Mr Skinner served them afternoon tea and his tense manner caused concern below stairs. He refused to divulge who the guests were and when they had gone, he was kept in the drawing room with the Broadbents for some time.

As Olivia plumped up the cushions on the chairs in the library, Mrs Hewlett came into the room, concern on her face.

'Olivia, your brother is in the kitchen asking for you.'

Surprised, Olivia frowned. 'Which one?'

'The youngest one. He said it's urgent and, well, he seemed very upset. Hurry along to him.'

She dashed out of the room and along the corridor and scurried down the back staircase to the kitchen where Lachie stood by the fire, dripping wet. 'Lachie? What's happened?'

'It's Father! You must come!' He broke down as she held him to her.

'I've fetched your coat.' Flora came running into the room, carrying Olivia's coat.

'Thank you, but...' She turned to Mrs Hewlett, needing permission to leave.

'Yes, go, go. It's obviously important.' The housekeeper went with her to the door leading to the yard. 'Send word when you can.'

Holding Lachie's hand, she dashed out into the rain. 'What's happened?' she asked, raising her voice as they ran through puddles.

'Father and Stu fought.'

'Fought?' She glanced at him as they ran through the field behind the stables. 'What about?'

'Stu's gone.' Lachie sobbed.

'Gone?' She hadn't run for a long time and soon had a stitch and the hem on her uniform was wet and heavy. She let go of Lachie's hand to pull up her skirts, ignoring the slap of wet material against her legs as she followed Lachie over the stile. Soon out of breath, Olivia had to pause for a moment and hold her side as they slipped through the gap in the hedge and onto the village road.

'Hurry, Liv!' Lachie raced ahead.

Tiredly, she sprinted after him, her wet coat growing heavier with every step. Mud splattered her petticoat and dress hem and covered her boots. The inclement weather had Mr Cleaver's window closed and curtains drawn. The rain turned into a downpour once again as she hastened down the road and through the gates to her home.

On the sofa by the fire lay her father. Mrs Bean from next door hovered over him, wiping his sweating brow.

'Father!' Olivia fell to her knees beside him. 'What's wrong?'

'Pain in my chest...' he grimaced, holding his chest.

Mrs Bean stepped back to give Olivia more room. 'I've sent my Alf for the doctor in Woolley to come, but who knows how long that will take?'

'Just rest and try not to move,' Olivia urged her father, frightened by the paleness of his face and the obvious pain he was experiencing. She didn't know what to do to ease his suffering.

'Stu?' Father muttered.

'He's left,' Lachie sobbed.

Olivia whipped around to her brother. 'What do you mean? Go and find him!' If he was in a pub drinking, or wasting time chatting to his mates, she'd have his guts for garters!

'He's left home, us,' Lachie wailed.

'Nay, lad, don't...' Father's face screwed up in pain again. 'Ah!' He groaned, gasped and fell back against the sofa.

'Father!' Olivia jerked forward to help him, but his half-opened eyes were sightless, his breath gone.

'Holy heavenly Mother of God.' Mrs Bean knelt beside Olivia and felt for a pulse on his wrist and then his neck. 'I think he's gone, lass.'

'No!' She refused to consider it. 'Father!' She shook him. No response. She shook him again harder. His head flopped on his neck.

'Olivia, lass.' Mrs Bean pulled her away. 'I'll check him again.'

Stunned, Olivia watched the other woman check her father's neck and wrist again before putting her ear to his mouth and chest. Sadly, Mrs Bean shook her head. 'There's nothing, my dears. I'm sorry.'

Lachie's sobs filled the room.

'Are you sure?' Olivia whispered, knowing the woman told the truth, but not wanting to accept it. How could she accept it? Her beloved father had died right in front of her.

'Aye, lass. I'm sure. The doctor will confirm it once he comes.' Mrs Bean's knees cracked as she pushed herself to her feet. 'I'll put the kettle on for a cup of tea.'

Staying next to her father, Olivia sat on her bottom, holding his hand for a long time. She couldn't think or feel. Numbness had settled into her body like a thick fog. While she held his hand, it stayed warm in hers and her father was still with her.

The doctor finally came some hours later. They lifted her father to his bedroom and Olivia stood at the end of the bed as the doctor examined him, asked them questions and pronounced the death from a possible heart attack. Mrs Bean paid him from the tin of money on the shelf above the fireplace that Olivia gave her.

It was dark by the time Olivia found her voice. Mrs Bean lit two lamps and a few candles, then returned home to fetch them some beef soup and bread, leaving Olivia at the table sitting next to Lachie, who was exhausted from crying.

'What did Father and Stu fight about?' she asked Lachie.

'Stu said he was leaving, going away. Father told him he couldn't go.'

'They've argued about that before. Why was it different this time?' She didn't understand it.

'Because Stu had packed his bag, and Father became annoyed and asked him what was he doing. He wanted Stu to go and collect a horse from Milton's Farm. Stu said no. Father got so angry, Liv, as angry as I've ever seen him.'

'Stu should have handled it better. Talked it over with Father properly, told him his plans.' She'd swing for her brother when she saw him again, *if* she ever saw him again.

'Stu shouted at Father and said he was done with being a

blacksmith's apprentice. He said Mr Parkinson had given him five pounds for repairing his motor car.'

'Five pounds?' Olivia gasped.

'Stu had kept it hidden from us until today.'

'Did he say where he was going?'

Lachie shifted on his chair. 'He said he'd saved enough money to get him a ticket to America.'

'America?' She closed her eyes, knowing Stu would do it as well.

'He wanted to work for a motor car company.'

'Couldn't he have done that in this country?'

'He wanted adventure, Liv.' Lachie sounded very grown up at that moment. 'He wanted out of this hamlet, out of Yorkshire.'

'Stu never came and said goodbye to me.' That hurt her, and she fought back a sob. Or perhaps he had? When he embraced her in the field that time? Maybe that was his goodbye? It seemed he had been silently planning his departure for weeks.

'It was awful listening to them yell at each other,' Lachie said with downcast, red-rimmed eyes.

'Stu doesn't know that his argument with Father caused him to have a heart attack and die. We need to find him, Lachie. Do you know where he might have gone for tonight?'

'No.' Tears welled in his eyes once more. 'I begged him not to go. To wait a few days. But he was so mad at Father. He said he was going and never coming back.' Lachie wiped away his tears. 'He gave me a hug and walked out with his bag. Then Father yelled and stomped about until suddenly he fell to his knees, clutching his chest. At first, I thought he was all right because he got back up to his feet and walked around a bit. He asked me to make him a cup of tea. I made it and he was cursing Stu, saying he was ungrateful, that Stu didn't know how good he had it here…'

Olivia rubbed his back, tears falling over her lashes. Poor Lachie had witnessed so much.

Lachie sniffed. 'I've never seen Father so upset. He said Stu would come back once he realised he'd made a mistake, and that the grass isn't greener on the other side, whatever that means!' Lachie wiped his eyes with his sleeve. 'I made the tea and gave it to Father, but he couldn't hold it. I put it on the table and the next thing Father was on the floor gasping for air, his face so red, his eyes bulging. I tried to help him, Liv! I did...'

'Of course, you did, love. It's not your fault.' She held him tightly, their grief uniting them.

'I ran to fetch Mrs Bean, and she came over and then she sent me to get Alf, who went for the doctor while I ran to you. I didn't know what else to do.'

'You did everything right,' she soothed as he cried into her shoulder. She let her tears flow, needing to cry as much as him. She loved her father deeply. To lose both parents was such a blow.

A knock came at the door, and they broke apart for Olivia to answer it. She expected Mrs Bean only to find a very wet Arnold on the doorstep.

'We were all worried, Olivia. I offered to come and check everything was well,' he said to her, taking off his dripping hat.

'Come in.' She opened the door wider. 'My father has died, Arnold.'

'Oh, I'm sorry, really I am.' Arnold glanced at Lachie sitting at the table.

'Will you tell Mrs Hewlett for me?'

'Aye, aye.'

Mrs Bean entered behind him, carrying a covered tray.

'I'll head back then.' Arnold stepped back to the door. 'Unless you need me for owt?'

'No, thanks for coming though. I'll return to the manor tomorrow and speak with Mrs Hewlett. Will you tell her that?'

Arnold nodded, his expression sad. 'Take care of yourself.'

Olivia closed the door on him and the black rainy night. She rested her head against the wood in despair. In one day, everything had changed.

She entered her father's bedroom and sat on the chair placed beside his bed. She took his hand that now held no warmth and stared at his dear face. 'I'll miss you,' she whispered, a sob in her throat making it difficult to breathe. 'Be happy with our mam. I'll look after Lachie, I promise.' She couldn't think just how she'd do that at that moment, but she'd do whatever it took.

The following morning, sunlight streamed through a crack in the curtains of the bedroom. Olivia had fallen asleep in the chair and her neck ached in protest as she straightened. She went out to use the lavatory and washed her face in the water butt beside the forge. She felt dirty, her dress hem had dried with caked mud.

Back in the kitchen, she softly squeezed Lachie's shoulder where he knelt before the range lighting the fire. 'Did you sleep?'

'Not much.'

'Are you hungry?'

He shook his head. 'Just some tea is enough. Father has shoeing booked in for today. Three horses from Osborn's foundry in West Bretton. I'm to take an order of nails to Watson's in Woolley this morning.'

She emptied the old tea leaves from the teapot into a bucket. 'I'll ask Alf if he'll go to Osborn's and tell them what's happened. Can you take the nails?'

'Aye.'

'You'll have to stop at the undertakers as well. Ask them to pay us a visit.'

He nodded with a deep sigh. 'They should have come last night.'

'I told the doctor no. Enough had happened yesterday.'

A slight knock on the door pre-empted Mrs Bean. She brought with her a plate of fried eggs, bacon and slices of bread spread with dripping and a sprinkle of salt. 'I thought you might not be hungry, but you have to eat to keep your strength up.'

'Thank you, Mrs Bean.'

'I've sent my Alf to the undertakers for you, too. I knew you'd not want to go out today if you can help it.'

Olivia clasped the woman's hand. Mrs Bean had been a good friend to her mam and always kept an eye on the family since her death. 'That's very kind of you.'

'Well, I know how it feels to lose those you love. I've buried five children and my parents. It's not an easy task. Lean on others if you can.'

'Someone is here.' Lachie went to the window. 'It's Mr Burns. He wants his horse shod it looks like.'

'I'll go out.' Olivia stepped outside to the man leading his horse. 'Good morning.'

'Morning, miss. Is your father about? Would he have time to take a quick look at Samson's back hoof?'

'I'm sorry but my father died last night.' She managed to say the words without a break in her voice. She lifted her head, refusing to acknowledge the pain of losing her darling father.

'He never did?' Shocked, Mr Burns stared at her.

'Heart attack.'

'Nay, I'm that sorry, lass.'

'Thank you.'

He tipped his flat cap at her and lead his horse back up the short drive.

Impulsively, Olivia marched up the drive and grabbed one of the gates. It wouldn't budge. She heaved and pulled, nearly toppling backwards when it finally gave and moved a few inches from the dirt encasing the bottom of it. Straining, she pushed the gate free and then worked on the other half which had years of grass growing around its base. After much tugging, it came free, and she dragged both gates to meet. The rusted chain left her hands filthy, but she secured it through both gates, locking out the world.

'Do we have some paper and a pen?' she asked Lachie,

entering the kitchen. 'I want to make a sign that we're closed, and Father has died. We'll put it in the gate.' A sign would save her the distress of telling each person who stopped by the forge.

'I'll do it.' Lachie sat at the small desk near the fire to write.

'Is there anything I can do, lass?' Mrs Bean asked.

'I need to go back to the manor and speak with Mrs Hewlett, change my clothes...'

'I'll stay here with Lachie.'

Lachie spun around on the chair to glare at Olivia. 'I'm not a child. I don't need looking after.'

'No one said you were, but things need doing. I'd feel better if Mrs Bean was here. The fire needs putting out in the forge and there is the nails order. Can you do that while I visit the manor and the vicar?'

'I can do all that,' he replied stubbornly.

'Someone needs to stay here in case people come wanting Father.' She grabbed her coat, gave Mrs Bean a nod of thanks. 'I'll be back as soon as I can.'

As she passed Mr Cleaver's closed window, she saw his look of surprise from where he sat inside by his fire. 'Olivia?' he shouted, loud enough for her to hear him.

She waited for him to struggle out of his chair and hop over to the window and open it, but didn't give him the chance to speak first. 'Mr Cleaver, my father died yesterday.'

'Oh, no. Oh, lass. No, not Fergus. Not my good friend.' Mr Cleaver's eyes filled with tears.

'I can't stay as I've got to get to the manor and back again to sort everything out. Will you tell others for me?'

'Aye, lass.' His expression grave, he reached out and took her hand. 'We'll give him a good send-off, lass. He deserves nothing less.'

'Have you seen our Stu?'

'No, lass.'

'He's left us. He scarpered before Father had his heart attack. I don't know where he's gone, but he needs to come home. Can you let me know if you hear about him?'

'I'll see if I can find out anything, lass. Don't you worry.'

The wet grass made trudging across the fields difficult. Her dirty hem became soggy and damp. She looked a state, her hair not neatly held in a bun, or a hat to cover it, her dress creased, and her boots encrusted in mud.

Her mind spun in many different directions. With Stu gone, there was no one to man the forge, Lachie was too young to keep the cottage, and he'd need to find work elsewhere, a live-in position. They'd have to give up their home. She stumbled at the thought. Her home...

Arnold saw her first, as though he'd been watching out for her. He dropped his spade and ran to her. 'Olivia? How are you?'

'I'm fine, Arnold. I need to speak with Mrs Hewlett.'

'I did tell them last night. They were all in the staff dining room having supper.'

'Thank you.'

'If you need owt, let me know. I'll help you.' He tried to embrace her, but she side-stepped him.

'I best get on, Arnold. There's a lot to do.' She hurried across the yard and into the scullery. Fanny was scrubbing pots in the stone sink. 'Fanny, is Mrs Hewlett downstairs?'

'Aye, she was talking to Mrs Digby just now in her office.'

Flashing a smile of thanks, Olivia went through the kitchen to the corridor and along it to knock on Mrs Hewlett's office door.

The door was opened by Mrs Digby. 'Olivia! We didn't expect to see you. Mrs Hewlett and I were just talking about you.'

'Come in, my dear.' Mrs Hewlett beckoned. 'We are most sorry to hear of your dreadful news.'

'Thank you.' Olivia blinked back emotion. She needed to keep a clear head. 'I understand this is an inconvenience for you, but I need some days off, Mrs Hewlett. Would that be possible?'

'Yes, absolutely. We'll manage. Mrs Broadbent is aware of the situation. I told her this morning when I took her breakfast up to her.'

Mrs Digby patted Olivia's shoulder. 'You're in my prayers, in all our prayers.' She turned to the housekeeper. 'I'll leave you with Olivia and we'll talk later.'

Alone with Mrs Hewlett, Olivia tried hard not cry. 'I was wondering if you knew if there was a position at the manor for my brother, Lachie?'

'Here?' Mrs Hewlett frowned. 'I'm not sure... Things are a little unsettled.'

'My older brother, Stu, he's left. Lachie has no one but me now.'

Mrs Hewlett tapped her fingers on the desk in thought. 'I'll see what I can do.'

'Thank you so much.' She swallowed the lump in her throat.

'Run upstairs and get changed,' Mrs Hewlett said sympathetically. 'I'll have Mrs Digby make you up a basket to take back with you. Send word when the funeral is happening so some of us may attend.'

'You're very kind, Mrs Hewlett.'

Olivia climbed the back staircase, again thoughts whizzing in her head. If Lachie could work at the manor, then they'd cope with their father's death and Stu's leaving.

In her bedroom, she stripped off her striped cleaning uniform that she'd worn for two days and had a good wash, not caring that the water in the jug was cold. After donning clean undergarments, she found in her wardrobe the black skirt and blouse of mourning she'd worn on her days off after her mam died. They smelt a little fusty as she pulled them on and fastened the buttons. A small brooch of a blue lily was pinned on the blouse. It'd been her mother's and Olivia had worn it for weeks until she stopped wearing mourning clothes.

Determined not to let the tears flow, she brushed her long hair multiple times and then plaited it before winding it up into a bun and securing it with pins. She would have to wear her boots back across the fields, but she put her house shoes in a bag and some other bits of clothing and toiletry items.

With a last look around her bedroom, she closed the door. Washed and dressed in clean clothes, she was ready to face the rest of the day.

She heard voices drifting up the back staircase, the clatter of feet on the stone pavers in the corridor at the bottom. Mr Skinner stood by the staff dining room, ushering everyone inside.

'Ah, Olivia, I was just about to send Molly up for you,' Mr Skinner said.

'What's happening?'

'The master and mistress wish to speak to us.' Mr Skinner frowned at Ray who came running in from the side door leading to outside. 'Walk, Ray,' he whispered harshly.

Olivia found the dining room packed with all the inside and outside staff. She stood beside Flora at the side, who seemed just as confused as she was. 'Why do they want to speak to us?'

Flora leaned closer. 'Bad news, I suspect. I've only heard bits.' She stopped talking as Mr and Mrs Broadbent entered the room and faced them.

'Thank you all for gathering.' Mr Broadbent cleared his throat. 'My wife and I have some news we need to share with you all as it affects your future as well as ours.'

Olivia tensed. She didn't want to hear more bad news.

'After much discussion, my wife and I have decided to sell Hawthorn Manor.'

A loud gasp filled the room.

Olivia couldn't believe it. Sell the manor! They couldn't. No one sold manors. They were inherited. Oh God, Spencer. He wasn't to have this as his home now? *He wouldn't be here.* Suddenly, she ached as though her chest was crushing inwardly.

Her world was spinning out of control. She swayed and Flora held her elbow to steady her.

Mr Broadbent continued, 'We shall be moving to Paris to be closer to our granddaughter, Anthea. We shall be leaving by the end of next week. The new owners of Hawthorn Manor, Mr and Mrs Peck, will be arriving a week or so later. I hope you all will show the same high level of service to them as you have done to me and my family over the years. However, the new owners have told me that they have their own staff, but may keep some of you, though your positions may change.'

Flora glanced worriedly at Olivia.

The master continued, 'My wife and I have written you all splendid references should you have the need of them. Mr Skinner will have them in his safekeeping until asked for.'

Olivia looked at Mr Skinner who stood stiff and pale. Mrs Hewlett, beside him, seemed ready to faint. Mrs Digby's chin wobbled in distress and the faces of the other servants revealed their upset. Olivia's hopes sank. This was her world. She'd never worked anywhere else.

Mr Broadbent seemed to sag a little. 'So, there you have it. Our hearts are heavy to be leaving, but we must embrace the future. Change builds character.' He turned on his heel and marched out.

Mrs Broadbent, hands clasped in front of her, struggled to smile. 'We wish you well and thank you for years of dedicated service.' She followed her husband out.

The silence lasted a few moments more, then voices rang out as everyone digested the news.

'Bring their own staff?' Flora scoffed. 'That's me out on my ear then. They'll have their own maids for everything, you mark my words. They'll not want strangers seeing to their private needs, not when they have people they know and trust. I knew something was up.'

Mr Skinner held up his hands to quieten the unrest. 'Naturally, this news is a shock to us all. There is no immediate rush to find new positions as the new owners will need us to help them settle. We know this house, this area, and we are the best people to serve them.'

'What about their servants? The Pecks won't want to pay for all of us. We need to know who is staying and who's getting the chop,' Mr Dennison, the head gardener grumbled. 'I'm too old to start again somewhere new.'

'When I know more, I'll inform you all.' Mr Skinner shifted uncomfortably.

'That's not good enough,' Flora blurted out. 'This is our livelihood. Do we have a position or not?'

Arguing broke out and Mr Skinner stormed out of the room.

Mrs Hewlett came to Olivia. 'Go home. You're needed there more than here. I'll let you know what develops.'

'This is my home, too,' she murmured sadly, devastated on many levels. She wished Spencer was here to talk to.

The housekeeper sighed heavily. 'We are all thrown by this sudden news.'

'Do you think they will keep us?' Flora asked Mrs Hewlett, fear on her face.

'Honestly? No.' The older woman shook her head. 'The little I heard when the Pecks visited doesn't sound good for us. Mr Peck has a large house in Birmingham, but his wife is from Yorkshire and wants to live here to be closer to her family. They are selling the Birmingham house and bringing at least fifteen servants here.'

'Fifteen?' Flora gasped.

'The outside staff might be safe, but indoor...' Mrs Hewlett shook her head. 'I understand from Mrs Peck, when I was helping her into her coat as she left, that her housekeeper was younger than me and she asked me if I was close to retirement.'

'The cheek!' Flora tutted.

'With this news now, I understand her question clearly. Effectively, she was telling me to retire.'

'What will you do?' Olivia put aside her own frantic concerns and placed her hand on the housekeeper's arm in comfort.

'Go and live with my sister. She's been asking me to go to her since she lost her husband last year. I didn't feel ready for that change, but I guess I'll have to be.'

'My aunt works in a candle factory in Leeds,' Flora said. 'I think it's time I gave up changing beds and try something new, like making candles.'

'What about you, Olivia?' Mrs Hewlett asked. 'Will you stay on and hope you still have a position?'

'I need to take care of Lachie.' Her thoughts were agitated. 'If they, the Pecks, won't keep us on, then I'll need to find another position in a house somewhere and hope they take Lachie on as well. Unless he boarded with Mrs Bean, but what work would he do? Maybe some labouring on a farm… Any position I take needs to be close to Lachie…'

'Go home and think about it,' Mrs Hewlett advised. 'I'll come and see you as soon as I can. I'll make a list of local houses that I know of who might be willing to take on a maid.'

'Thank you.' Olivia hugged her and then Flora.

She left the manor feeling even more low and desperate than when she entered it, and she thought that would have been impossible.

CHAPTER 7

Olivia stood by her father's grave and threw a handful of soil onto the coffin below. The thud made her wince. Lachie stood beside her and threw his handful of dirt and then she turned away.

Many of the hamlet's residents, and a good many farmers further afield, surrounded the grave, each telling her how sad they were of her loss and what a good man Fergus Brodie had been. She nodded and thanked them, all the while wanting to run away and hide. Three years ago, before she buried her mam, they'd been a happy family of five. Today, there was just her and Lachie. Her mind couldn't accept it.

'Can we go home?' Lachie murmured.

'Yes.' They walked out of the churchyard and down the road, waving away Mr Cleaver's offer to buy them an ale in the pub. Olivia didn't want to sit in the pub's snug and listen to stories about her father. It was too soon, too raw.

At their cottage, Lachie opened the gate which had remained shut and tied with black ribbon, the wind having blown his sign off.

'Miss Brodie?' A man on horseback rode up to them.

'I'm Miss Brodie.' Olivia stared up at him and realised he was their landlord. She'd not seen him for some time. He'd grown fat and sported huge whiskers. 'Mr Flint.'

'I am too late for the funeral?'

'You are.'

He dismounted, his gold fob watch glinting in the sun, and took off his hat. 'My sincere condolences. Your father was a good man.'

'He was.'

'May I have a moment of your time? There are things to be discussed.'

'Come inside.' She led him down the drive.

'I'll water your horse, sir.' Lachie took the reins and walked the horse over to the trough.

In the kitchen, Olivia raked the coals and added wood to heat the kettle. 'Tea?'

'No, thank you.' He looked about the room.

Olivia faced him, wondering if her father was behind on the rent. 'Have you come for the rent?'

'No. Your father had paid up until the end of May.' Mr Flint turned his hat in his hands. 'I've come to ask if your older brother is to continue blacksmithing here.'

'No. He's gone. America, we think.' It hurt to say the words. They'd heard nothing from Stu. Even Mr Cleaver, who knew all the gossip, hadn't been able to find out where Stu had gone.

'Right.' He turned his hat some more. 'The thing is, Miss Brodie, this cottage and the forge are in good condition and the field behind, which also belongs to me, adds to its appeal. I have decided, with your father's demise, that I'm selling the cottage and land immediately.'

As though he'd dealt her a physical blow, the air left her lungs, and she staggered back. 'Sell?' She swayed, light-headed. She wasn't ready for such another shock.

'I'm sorry to impart such news but as soon as I heard about

your father a few days ago, my decision was made, and I contacted a selling agent the next day. He assures me a buyer will be found quickly.' He turned his hat some more in his hands. 'I'm sorry to say this but I must ask you and your brother to pack up your things and leave by the end of the month.'

'The end of the month? That's two days away.' She had to hold on to the edge of the table for her legs were ready to buckle under her. 'My father has only been dead a week, Mr Flint. We haven't decided what to do...'

'I'm sorry, Miss Brodie.'

'Our father's tools, they are worth something. We need to sell them and that'll take longer than two days.'

He scowled. 'I want no delays... Perhaps I will give you some money in lieu of the tools.' The hat went on his head. 'Shall we inspect them?'

Olivia walked into the forge with him. Lachie stood in the open doorway, his expression puzzled. 'What are you doing?'

'Mr Flint is buying Father's tools.'

'Why?'

She didn't answer him and instead watched as Mr Flint strolled around the forge, lifting a hammer, inspecting a set of tongs, the anvils, the array of other tools hanging on the walls. Olivia fought the urge to tell him to leave, to not touch her father's things, his precious tools, but what purpose would that serve?

'I'll give you three pounds for the lot and that's being generous. A lot of these tools were made by your father, costing him very little and are much worn.'

'It cost him time and materials,' Olivia argued.

'Three pounds or you take them with you and sell them at a market for pennies.'

'No, Liv, you can't sell them!' Lachie cried.

'We have no choice,' she said unhappily. She shook Mr Flint's hand. She couldn't afford to argue with him, but a burning anger simmered in her chest at the unjust fates that were robbing her of everything.

'I'll be back tomorrow with the money. Good day.' He untied his horse, mounted and rode up to the road.

'What was all that about?' Lachie demanded, following her back inside the kitchen.

'Mr Flint is buying Father's tools.'

'You can't do that! They were Father's tools! They belong to me now.'

'We have no need of them. You're an apprentice, or was. Those tools are worth more sold than sitting in a bag waiting for you to use them when you become a man. The three pounds he's paying will come in handy.'

'Stu might come back.'

'He won't.'

'He might!' Lachie shouted.

'Well, if he does it'll be too late because we have to *leave*,' she shouted back, frustrated and angry.

'Leave?' Lachie's eyes widened. 'Why?'

'Because Mr Flint is evicting us. Selling the cottage.' She could barely say the words.

Lachie's face paled. 'Our home?'

'*His* cottage. We don't own it.' She had to sit down. She was too stunned to cry. How was it possible that in one week she'd lost her father, her brother, her home and possibly her position at the manor? She couldn't add Spencer Middleton to the list. Seven days had twisted her world inside out. Seven days…

'This is our home.'

'We pay rent to live here, and we have no means to pay that rent now Father and Stu are gone and I might not be up at the manor anymore. So, we have to leave.'

'I don't want to live anywhere else,' he mumbled.

'Do you think I do? This cottage and the manor are all I've ever known.'

'You should have told Mr Flint we'd buy the place.'

'With what money?' she snapped.

'I won't go.'

'Don't be a child, Lachie.'

'I'm not.' He wore a rebellious expression.

'You say not to treat you like a child, so start acting like an adult. I need you to work with me in this, to find a solution, not throw a tantrum like a baby.'

'Go to hell!' He crashed back his chair and climbed the ladder to his bedroom in the loft.

Before she could follow him, a knock sounded at the door. She opened it to reveal Mrs Hewlett and Flora. Both of whom had been at the funeral. Surprised to see them again, Olivia held the door open wider. 'I thought you'd returned to the manor?'

'We did.' Mrs Hewlett had aged in a week. The hair under her hat was more grey than black and she had shadows under her eyes.

'Please, sit down,' Olivia invited. 'I'll make us some tea. Something has happened, hasn't it?' Dread filled her. What more did they have to take?

'No tea for me, ta. I can't stay.' Flora smiled sadly. 'And aye, something's happened. I've come to say goodbye as I've got a lift to Wakefield waiting on the road.' She placed a bag by the door.

'You're going to Wakefield?'

'To Leeds, I'm catching the train in Wakefield to travel to Leeds. I'm going to stay with my aunt.'

'You've decided then?'

'It was decided for us,' Flora huffed.

Mrs Hewlett sat at the table. 'When we returned to the manor after the funeral, the Pecks were there. It was announced that they would have no need for any of us, except the outdoor staff.'

'They *kindly* gave us two weeks to find another place and leave,' Flora added sourly. 'I told them I was going immediately.'

'But the master and mistress are still there for another few days, aren't they?' Olivia couldn't take it all in. 'You'll be needed.' She still bore loyalty to the Broadbents.

'The Broadbents leave on Friday for London,' Mrs Hewlett said.

'And they can make their own bed until then!' Flora snapped. 'I ain't staying where I'm not wanted. None of them care about us, so I'll look after myself for a change.'

'Enough, Flora. The Broadbents aren't to blame for the Pecks not wanting us.' From her black bag, Mrs Hewlett brought out two envelopes and a piece of paper and laid them on the table. 'Your references, Olivia. One envelope has Mrs Broadbent's reference for you and your final wages, and the other envelope has my reference for you. I thought you might as well have them now to save you coming to the manor to collect them as there's no point for you to return to your position. I am leaving in the morning myself. Mr Skinner is looking after the Broadbents until Friday.'

'This is happening so fast!'

'Too fast,' Mrs Hewlett agreed. 'The Pecks have moved forward with lightning speed. As we speak, the house is getting packed up, and the furniture is being put on wagons and taken to the auction house. I couldn't bear to watch it happen. Mr Skinner understood that I needed some air. I used you as an excuse to leave the manor. He has Molly and Ray to help him.'

'I can't take it all in,' Olivia murmured. 'I understand now why we had to itemise all the furniture, for the auction house.' That happy memory with the captain was tainted now. That task had been done with her not knowing that soon she'd lose her position. Captain Middleton's handsome face came to mind and her heart ached.

'I have to go.' Flora sniffed and hugged Olivia tightly. 'That bag over there is all your belongings from your bedroom. I took the liberty of packing it for you. Take care of yourself. If you're ever in Leeds, look for a candle factory and come and see me. Goodbye, Mrs Hewlett.' Flora left the cottage.

Olivia sat down again with a thump. She'd lost her friend as well. Her old world was evaporating like mist in the wind. 'I'm speechless.'

'We all feel a bit that way.' Mrs Hewlett rubbed her forehead as though she had a headache. 'We are all tired, confused and upset. Everything we thought was safe has been pulled out from under us.'

'I thought the manor was to be Captain Middleton's inheritance?'

'The Broadbents are bankrupt. They've had to sell everything just about.'

'The poor captain.' She knew this would affect him greatly. He'd be concerned about his elderly grandparents, about losing the manor. She was desperate to see him.

'Don't waste your worries on him. Captain Middleton will be fine. He's likely in Ireland by now.'

'He said he was coming back.' Olivia made a pot of tea, needing to keep busy.

Mrs Hewlett shook her head. 'I doubt it. He'd see his grandparents in London, if he's still in the country.'

Olivia didn't want to think of not ever seeing him again. He said he'd come back, but without his grandparents and the manor to return to, would he? Were those precious moments they shared enough for him to seek her out, or would he walk away supposing there was nothing to come back for?

Mrs Hewlett accepted the teacup Olivia gave her. 'The Broadbents nor any of their family are no longer our concern. We, on the other hand, need to focus on ourselves. What will you do? Stay here?'

'That's impossible. We've been evicted.' Olivia had the insane urge to laugh. It really was all too much.

'Goodness. I'm very sorry to hear that, Olivia. What a time you've had. Where will you go?'

She shrugged, overwhelmed.

Mrs Hewlett pushed the piece of paper forward. 'That's a list of nearby houses who have staff. You might get a place with one of those.'

'If I didn't have Lachie to think about, I would visit each of them tomorrow, as I'd like to stay close to my parents' graves and the hamlet.'

'You don't want to leave this area?'

'Not if I can help it. This hamlet is my home.' It was the only place where the captain would find her if he ever came back for her. But would he? She didn't know for certain if that was his intention. Everything was such a mess.

'Now might be the perfect time to try somewhere new, if you're brave enough, which you are.' Mrs Hewlett gave a confirming nod.

'I don't feel very brave at the moment. I'm terrified.'

'That's because you've just lost so much in one week. It's bound to scare you, but underneath, and in time, your courage will rise again, Olivia. I know it.' Mrs Hewlett sipped her tea.

'What are the chances of both me and Lachie being taken on together at the same place?'

'Slim, I would trust. What experience does Lachie have?'

'He worked with Father in the forge. He's good with horses.'

'Yes, but most of the bigger houses are replacing horses with motor cars. Groomsmen aren't in great demand anymore, same with blacksmiths I would assume. He might get taken on by a farmer? Even if he did, you'd not be together. You'd be in a big house somewhere and he at a farm.'

'We can't be split up, not yet, not until he's a bit older. We need to stay together. All we have is each other.' Olivia fought back the tears. 'It's all so worrying.'

'Go to Wakefield, Huddersfield, or Leeds, like Flora. The towns and cities have work if you're not too picky about what you do. That's what I'd do if I was you.'

'You don't suggest I find a housemaid position in another big house?'

Mrs Hewlett shook her head. 'There's more money to be made in the towns and there is more of a chance that you and Lachie can stay together. Find a job where you can go home at night to your own bed. Something that allows you some freedom. Yes, factories are hard work, twelve-hour shifts, but that's no different to working in a big house, except you get to be in your own home, not living in a place where you own nothing, not your bed, not a kettle for a pot of tea, not your time. Do you understand?'

'I think so.'

'A big house is usually miles from anywhere. So, you have to stay close by even on your days off. Change your life, Olivia.' Mrs Hewlett smiled encouragingly. 'I was scared of leaving the manor but the more I think about it, the more I realise I finally get to be my own woman at last. I'm not bound by the clock in staff dining room, or by Mrs Broadbent's bell.' Her smile grew wider. 'Excitement is building in me that I'm starting this new life I'm about to lead. My sister answered my note telling her I'll be with her soon and she's very pleased.' The older woman finished her tea and stood. 'I best be getting back. I've a lot of packing to do and I leave in the morning. Besides, Mr Skinner will want some moral support after the day he's had. He's taken this hard.'

'Thank you for coming to say goodbye and for the references.' Olivia walked with her to the door.

'Take care, Olivia. You're a smart young woman.' Mrs Hewlett embraced her. 'Good luck.'

'And you as well. Enjoy your retirement.'

Mrs Hewlett grinned. 'After this conversation, I think I just might!'

Lachie slowly came down the ladder as the other woman left. He watched Olivia as she cut up vegetables for the pot, using the last of the food they had. 'What will we do?' Lachie whispered, eyes shining with unshed tears.

'I'm going to give it some thought tonight.' Olivia chewed her lip, her mind abuzz with ideas after the talk with Mrs Hewlett. 'If Mrs Hewlett and Flora can start a new life, I'm certain we can,' she said to Lachie.

'Where?'

'Shall we start asking at some of the big houses around here?' She injected enthusiasm in her voice despite feeling wobbly inside at the decision. 'I'd rather stay close to the hamlet then venture into one of the towns straight away.'

'One of the towns?' He grew excited at the idea. 'I'd like to do that.'

She scowled. 'You want to live in a town not stay in the country?'

'Aye, it'll be exciting, different.'

'All we know is this area, Lachie. We know nothing about living in cities.'

'We can give it a try, can't we?' His face lit up. 'I want to do that, Olivia, live in Wakefield or Huddersfield. There'll be more jobs for us.'

'Will there be? It's a gamble.' She was amazed by his enthusiasm.

'I went with Stu a few months ago for the day to Wakefield.'

She frowned. 'I never knew that.'

'We told Father we were going fishing, but we caught a lift on a farmer's cart and travelled into town. Stu said he had things to do there, but we couldn't tell Father, or he'd go mad.'

'What did you do in town?'

'Walked the streets. Stu met up with some of his mates and

they went into some office, but he gave me some pennies and sent me to go and get some sweets while they were in the building.'

A flash of annoyance at Stu made her grimace. 'So, Stu had been planning on leaving us for a while. Why else go into a building with his mates and send you out? What kind of building was it?'

'I don't know, but it had a large poster of a ship on the front window like the *Titanic*.'

Olivia's hopes sank. 'A ticketing office for the shipping lines. Stu kept the visit to town a secret because he knew he was leaving. He was getting the information about how to emigrate.' It hurt that he'd been so cagey about it all. Why hadn't he told her?

'Stu's not coming back, is he?' Lachie added a piece of wood to the fire.

'No, I don't think so.'

'I'm glad we're going to town to live. I don't want to stay here if we're not in our home and Father and Stu aren't here. I keep thinking I'll see them walk in.'

Olivia looked around the cottage. Memories of people gone filled it. 'It'll be a big change, Lachie. We've never lived in a town before. We're country people.'

'I want to go. Nothing is the same here anymore.' His shoulders slumped.

She hated to see him upset. 'No, that's true.'

'I'm sorry I yelled earlier.'

She pulled him to her and held him. 'We've got to stick together, Lachie. It's just the two of us now.' She kissed his cheek and went back to the range. 'Set the table. We need to eat and plan.'

'Are you sad you've lost your position at the manor?' he asked, putting out knives and forks.

Olivia sliced the small leg of ham Mrs Bean had gifted them. 'I'm very disappointed not to be returning to the manor. I liked it there.' She placed the slices on a plate, her mind drifting to Spencer Middleton. She'd never see him again and the hurt that had been coiling inside her like a hideous snake twisted around her heart until she couldn't breathe.

To never see him again...

She pictured him laughing with Father outside, the sun shining, the happiness she'd experienced, and it seemed a monstrous joke that it'd all been taken from her. He'd hinted at something between them with his words, his looks. Now he was gone, and she didn't know how to reach him. Should she even try to reach out to him? He'd be in Ireland by now and he'd made no suggestion that they should write to each other. She'd been foolish to think someone like Captain Middleton would seek her out, that he might feel the same as she did. But she thought he had...

She turned away from the table and gulped for air.

'Liv?' Lachie came to her side. 'Liv?' He put his arms around her. 'We'll be all right. We'll find jobs in town and somewhere to live.'

She nodded and sniffed, wiping her eyes, trying to believe him. 'Course we will.' She rubbed her face. 'Eat up. We've got to pack.'

After their meal, Olivia asked Mrs Bean if she'd come over and select any furniture she wanted.

'I don't think we need anything, lass.' Mrs Bean shook her head, gazing about the kitchen and living room. 'My, I've had some fun times in this cottage. Me and your mam would spend hours chatting, sewing, raising babies and laughing together. Lord, did we laugh. Rebecca had a right giggle on her, didn't she?'

Olivia smiled, remembering her mam's laugh.

Alf, Mrs Bean's husband, nodded sagely. 'Always in each other's houses they were.' He frowned. 'Nothing stays the same though, does it? It's a sorry state of affairs and no mistake.'

'What will you take with you?' Mrs Bean asked, helping Olivia to wrap cups and plates in newspaper.

'What we can carry.'

Alf held up his hand in protest. 'Nay, lass, you'll not be carrying nowt. This hamlet won't see you off as though you were a pair of beggars. We can do better than that. I'll borrow Tom Green's wagon in the morning, and we'll load it up with your belongings.'

'Really? He would allow you to do that for me?' Olivia sagged in relief.

'Aye, he's a good man is Tom. He and your father often had a drink in the pub. I'll go and ask him now.' Alf left them to the packing to visit his neighbour on the other side of the Bean's cottage.

'Take everything you can, lass,' Mrs Bean advised. 'The more you take the less you'll need to buy elsewhere.'

'I don't even know where we're going yet.' A flicker of fear froze her for a moment.

'Mr Flint's money will rent you a flat in town for a bit, I'm sure.' Mrs Bean placed a wrapped plate in a crate which Olivia had lined with bedding.

'I really wanted to stay close to the hamlet, but Lachie is keen to be in a town.'

'He's a lad. Of course, the thought of living in a new town will seem exciting to him.'

'And frightening to me,' she murmured. 'I really don't want to go, but I want him to have some happiness after everything we've gone through.'

'You'll be fine, lass. You're doing the right thing by Lachie, giving him a fresh start with more prospects. The lad could end up doing all sorts. He's a clever one with his book learning. You, as well. You're smart. Whatever town you end up in could be the making of you both. Grab every opportunity you can, Liv.'

Olivia pondered on those wise words. Not that they helped to rid her of the tension she suffered as she packed. She didn't have many belongings. Living at the manor for so long, her childhood trinkets had been given away or lost over time. She had two bags, one of clothes and the other that Flora had brought her, which held her sewing kit, her knitting needles, her winter woollen hat, and the presents the Broadbents had given her at Christmas over the years; a small Bible, handkerchiefs, hair ribbons and combs, a stationery box that contained pencils and writing paper, and a little case of shoe-polishing tools.

Lachie, on the other hand, had numerous things he didn't want to leave behind, several sized balls, a cricket bat, old books, drawings, favourite bits of metalwork he'd made with Father's help, smooth stones he'd collected from the river, tatty and worn coats, hats and boots.

'Lachie, we can't take all that,' Olivia admonished when he came down the loft ladder struggling to hold on to another large box. She took it from him and sorted through it.

'I can't leave it behind,' he defended. 'They're my things.'

She agonised over depriving him of anything. 'We have to be sensible.'

'I need my fishing rod as well.'

'We don't know if we'll be living close to a river or anywhere you can fish.'

'Father bought me that rod!'

'Listen,' Mrs Bean interrupted. 'Why don't I keep some of your things, Lachie, and when you're settled, you can come and get them?'

Olivia waited for Lachie to argue.

'You'll keep it all for me?' Lachie wavered.

'Every item. I'll get Alf to put it all up in our loft where it'll be safe.'

He accepted the deal and climbed back up to the loft to continue packing.

In her parents' bedroom, Olivia hesitated. She didn't want to go through her father's things. It'd been hard enough when she gave away her mother's clothes, and to do it all again for her father was too much.

'Lass, let me do that after you're gone,' Mrs Bean said, standing behind her. 'It'll not hurt me to do it as it would you.'

'Thank you.'

'I'll clear out Stu's things as well and keep them in case he comes back.'

Olivia hugged the other woman. 'I don't know what I'd have done without you in my life, Mrs Bean.'

'Well, lass, you'll soon find out as I'm not coming with you.' Mrs Bean grinned. 'But you'll write and let me know when you're settled?'

'I will.'

Later that night, Olivia slept in Stu's bed, which had originally been her bed before she went to live at the manor, and he'd shared with Lachie in the loft. The cottage creaked as old buildings do and somewhere a fox howled, an eerie sound in the quietness.

Turning in the bed, Olivia adjusted the pillow. Tiredness burned her eyes. She thought fleetingly of Captain Middleton, but the heaviness of leaving her home in the morning pushed all other thoughts away until finally she fell asleep.

She woke at a noise. The bedroom was dark, telling her it wasn't yet dawn. She lifted her head, wondering if it was Lachie. The noise came again. She heard a horse whickering, the jangle of a bridle. Was it the horses in the field? Had they come up closer to the cottage? She listened a bit longer but couldn't define any particular sound. Lachie coughed above her head in the loft. He was still in bed.

She snuggled down again as a horse snorted, but she gave it no heed and closed her eyes. When a bang echoed, Olivia jerked up. Sitting in bed, she listened intently. Was that a voice? Someone on the road? Yes, there came the distinct sound of cartwheels.

She settled back down with a yawn, deeming it was someone in the hamlet going to work or a farmer making an early start. She needed more sleep. The morning would come soon enough.

'Liv!'

Olivia frowned, annoyed at being roughly shaken. 'Lachie, stop it.'

'Liv! Get up!'

She rubbed the sleep from her eyes. Morning light seeped into the room. Somewhere a rooster crowed. 'Why have you woken me? Have I slept late?'

'Aye, we both have, and someone's been in the night and stolen all father's tools!' Lachie cried, his face distraught.

Wrapping a shawl over her nightgown, Olivia raced out of the cottage, down the yard to the forge. She lurched to a stop in the doorway and gasped in disbelief. The walls were bare of tools, the heavy anvils no longer stood on their wooden blocks. The large bellows had been taken off the supporting frame and all the small tools her father had kept in crates or on the shelves under the work benches had disappeared.

'We've been robbed,' Lachie's voice broke as he spoke. 'It's gone, all of it. Gone.'

The blow added to the others she'd been dealt recently, and she staggered under the enormity of what had occurred. No one stole things in this part of the countryside. Everyone knew each other. Who could have possibly done this?

Lachie picked up a fallen nail. 'Do we fetch the constable?'

'I don't know.' She couldn't think properly. Her father's belongings all gone. It didn't seem real. Staring at the empty spaces on the wall didn't make any of it true.

'Morning,' Alf called coming down the side of the cottage. 'You're up early. I've brought you some eggs for your breakfast. The missus will be along shortly...' His words died away on seeing their faces. 'What's happened?'

'We've been robbed,' Lachie told him.

'Jesus above.' He ducked his head inside the doorway to see for himself. 'Who'd do that to you?'

'Someone who knew Father was gone,' Olivia murmured, wrapping her arms around herself.

'It'd be no one in this hamlet. Your father was too well respected.'

They turned as a horse and rider came down into the yard. Mr Flint dismounted. 'Good morning, all. Isn't it a beautiful morning?' His cheeriness grated on Olivia. She had nothing to be happy about.

'I'm sorry, Mr Flint, but we've been robbed during the night. The tools are gone.' Anger replaced her misery. They didn't deserve this.

'That is a terrible shame, Miss Brodie.' Mr Flint clasped his hands behind his back and rocked on his heels. 'I'll just have to keep my money then, shan't I?'

Something in the way he spoke made Olivia stare at him. She wrapped her shawl around her tighter. 'Do you know anything about it?'

'Me?' He feigned a look of innocence. 'How is it possible that I would know anything about it when you've only just told me?'

'You don't seem surprised,' she accused.

'Nonsense, dear girl. I'm deeply stunned. Such a terrible crime to be committed out here in the middle of nowhere.'

She didn't trust him. His surprised tone wasn't genuine. His shock artificial.

'So,' he continued, rubbing his hands together, 'are you ready to depart?'

'We have until tomorrow,' she reminded him.

'Ah, why wait?' His wolfish smile didn't reach his narrowed eyes. 'You mustn't have much to pack, just the two of you?'

'We'll be gone by the morning, Mr Flint,' she said stubbornly.

He bowed. 'Then I wish you well, Miss Brodie.' He mounted his horse and trotted up the drive.

'I've never liked that man,' Alf stated. 'I know he's thrown several families off their farms and sold the land. Sadly, there are too many men such as him in the world. Greedy and self-serving.'

Olivia walked inside, deflated and worried. 'We needed that money. Three pounds would have found us a decent place to stay for a bit until we got some work.'

'Listen, lass, stay with Mrs Bean and me,' Alf said with concern. 'We don't want to see you struggling.'

'There's no work here in the hamlet, Alf, but thank you for the offer.' Olivia found a weak smile for him.

'What will we do without money?' Lachie asked, taking a frying pan from a shelf and putting it on the range.

'I have some…' She rubbed her forehead in thought. Did she have enough to last them until they found work? Her wages for the previous quarter were five pounds. She had a few shillings saved from the quarter before that, but she'd bought Father's penknife and new stockings and more hair pins. At Christmas she'd bought good presents for Father and her brothers. Never did she think she needed to save her money because the Broadbents would sell up. She expected to be in that position for years to come, maybe one day becoming the housekeeper. She'd started to earn twenty pounds when the head parlourmaid left to get married, before that she earned fifteen pounds a year and when her mam was alive, she'd give her most of that money to help the family at home.

Her head pounded with a dull ache. Why hadn't she saved her money? Instead, she'd spent it willy-nilly buying a new straw hat for the summer, a linen petticoat with lace at the hem. All things she could have done without if she'd known what was happening at the manor. Anger at the Broadbents fired through her veins. They should have warned the staff of the impending disaster of losing their positions.

Lachie added wood to the range fire. 'I might get an apprenticeship at a blacksmiths in one of the towns.'

She nodded and took a deep breath to calm her racing mind. 'I'm sure you will.'

She walked into the bedroom to dress and so that Lachie couldn't see the uneasiness on her face. The desire to cry was so strong she had to cover her mouth to stop a wail. She had to be strong for Lachie. He relied on her, needed her strength to get him through this great upheaval in their lives. Only, she didn't feel strong or reliable at that moment. Her world that had once been safe and familiar was shredded into pieces and she didn't know how make it whole again.

CHAPTER 8

With a cold gale more suited to November than May, and which nearly took his cap off his head, Spencer hurried from the hansom cab up the steps to the manor's front door.

Mr Skinner opened it, welcoming him in, taking his cap and greatcoat. 'Welcome, sir. It's a frightful day, isn't it?'

'Not a May day we usually have. Where has spring gone?' Spencer smoothed down his hair, glancing around at the empty hall. He hoped to see Olivia while he was visiting. 'My grandparents? Are they still here or have I missed them?'

'In the library, sir. They leave in an hour.'

Spencer glanced at the reception rooms as he passed, bare of furniture the house seemed cold and uninviting. The drawing room had workers in there stripping the walls, ready to redecorate. There was no sign of Olivia.

In the library, he found his grandpapa sorting through papers while his grandmama sat before the fire, searching through her bag. They hadn't seen him. He noticed how stooped their backs were. Theirs faces heavily lined, hair snow-white. His heart twisted at the pitiful sight of them surrounded by hundreds of books they'd be leaving behind.

'Spencer!' Gran saw him first. Her smile was wobbly, but her chin remained high as he bent to kiss her cheek.

'How are you faring?' he asked.

'Oh, I'm fine.' She waved away his concern.

He nodded but saw through the lie. He shook Grandpapa's hand. 'Is there anything I can do?'

'No, lad.' Grandpapa turned away to place the papers into a leather satchel.

'We didn't think we'd see you before we left for France.' Gran held his hand. 'Your last letter said you were sailing for Ireland this week.'

'I am. Tomorrow. I begged for leave to come and see you. I only have a few hours and must return by midnight.'

'You shouldn't have bothered. The journey is too much to do twice in one day and we must go soon.'

'Don't worry about me. I wanted to see you both. I don't know when I'll get the chance to visit Paris.' But looking at them he was concerned he may never see them again for they looked beaten and dreadfully old. He'd be in Ireland for a couple of years he suspected, unless the Balkan crisis reared its ugly head again, and he doubted if his grandparents would last long enough for him to visit France. Unless living in Paris gave them a new outlook on life and they found the energy to survive the upheaval. He certainly hoped so.

'The carriage takes us to the train station in an hour.' Grandpapa tucked the satchel under his arm. 'I'll go and put this with our luggage and make sure everything is loaded onto the carriage.'

'Skinner will do that, dearest,' Gran said.

'Yes, but I want to make certain it is done properly and nothing is left behind.'

'Do you want some tea first?'

Grandpapa shook his head and left the library.

Gran's downcast eyes matched her long sigh.

Spencer sat opposite her and took both her hands in his. 'I suspect this has been a very difficult time.'

'Anthony and I have been through a lot. We've buried three daughters…' Gran shrugged. 'I feel as though I am a cork in the sea, tossed about, unseen, forever lost…'

'Gran, you mustn't let this ordeal beat you. Anthea will welcome you with open arms. You'll be seeing the delights of Paris shortly. The museums, the art galleries and think of the food and wine, but most of all, you'll have Anthea's children to love and to watch them grow. Anthea wrote to me only a few days ago saying she's so excited to have you both there with her. She hasn't had any family close by for years.'

'Well, she shouldn't have married a Frenchman then, should she?' Gran sniffed with disapproval.

'She married a good man she loves.' Spencer squeezed her hands gently. 'You like Jean-Pierre.'

'I do, yes.' She sighed heavily. 'I'm just tired, Spencer. Tired and old and desperately unhappy to be leaving my home. I came here as a young married girl. I never considered I would not die here in my own bed. Now I will die in a foreign country.' She shivered. 'I truly loathe the thought of that.'

'Is it too late to find a place in England to live?'

'Yes. Anthony has tried everything, but if we sold the apartment in Paris and bought something here, his creditors would have it taken from us. That is his fear. The apartment is in my name and not in England. We'll be safe over there.'

'Lean on Anthea. She wants to help.'

'I know. She's a dear girl. Very much like her mother, *your* mother.' Sadness entered Gran's eyes. 'It hurts me every time I think of Anthea's birth, of my beloved daughter dying and never seeing her new baby, her own little girl. My darling Victoria left behind you, Ralph and Anthea, and you three sustain me.'

'I only remember small things of Mama.' It upset him that the memory of his beautiful mother was fading as he grew older.

'A mother should never have to bury her child. To witness the life I gave to her be snuffed out like candlelight.' Gran shook her head. 'Enough of such maudlin talk. Tell me of your plans? Will you be in Dublin?'

'Yes, to start with but with all this Ulster business, I suspect we'll be sent to Belfast. We are to show a presence.'

'You're not looking forward to it, are you?'

'They should just pass the Home Rule Bill and be done with it. Give Ireland to the Irish to rule.'

'Are you becoming a radical?' Gran frowned.

'Of course not. But it makes sense to me.'

'The British Empire wasn't built by simply giving the countries they ruled ownership.'

'The world is changing, Gran. Didn't we see the consequences of that in southern Africa? Look at the troubles in the Balkans. Most of Europe is banging on each other's boundaries demanding to be let in. Austria and Hungary, Germany, Serbia and Russia, they are all playing with people's lives, Gran, without care of the ultimate deaths of innocents.'

'I do read the newspapers.' She tilted her head in question. 'Why are you speaking like this? You knew what you'd experience once you decided to join the army.'

He stood and stepped to the window. The wind whipped the trees. Memories surfaced of other places, other times, far away from this little pocket of Yorkshire. 'Because I am tired of seeing unnecessary death. I'm trained to kill or to give orders for others to kill an enemy, but in the colonies women and children died due to the fighting.'

'That is war, my beloved. Innocents die.'

He stared at nothing, reliving the moments of finding dead children in a concentration camp in South Africa.

'The Boer War was years ago, Spence,' Gran said gently. 'You must put what you saw and did from your mind.'

'I wish it was that easy, Gran.'

'Going to Ireland has brought this mood on you, hasn't it?'

'I can cope with facing an enemy across a battlefield, but Belfast or Dublin isn't a battlefield. It's streets and roads and houses and schools. People shopping, going to work, and the enemy is hiding within in, undetected. As a younger man it was all part of the excitement, but I'm in my thirties now and I realise it's becoming harder to be positive about soldiering, especially now I won't have this manor, a home, to return to.'

'Then leave the army. Come to France with us.'

He turned back to her with a smile. 'And what would I do with my life? Soldiering is all I know.'

'Learn something else. Buy a business, buy property, anything. I would adore it if you were to come with us.'

'Perhaps, one day.' Movement out of the window caught his eye. A gardener was struggling to carry a long branch that had been snapped off in the gale.

He gave himself a mental shake and squared his shoulders. Enough of the bad memories, the maudlin talk. He had to break out of these strange moods when they came upon him and think of other things, be active, make plans. He wanted to see Olivia. 'When do the Pecks arrive?'

'Tomorrow.'

'They've wasted no time.' He sat opposite his gran.

'The wife is pulling all the strings. She's the one with all the power. Her husband merely nods and gives her the control to do whatever she likes. The ink was barely dry on the sale contract when she was giving out her orders for changes to be done here.'

'How are the staff dealing with it?'

'What staff?' Gran mocked. 'They've all gone. Only Skinner and Mrs Digby remain, and they are to leave this afternoon.'

'The staff are all gone?' The news shocked him. Olivia has

already left the manor? She would have gone to her father and be living at the forge. He felt relief that would she, at least, had a home to go to.

'The outdoor men are still here. The Pecks wanted to keep only them.'

'I wasn't expecting such a large transformation.' He was sorry for the staff who'd now have to look for other positions.

'No one was. Anthony and I did our best for the staff, gave them excellent references and wages owed. We personally wished them well for the future.' Gran stared into the flames of the small fire. 'One by one they left, and the house grew quieter, emptier. Until the builders and decorators arrived yesterday. Now the house is filled with noise, dust and strangers. I cannot bear it, Spencer.'

'Soon you'll not have to.'

'And the weather has prevented me from one more walk in the garden.' Tears filled her eyes. 'I wanted to see the gravestones of Socks and Terry,' she spoke wistfully of her cat and little dog that had died several years ago.

He could see how much today was affecting his gran, and so he sat down again and turned the conversation to lighter topics, tales of acquaintances, the antics of his fellow officers, anything to take her mind off the moment she would have to leave.

However, when Skinner knocked on the door and said the carriage was out the front, her face fell, and she appeared to shrink inside herself. Spencer helped her up, aided her in donning her black sable coat while Grandpapa fussed about, doing nothing but mumbling about final preparations for Skinner to see to, and when Spencer glanced at Skinner, he knew they wouldn't be done. Skinner no longer had to care for the manor. It wasn't his responsibility anymore.

'Will you not ride with us, dear boy?' Gran asked at the top of the steps after wishing Skinner good fortune for the future. The wind had died momentarily.

'No, Gran. I've booked a hansom to collect me.'

'What will you do while you wait?'

He kissed her cheek. 'I'll go and visit Socks and Terry's grave for you.'

Tears slipped down her papery cheeks. 'You are the best of men. I'm proud to call you my grandson. Write as much as you can.'

'I will. Take care of yourself.' He helped her into the carriage loaded with trunks on the top. He gripped his grandpapa's hand. 'Stay safe.'

'And you, lad. No heroics, understand?' Grandpapa slapped him on the back. 'Visit us soon. Your gran will appreciate that.'

'I'll try.' Spencer stepped back and watched the carriage rattle down the drive until it was gone from sight.

'Sir, would you like a mug of tea?' Skinner asked. 'There's no food, I'm afraid and Mrs Digby is packing her final belongings, but I'm sure she'd manage something for you?'

'No, please don't trouble yourself, Skinner, or Mrs Digby. My hansom isn't due for two hours, so I might go for a walk and let you two finish up.'

'Thank you, sir. I'll fetch your cap and coat.'

Spencer looked around the empty hall. This manor was meant to be his. He'd grown up believing it. After today he'd never see it again and that gave him a dull pain in his chest. It was more than just a house, it contained memories, nice memories for him as a boy when he visited, then as a young man and finally as an adult. This manor had been his mother's home and strangely he sensed her presence here more than at the York house where she'd died in childbirth.

He shook Skinner's hand when he returned. 'Don't stay on my account. I'll leave as soon as the hansom arrives. Good fortune to you, Skinner.'

'Very good, sir. Thank you, sir, and to you.'

The wind although still blowy wasn't the gale it was when he arrived, thankfully. Spencer donned his military cap and service coat over his uniform and headed across the fields towards the hamlet.

He was desperately keen to see Olivia. She'd been on his mind ever since he left. This time he'd ask her if he could write to her and see where that took them. If they exchanged letters while he was away, he'd learn more about her and she him, which in turn, would lead to them growing closer.

Entering the hamlet, he was surprised to see Mr Cleaver's window open, despite the wind, but the old man was having a conversation with another equally old man.

'Captain!' Cleaver waved him over.

'Good day, Mr Cleaver.' Spencer also included the other man in his greeting.

'We never thought we'd see any of your family about here again.' Cleaver frowned as though Spencer's appearance was a personal slight. 'I heard your grandparents were leaving today?'

'They are. They've just gone.'

Cleaver and the other old fellow shook their heads. 'A sad day indeed, Captain. One I never thought I'd see.'

'Nor I, Mr Cleaver,' Spencer admitted.

'What are you doing wandering about here?' Cleaver seemed confused.

'I thought I'd call at the blacksmith's cottage.' Spencer didn't really want to tell him his business.

'Why would you call there? It's empty.' The other old man spoke for the first time.

'Empty?' Spencer stared from him to Cleaver. 'What do you mean?'

'You don't know?' Cleaver rubbed his whiskery chin. 'A sorry state of affairs.'

Dread filled Spencer with alarming speed. 'What has happened? Is Olivia well?'

'Olivia, nay I would like to think so, wherever she may be...'

The breath left Spencer's lungs. He wanted to shake the information out of Cleaver. 'Where is Olivia?'

'No one knows, Captain. She and Lachie could be anywhere by now.'

He didn't understand. 'Why aren't they with their father?'

'He died.' Cleaver nodded with a thoughtful expression. 'Fergus died from a heart attack after Stu decided he wanted some adventure and went on his merry way, not realising the chaos he'd leave behind.'

'Chaos?' Spencer echoed.

'Their landlord threw Olivia and Lachie out. The poor lass had buried her father, her brother was nowhere to be seen and to top it all she lost her position at the manor.'

'Where has she gone?' He couldn't comprehend it.

'Mrs Bean told me she was going to try one of the bigger towns for work, perhaps Huddersfield, or Leeds, maybe Wakefield. There's no work out here. They packed up a cart and away they went two days ago.'

'Two days ago?' He took his cap off and ran his fingers through his hair. He'd missed her by two days. He could have helped her in some way he was sure of it.

'It's a shame to see the young 'uns go off to new pastures,' the other old man muttered. 'This hamlet will be nothing but vacant shells soon, or just us old folk shuffling about.'

'Aye,' Cleaver agreed. 'There's nowt here to encourage people to stay or to move here.'

Spencer didn't care about the hamlet. He only cared about Olivia and now she'd gone, he realised exactly how much he truly did care. 'You have no idea where Olivia has gone? No forwarding address?'

'You could try Mrs Bean, the cottage next to the blacksmiths, but I told you, Olivia and Lachie were undecided.'

'Thank you for your time.' Spencer marched away quickly, eager to speak with Mrs Bean. He had to find out where Olivia was. Why didn't he ask her to write to him the last time he saw her? He'd been complacent, expecting she'd always be at the manor or the blacksmiths. What a senseless fool he'd been.

When he knocked on the Beans' cottage door, Mrs Bean answered it while wiping flour off her hands. 'You must be Captain Middleton? I saw you visiting next door a couple of weeks back.'

'I am, madam, and I'm looking for Olivia.'

'You're too late, sir.'

'Do you know where she's gone, an address perhaps?'

'I wish I did, but Olivia hadn't made up her mind where she'd go. She said she'd write to me once she's settled.'

'She did?' A spark of relief flickered.

'Aye.'

'Would you mind very much to send me her address once you have it?' He took out his card that informed her of his headquarters' address. 'Any post will be sent on to me in Ireland.'

Mrs Bean took his card. 'I'm not good with my letters, sir, but I'll get word to you somehow and only because Olivia spoke well of you. Anyone else, and I'd not be doing it.'

'I appreciate it,' he said gratefully. 'Thank you.'

'May I ask, sir, why you want to know where she is?'

Her questions made him pause from turning away. 'We got along quite well, and she was kind to me, her whole family was. It's a terrible shame that in such a short time the family has crumbled into fragments. I want to know she is all right.'

Mrs Bean pursed her lips. 'She's a good girl is Olivia. Not the kind you can play loose and free with, if you know my meaning?'

'I have only respect for her, Mrs Bean, I assure you.' He didn't blame the woman for wanting to know his intentions. She seemed a good friend to Olivia.

Mrs Bean started to close the door but hesitated. 'I wish you'd been here a few days earlier, sir. Olivia and Lachie could have done with your help.'

'I wish I had been as well. I wish I'd known what had happened.'

'Good day, sir.' The door closed.

Walking back along the road, Spencer experienced a deep sense of loss, a sensation he'd not felt for a very long time. How quickly life could alter. Months ago, he'd been content as a soldier, knowing his family were in fine health and his inheritance of the manor there for him when he retired from the army. Now, he remained at odds with everything he once took for granted. He had no inheritance, his grandparents would be living in another country, and being a soldier had begun to lose its appeal.

Then there was Olivia. A young beautiful woman he'd become attracted to, wanted to know more about... Someone who took up much of his thoughts. A change of circumstances no one saw coming had taken her from him. She was out there somewhere, starting a new life and he didn't know where or if he'd ever see her again. A part of him couldn't accept it. He'd been too slow to make his intentions known to her. But then, what exactly were his intentions? He hadn't the chance to find out, to explore his feelings and now he probably never would.

CHAPTER 9

*R*esting in the bed of the rented room of a lodging house in Westgate, Olivia wiped her nose with a handkerchief and sniffled. Her aches and pains had lessened somewhat in the last few hours giving her some relief from the illness that had kept her bedridden for over a week.

After arriving in Wakefield, she'd spent the first two days looking for work with Lachie, but on the night of the second day, a fever took hold of her. Stripped of her energy, unable to leave her bed, she feared the worst. She couldn't remember a time when she'd been so ill, certainly not for years. She begged Lachie to stay away in case what she had was contagious, but he refused, helping to nurse her through it. Thankfully, their landlady, Mrs Marsden, was a kind and considerate woman. She tended to Olivia when she could, especially when Lachie was out searching for work.

Weak, yet considerably better than she had been for many days, Olivia shuffled out of bed to stand at the window, which overlooked the small yard. In the corner, covered with a waterproof sheet, were their boxes of belongings from the cottage. The setting sun cast long shadows across the rooftops. It had been fine weather recently, or so she was told by Lachie and Mrs Marsden. She wished she hadn't become ill, their future depended on her securing a position. Money was tight. Lachie had told her this morning he'd paid for another week's lodging and board, including washing.

A slight knock prompted Mrs Marsden, who came in carrying a tray of tea things and a plate of buttered bread. 'What are you doing out of bed, lass?' Mrs Marsden tutted.

'I needed to stretch my legs.'

'Are you feeling better?'

'A little, yes.'

'Good.' Mrs Marsden put the tray on the small table next to the window. 'I thought you might like some tea? You need to start eating. You're skin and bone.'

A stirring of an appetite was returning. 'I might be able have a bit of bread.'

'That's the spirit, lass.' Mrs Marsden poured the cup of tea for her. 'Your Lachie seems to have got another day with Tomlin then.'

'Tomlin?' Olivia didn't know the name. She sat on the wooden chair at the table.

'The coalman. Isaac Tomlin.'

'He's hired Lachie?' Had Lachie told her and she'd forgotten?

'Lachie did a half day yesterday with him and he's gone out with him on his deliveries again today.' Mrs Marsden gave Olivia a plate of bread and butter and put the teacup closer to her. 'Tomlin's son fell down some cellar steps carrying a sack of coal. Landed funny and twisted his ankle. Isaac was telling me yesterday, and I said how your Lachie was looking to make a bit of money, so he took Lachie out with him for a few hours.' The landlady frowned. 'Did Lachie not tell you?'

'I can't remember if he did.'

'You've not really been with us, have you? This illness came quick and strong and knocked you off your feet.' Mrs Marsden headed for the door. 'It's fish for your meal tonight. Just what you need. A bit of fish will see you right, lass.'

Left alone, Olivia tried to remember if Lachie had mentioned the coalman and was sure he hadn't. She ate her bread and drank the tea before visiting the lavatory downstairs in the outhouse. The journey down and back up the staircase took what remaining energy she had, and she needed to lie on the bed for a while.

She woke to the bedroom lit golden by the gaslight wall sconces. Lachie was lying on his single bed, reading the newspaper.

He looked up as she moved. His hair was freshly washed, still damp at the ends. 'Had a nice sleep? Mrs Marsden said you've been out of bed, and you've eaten?'

'I did.' She smiled, knowing he'd been so worried about her, and been fearful of being left alone in the world if she died. 'Mrs Marsden told me you've been delivering coal?'

'Aye.' He shrugged his thin shoulders. 'He doesn't pay much, and it's only until Mr Tomlin's son is walking properly again. I might get a few more days, but he can't keep me on after that.'

'At least it's something.'

'I'll go down and fetch our trays. We're having fish again.' He rolled his eyes and gave her the newspaper. 'There are some positions wanted for maids. You could write to them when you're better.'

She took the newspaper from him and read down the column. Several of the maid positions were for in town and although they were for general housemaids, she would apply for them. They needed regular wages coming in and a permanent home.

While she picked at the fish and boiled potatoes, she used some of her stationery and wrote letters in reply to seven advertisements.

'I'll post them in the morning before I go to the coal yard,' Lachie said.

'No, I'll do it. I need some fresh air and to get out of this room for a bit.'

'Are you well enough?' He looked concerned. 'I can't have you sick again, Liv. I thought I was going to lose you.'

'I'll be well, don't worry. I'm stronger than you think,' she jested, trying to make light of his doubts.

'You weren't strong last week, gasping for breath and burning with fever.'

'But I overcame it, didn't I? The sickness didn't win, I did.' She gave him a loving smile. 'See? I'm stronger than I look.'

He nodded, not completely convinced. 'I couldn't bear to be left on my own.'

She saw the scared young boy in him where usually he was a joyful, carefree youth. All that had happened in the last month had shaken him deeply, shaken them both. They only had each other.

Gathering their trays, she didn't like seeing his downcast expression and wanted to make him happy. 'It's your birthday in three days. We should celebrate it in some way.'

He perked up slightly. 'How?'

'I'll ask Mrs Marsden for some ideas. We might stretch our pennies for a nice meal, maybe a bit of cake?'

'Trifle like Mam used to make?'

'We'll see.'

The following day, Olivia was accompanied to the post office by Mrs Marsden who needed to do some shopping but who was also alarmed at Olivia not only being out of bed but walking outside.

'If you collapse on the street, don't be shocked when I say I told you so,' Mrs Marsden warned.

'I'm feeling much better today, especially after having a good wash and getting out of my nightgown.' Olivia wore her best dress, the cream cotton and straw hat. She'd woken early and washed her hair with Lachie's help before sitting at the window drying it with a towel and brushing it in the sunshine.

Walking along Westgate, she took note of the shops and public houses. She intended to ask for work in each and every one. She didn't have any experience in working in a pub or a shop, but she was determined to learn. Any job was better than none at all. They needed money.

The first two days after they arrived, she'd gone to the mills and factories asking for work, but had been turned away due to lack of experience. A mill overseer had laughed at her, saying it'd cost *him* money to teach her how to work at the loom, and that young girls grew up working alongside their mothers and older sisters and knew how to weave in their sleep. Why would he take on a lass who knew only how to polish furniture? She'd argued that she wouldn't gain experience if no one took a chance on her. Again, he'd laughed and said the time it took to gain experience cost money.

She'd been too unwell to argue with him further.

Now, while they waited in line at the post office, Mrs Marsden chatted with her neighbours who were in the queue. She pushed Olivia forward in front of her as she continued gossiping.

Paying for the postage, Olivia prayed she'd get some positive answers back to her letters. A thought crossed her mind that maybe she should write to Captain Middleton, but she didn't know where he was stationed in Ireland or even where his barracks were in England. Would he want to hear from her? Surely if he had wanted them to correspond, he would have suggested it? But had he seen her just as a maid to pass the time with while he was at the manor? She liked to think it was more than that, she wanted to believe their connection was as important to him as it was to her, but how could she truly know? The uncertainty of it all made her shy away from writing a letter to him. Perhaps the captain should stay in the past along with everything else from her old life?

'I think I might call in at some of the pubs and ask if there is any bar work,' Olivia told Mrs Marsden after they left the post office and Mrs Marsden was in the greengrocer's buying vegetables.

'A pub?' Mrs Marsden blurted out. 'Nay, lass, you'll not be wanting to do that.'

'We need money, and until I hear back for the advertisements, I have to do something.' She gave her a reassuring smile. 'I'll see you back at the house.'

She left the grocer's before the older woman could utter another word and hurried down Westgate. At the entrance of The Wheatsheaf pub, she paused, adjusted her hat slightly and opened the door.

'Hey up, lass, you're not allowed in here. No females in the main tap room,' the man behind the bar informed her.

'I'm here to ask for some shifts,' she asked nervously, never having been inside a pub before. The smell of stale beer tickled her nose.

'I don't have any work.' He scowled. 'And even if I did, I'd want a man who can lift barrels and throw drunks out, not a scrawny lass like you.'

Determined not to be put off by the man's blustery attitude, she ventured further down the street to the next pub.

The man wiping down tables stared open-mouthed at her. 'Give you some shifts?' He chuckled. 'Not on my life, love. Have you seen how you look? Jesus wept, you'd have my customers fighting over you every night. Sorry, love, but a pretty face in a pub is a recipe for disaster.'

Undeterred, she tried at the next pub, The Black Horse. The woman sweeping the floor eyed her suspiciously. 'You?'

'Yes.' Olivia smiled enthusiastically.

'Not bloody likely.'

Shocked at the language, Olivia blinked, her smile fading.

The woman banged her broom with a grunt. 'My old man has a wandering eye as it is and with you under his roof, well, murder would be done to either him or you by me.' The woman shrugged as if it was a foregone conclusion. 'I ain't putting temptation right under his nose. Go on, get out.'

Deciding that perhaps a pub might not be her best chance to find work, Olivia entered the confectioner's shop across the street.

The man serving sweets to two children had a kind face. 'Ah, sorry, lass, no. There's me, my wife, my son, his wife and two granddaughters working here. Some days there are more people behind this counter than in front of it. Good luck though.'

The painters and decorators next door turned her away when she told them she had no experience of wallpapering or plastering. The cobbler and also the milliner said the same. Lack of experience in anything but cleaning a house, proved to be a hindrance.

Her confidence knocked slightly, Olivia returned to the lodgings tired and concerned. She would wait and hope to hear from the advertisements.

She needed to lie down for a bit and fell asleep straight away.

The next morning's post brought two replies which Mrs Marsden was quick to bring up to her. 'What do they say, lass?'

Olivia opened the first one. 'I have an appointment at two o'clock this afternoon in Pinder Fields Road.' She beamed and opened the next envelope. 'This one is an appointment for tomorrow afternoon at four on Leeds Road.' She was both relieved and anxious. 'I don't know where these streets are.'

'Right, I'll draw you a map.' Mrs Marsden bustled out of the room. 'Come with me.'

Later, with her map in hand and butterflies flapping in her stomach, Olivia walked along the unfamiliar streets until she found Pinder Fields Road. The sun warmed her back. She checked the numbers of each house until she found the one she needed. The red-bricked house was similar to many others in the street, but the brass knocker was tarnished and the front step not swept.

It took an age before the door opened and the yapping of a dog greeted Olivia when an older woman with thin grey hair stood before her, the dog in her arms barking like something crazed. 'Olivia Brodie?'

'Yes. Mrs Ainsworth?'

'Come in, come in.'

The little white dog wiggled and squirmed in her owner's arms, snarling at Olivia. 'Don't mind, Sinbad. He doesn't like strangers. It's nothing personal.'

Olivia followed the woman as she shuffled into the front room, barely keeping a hold of the overwrought dog. A ginger cat sat on the back of a velvet couch and hissed at Olivia or the dog, she wasn't sure.

With a practised eye, Olivia noticed the neglect of the room. Newspapers stacked untidily on the little round table under the window. The window itself needed a good clean and the same for the net curtains. Stains on the carpet caught her eye as she sat down on a chair by the fire which hadn't been set and still held dead ashes.

'Now, your references?' Mrs Ainsworth held out her hand.

From her small black bag, Olivia gave them to her but as she reached over, the scruffy little dog snapped at her, just missing her fingers.

'Enough of that nonsense, Sinbad,' the old woman crooned sweetly. 'Behave.'

Olivia had never been frightened of dogs. She had no need to be. The Broadbents' dog had been sweet and loving. Yet, the growling coming from Sinbad had her sitting on the edge of the chair. Even the cat stalked along the couch, its beady eyes on her as if in warning.

'Very good.' Mrs Ainsworth handed the references back to Olivia. 'Now, the position is a live-in one. Eighteen pounds a year.'

'Live-in?' She baulked at that. 'I don't need a live-in position, Mrs Ainsworth. I have my brother to care for.' She didn't add that eighteen pounds a year was below what she'd been earning at Hawthorn Manor.

'But I need someone here every day, all day and night!' Mrs Ainsworth snapped. 'I'm getting too old to be going up and down the stairs to let Sinbad out for his nightly excursions.'

Olivia glanced at the dog and its top lip lifted in a snarl at her. 'Would there be a place for my brother? He's fifteen soon and very useful. He'd be handy about the house.'

Mrs Ainsworth waved her hand. 'I think not. I can't afford two people. Now, you'll cook all my meals, wash all my clothes and bedding and iron as well. Keep the house clean and tidy, which includes the small yard out the back. The outside lavatory must be scrubbed once a week. You are to run errands for me, as well as do all of my shopping, run my bath, polish my shoes and trim my hair when needed. You'll sleep in the back bedroom close to my bedroom so you can hear me when I call. Your duties will include walking Sinbad three times during the day and once in the late evening. In the spring he has his big bath, but other than that his paws are to be wiped after every walk, and he must be thoroughly dried if it's been raining. You are to feed and groom both him and Ginger.' She nodded at the cat that now sat on the windowsill.

It took all of Olivia's good manners not to gasp at the enormous list of duties.

'Oh, and you may have every Sunday afternoon off, but I'll not allow any visitors to the house as it upsets Sinbad.'

Olivia could have laughed. As much as she was desperate for a position, she couldn't see herself working for this woman.

'Your thoughts?' Mrs Ainsworth asked.

'Well, I do have other appointments, so if you could give me a few days to consider your offer?'

'You'll not take the job today?' Mrs Ainsworth's expression altered. In an instant Sinbad shot off her lap and attacked Olivia's ankles. She screamed and jerked away as the dog bit into the top of her shoe, tearing a hole in her stocking.

'Sinbad!' Mrs Ainsworth struggled to get off the couch. 'Sinbad.'

'Get off!' Olivia kicked at the dog, which incensed it even more. The cat raced out of the room and Olivia did the same, running for the front door.

'Don't run! It makes him worse,' Mrs Ainsworth yelled.

She didn't care. She jerked opened the door as the demented dog snapped at her heels. She screamed as he bit her leg. Sinbad chased her down the street, yapping like it had lost its mind.

A boy riding a bicycle skidded to a halt and shouted at the dog, ready to kick at it as Sinbad launched himself at the youth, but it hit the bicycle wheel instead and fell backwards with a thump.

Hiding behind a stone wall of someone's front garden, Olivia gulped in air, watching wearily as Sinbad slowly walked back home. Now and then the dog would turn and bark at them.

'Are you all right, miss?' the youth asked.

'Thank you so much for helping me. Yes, I'm fine, I think.'

'Nasty little rat that one.' The lad checked the road for Sinbad, but he'd gone. 'You're bleeding.'

'Am I?' She looked down at her ankle and saw spots of blood seeping through her stockings. 'I'd best get it cleaned up. Thanks again.'

When she told Mrs Marsden of the incident and the interview, the landlady shook her head in dismay. 'You can't work there, lass. That dog will savage you at every opportunity.'

'And Mrs Ainsworth, I feel, would be a difficult mistress. I can just tell I'd be run off my feet with her constant demands on top of all the cleaning and list of things she wants me to do.' Olivia dabbed iodine on the bite mark on her leg.

'You'd be better off working twelve-hour shifts at one of the factories.'

'I agree.' She sighed heavily, not wanting to work in a filthy factory or hazardous mill, but maybe she'd have no choice. She'd been a parlourmaid all her adult life, and she enjoyed the cleanliness and orderly routine of preparing rooms, polishing beautiful furniture and making an area of comfort and style. It's all she knew how to do, all she wanted to do. 'I'll go visit some of the factories tomorrow.'

'Don't be too hasty, lass. See if some of those replies come back and you've that interview tomorrow.' Mrs Marsden passed her a cup of tea.

After a restless night where sleep seemed impossible and her worries about the future grew with each passing hour, Olivia became even more nervous and edgy when she rang the doorbell for her four o'clock appointment the next day.

A stiff-looking butler answered the shiny black door of the stone-built house with its prim front garden. 'Yes?' His brusque tone matched his chilly stare.

'I'm Olivia Brodie, here for the interview for the parlourmaid position.'

'You should have gone to the back entrance. Do you not know any better?'

'Sorry. Yes, I should have.' She glanced over her shoulder at the narrow drive that went down beside the house.

'Come in, come in! I can't be standing on the doorstep all afternoon!' he commanded.

She followed him into a square hallway, and he jabbed her in the back to go down the narrow corridor to the back of the house. That he touched her so roughly shocked Olivia. Mr Skinner had never touched her. No one had ever pushed her but her brothers when they'd been playing as youngsters.

'Mrs Carmody. Your four o'clock,' the butler announced at the doorway of a small office. 'She came to the *front door*. Obviously badly trained.'

Offended, Olivia glared at him. 'I was trained by the best, sir!'

The housekeeper tutted. 'I doubt that. If you were, you'd be employed by a larger house and not be begging for a position here.'

'Hawthorn Manor was a fine establishment with the best of staff who trained me well,' she defended.

'The master was declared bankrupt, so I heard. Such a disgrace.' The housekeeper nodded to the butler, who left the room with a smirk at Olivia.

Olivia stood stiffly for she wasn't invited to sit on the chair opposite the desk. The small room was bare of comfort or personal touches, resembling a prison cell.

'The housemaid position requires you to live-in,' Mrs Carmody stated.

'I—'

Mrs Carmody held up her hand to silence her. 'You'll be responsible for all the upstairs and downstairs rooms. Four bedrooms above, two reception rooms and the dining room. You do not enter the master's study. He is an important man, and you are not worthy to be in such a room where significant business is conducted. You do not touch the silverware or crystal, only Mr Granger, the butler, or myself are in charge of handling those. You are to be paid monthly, and you must purchase your own uniform. All breakages will come out of your wage. Absolutely no visitors. You will receive a half day off every week and a full day once a month. You are never to be seen or heard by the family. If they enter a room, you must leave immediately.'

Angered that Mrs Carmody assumed she didn't know the rules, Olivia glared at her. 'I know my place. I know how to behave in front of the family.'

Mrs Carmody's top lip curled back revealing stained teeth. 'Speaking out of turn now shows me the opposite.'

'I can't live-in.'

The housekeeper gasped. 'Not live-in?'

'That's correct.' Olivia stood tall, shoulders back. She'd not be cowered by this awful woman, who she knew instinctively would be a nasty person to work for, and the same regarding the horrid butler.

'You must live-in.'

Olivia gave a slight nod. 'Then this position isn't for me. Good day.'

'You wouldn't have suited us anyway,' the other woman scorned. 'Having airs and graces when you're nothing but a maid. You'd have had that beaten out of you under my rule.'

At the door, Olivia turned and tilted her head slightly. 'It's a good thing I'm not staying then, isn't it?'

Head high, Olivia walked out of the house, the way she came in, through the front door and past the startled butler.

All the way back to the lodging she kept her chin up, determined not to become upset. If she had to work in a mill or a factory, then she would. She'd start at the very bottom and work her way up. She could do that, of course she could.

Mrs Marsden met her in the hallway before she had a chance to go upstairs. 'How did it go?'

'Awful.'

'Why?'

'The butler jabbed me in the back as soon as I walked in, and the housekeeper was a nasty woman. Working there would have been torture, and I had to live-in. I walked out.'

'Never mind. You did the right thing. You're not that desperate yet.'

'I hope I'm never desperate enough to work for people like that.' She unpinned her hat and slipped off her gloves.

'Look, the late post has come while you were out and you've another letter.'

She groaned but took the letter and opened it. She read the few lines. 'I have an appointment tomorrow at noon.'

'Where?'

'College Grove Road.' Naturally, Olivia had no idea where that was.

'I'll draw you another map,' Mrs Marsden said excitedly.

'I hope this has a nicer housekeeper than the last one.' She didn't have high hopes of it after the last two places she'd been to.

The door opened behind them and Lachie came in whistling.

Olivia smiled. She'd not heard him whistle since before their father died. 'You seem cheerful.'

'I am. I've got a job.' He grinned, puffing out his chest.

'You have! That's brilliant.' Olivia hugged him. 'Where? How did you get it?'

He laughed. 'Hey up, Liv, I haven't finished. I've also got us a place to live!'

Mrs Marsden came back with a piece of paper, Olivia's map. 'You look pleased with yourself, lad.'

'He's got a job, Mrs Marsden, and a place for us to live.' Olivia could burst she was so proud of him.

'Nay, you never have?' Mrs Marsden patted him on the back. 'What are you doing, lad, and where's this place?'

'I'm off down the pit,' Lachie declared. 'The pit foreman told me of a house that's empty.'

Olivia stepped back in shock. Their mam never wanted one of her boys to work down a coal mine. 'The pit?'

'I start this evening, and we can move into the house in the morning.'

'No, Lachie. Anything but the pit…' She was horrified he'd be spending his days and nights down a filthy and dangerous black hole.

He shrugged, his expression changing at her disapproval. 'We need money, Liv, and I need a job.' He climbed the stairs to the room.

Mrs Marsden put her hand on Olivia's arm. 'He's doing his bit, lass. You can't ask for more.'

'I don't want him down the pit!'

'Happen he has a right to choose for himself.'

'He's a boy,' she argued.

'He's fifteen tomorrow and now a man.'

Olivia climbed the staircase, her heart and mind at war. She felt sick to her stomach that her brother was going down the pit, but also angry that they were in this situation. If Father's tools hadn't been stolen and they'd received the money for them, they could have waited a bit longer for Lachie to find a better job. If the Broadbents hadn't gone bankrupt, she'd still have her position. If Captain Middleton had asked her to write to him, he might have been able to help them. She leant her head against the wall at the top of the stairs. If, if, if!

CHAPTER 10

Pacing the front room of the lodging house, Olivia kept glancing out of the window for Lachie. He'd gone to work the evening before at six and now it was past seven o'clock the next morning. Where was he?

Other lodgers had left the house on their way to work and Mrs Marsden came in and out of the room many times seemingly just as concerned as Olivia.

'Happen they've kept him back?' Mrs Marsden said on her fifth time of coming into the room.

'He's worked all night, why would they keep him back?'

'Maybe they haven't. Park Hill Pit is two miles away. It'd take him an hour to walk back here when he's tired after doing a twelve-hour shift.'

'Yes, I hadn't thought of that.'

They both turned as the front door opened and Lachie walked in as filthy as Olivia had ever seen him. He was covered in coal dust, the whites of his eyes bright in a black face.

'Yee Gods, lad!' Mrs Marsden squawked. 'Get out and go around to the backyard. You'll need a scrub before you come in this house.'

Lachie nodded and left as quietly as he came in.

'I'll put some water on to heat. He'll need a proper wash.' Mrs Marsden hustled out while Olivia hurried along the corridor and out the back door to greet Lachie as he came in through the gate.

'How was it?' Olivia asked.

'All right.' Lachie sat on an upturned crate and pulled off his boots. 'I'll get a wash and then we can go to the rented place. I've got the keys.' He pulled them from his pocket and gave them to her.

'Lachie, was it very bad?' she asked.

'Horrible.'

Her chest tightened in dread for him. 'Were you frightened?'

'Aye. It's pitch-black, dusty, noisy and full of men who don't care about you unless you're costing them money and then they hate you and knock you on your arse.'

'Lachie!' She'd never heard him swear before.

'And that's the polite way to describe it.'

'What did you do on your shift?'

'I pushed carts full of coal out of the tunnels… and other stuff.' He sounded as dejected as he looked.

'You don't have to go back.' She hated to see him so low.

'Yes, I do. It's a job.'

'There are other jobs.'

He looked at her, seemingly much older being caked in coal dust. 'I've got this job now. Besides, there's a chance I can work with the pit ponies. The foreman now knows I'm used to horses.'

'Would that be better, working with the ponies?'

'Aye, hopefully.' He yawned. 'We need to go and see the place we can rent and then I need to sleep before tonight's shift. You get a good bashing if you fall asleep down there.'

'Don't go back. The place sounds like hell. We can wait for another job and another place to live.'

'Liv, I've given my word I'll be back tonight.'

'Who cares? We'll move away somewhere else. We'll try Huddersfield or Leeds.'

'I care!' He dragged off his filthy socks. 'I'll get used to it. We need the money and a home of our own.'

Mrs Marsden came down the back steps carrying a basin of warm water, a bar of soap and a towel. 'There's more water on the heat. I'll make you a cup of tea, lad, while you wash.'

'Thanks, Mrs Marsden.' Lachie took the basin and placed it on the crate, his movements sluggish with tiredness.

Olivia felt so torn. She didn't want him to work in such a place but how could she stop him? He needed her support, not censure. 'I can go on my own to visit this house, if you'd like?'

'Really?' Lachie pulled off his shirt. His skin startlingly white against the areas blackened by coal. 'I'm dead on my feet.'

'My appointment isn't until later, midday. I can go and have a look now. See what it's like while you wash and have a sleep.'

Lachie nodded and yawned again. 'One of the men pointed out the street leading to it as we walked past. Go along Stanley Road until you get to Norton Road. Woodcock's Square is off Norton. The house is number seven.'

She nodded and gave him a slight smile. 'By the way, happy birthday.'

He grinned, the old Lachie appearing for a moment. 'Thanks.'

'When you've had a sleep, we'll have some cake.'

'Cake?'

'Mrs Marsden is baking one for you today.'

'That's nice.'

She left him to it and went back upstairs to grab her hat, gloves and a little black bag. Although they couldn't afford it, she wanted to buy him something for his special day.

With Mrs Marsden's map in hand, Olivia walked away from Westgate, past the towering Cathedral Church of All Saints and east along Warrengate until she came to Stanley Road running north on the left.

Businesses lined Stanley Road, and also there were plenty of public houses and behind them, through archways, Olivia spied mean little alleyways leading to open yards surrounded by dilapidated dwellings where the poor lived.

After twenty-five minutes of walking, she came to Norton Road on the left. Another pub was on the corner and at the end of road were fenced garden allotments and a working men's club, but it couldn't detract from the ugliness of the entrance to Woodcock's Square on the right.

Plain brick two-storey terrace houses lined two sides of the cobbled square, the third side being the back of the shops and a pub facing Stanley Road. The fourth side was open to Norton Road. Washing hung on ropes stretched across the open area. Overflowing rubbish bins gave off a stench and young children played while some of the mothers leant against their front doors chatting, wearing aprons and suspicious expressions when they saw Olivia.

'You lost, hinny?' one woman asked, a baby on her hip.

'I'm looking to view number seven.' Olivia held up the keys to show the woman and her friend standing beside her.

'Are you just?' The first woman raised her eyebrows at her friend who held a broom. 'Did you hear that, Sadie? She's here to *view* number seven, if you please?'

Olivia's stomach quivered. They were making fun of her already.

'Come on then.' Sadie leant her broom against the wall. 'I'm in number five.'

Both women came towards her. They looked only a little older than Olivia. Sadie held out her hand. 'Sadie Watson and this here is Winnie Briggs and her little lass, Martha.'

'Olivia Brodie.' She shook their hands.

'You're new to the area?' Sadie asked.

'Of course she is, Sadie,' Winnie scoffed, her dark hair

hanging in a messy half knot. 'Look at her dress. That wouldn't stay clean around here.'

Olivia blushed and smoothed down her cream and pink-flowered dress. 'Yes, I'm from a hamlet between Bretton and Woolley.'

Winnie frowned. 'Where the 'ell is that?'

'Some miles south of Sandal Castle,' Sadie informed her. 'Me mam's cousin left to work at Bretton Hall.' Sadie looked at Olivia. 'That's right, isn't it? South?'

Olivia nodded and covered her nose suddenly when hit with an awful smell.

'That's the drains and the privies. The privies get blocked up because the drains are blocked or broken.' Sadie laughed. 'You'll get used to the stink.'

Olivia doubted she would for she wasn't going to live here. The houses appeared ready to collapse at any moment. Shingles were missing on the roofs, glass was broken in some of the windows and rubbish was piled in corners of the square.

'Here's number seven.' Winnie stood in front of a plain wooden door that needed a fresh coat of paint. 'Welcome to paradise.'

Olivia inserted the key and turned it, the door opened with a loud creak. She stepped into the front room, a small square that had only one window and a tiny fireplace. Bare floorboards and dirty yellow paint gave the room a sad, unkempt appearance. Mould grew like a cobweb in one corner of the ceiling.

A doorway on the back wall led into a kitchen as equally small as the front room with an old range and a built-in copper boiler for washing clothes on the far wall.

Two doors led off the kitchen. One door to the outside and a backyard which was an area measuring roughly ten feet by ten feet and held a narrow outhouse and a gate to the alleyway behind. The other door led down to a cellar which smelt of damp and other unidentifiable unpleasant aromas. It was too dark to see anything clearly from the top step and Olivia wasn't venturing down any further.

'A mansion, isn't it?' Sadie laughed as Olivia closed the cellar door.

'Upstairs ain't much better,' Winnie added. 'Two tiny bedrooms.'

Olivia climbed the steep dim staircase to the rooms above and agreed with Winnie. The two bedrooms were so small she doubted there would be room to move once a bed and a wardrobe was in them.

'It's cheap though.' Sadie led the way back down to the front room. 'And we all look out for each other in this square. It makes it bearable.'

'Got a husband?' Winnie asked.

'No, it's just me and my brother.' Olivia looked around the front room, eyeing the damp on the walls and shivered. The place was like a dungeon.

'What's your brother do for work?' Winnie asked.

'He's started at Park Hill Pit.'

'Oh, that's where my Gerry works,' Sadie said proudly. 'It's not a bad pit.'

'My fella, Norman, is a foreman at Mount Clay Brick Works.' Winnie supplied. 'What work do you do?'

'I'm a parlourmaid.'

'Fancy,' Winnie cooed. 'Are you in some gentleman's residence?'

'I was at Hawthorn Manor, but the family sold and moved to Paris. My father died at the same time, so my brother and me are looking for a new home and jobs.' She didn't know why she was explaining everything to these two women. She liked Sadie but Winnie seemed the pricklier of the two.

'Are you going to take the house?' Sadie asked as Olivia locked the door.

'I don't know.' In all honesty she'd rather never step foot in the square again. Surely, they could find somewhere better than this awful place?

'It's no palace, but the people are nice and it's close to Park Hill Pit for your brother. He's only got to walk across the fields.' She pointed to the east. 'He'll appreciate that when it's six foot of snow in winter.'

Olivia hadn't thought about any of that. She didn't want to be selfish and make Lachie walk further than he had to, especially in winter, but the very idea of living in that dreadful little house made her shudder with revulsion. 'I'll discuss it with Lachie.'

'Don't wait too long. Places like these go quickly as its cheap rent,' Winnie warned. 'It's a roof over your head and that's all you need.'

Olivia didn't agree. She wanted more than just a roof, she wanted a home to be proud of, clean and welcoming.

'And you know us two now,' Sadie added. 'So, that's a start.'

Olivia smiled and nodded. 'I'd best go. I've an appointment at noon.'

'*An appointment at noon*,' Winnie crooned again, making fun of her. 'You might be too posh to live here after all.'

'Leave her alone, Win.' Sadie nudged her friend in the side. 'Hopefully we'll see you again, Olivia.'

'Goodbye.' Olivia hurried out of the square and into Norton Road and glancing at the map headed down Stanley Road, before turning sharply right onto Jacob's Well Lane.

She pushed the house and Sadie and Winnie from her mind as she walked towards College Grove Road. She needed the position and hoped the family were nice. If the establishment was large enough, she might be able to get Lachie a job there as well. No matter what he said, she was determined to get him out of the pit as soon as possible.

She stopped to ask a gentleman the time and was relieved to find it was ten minutes to noon. College Grove Road was at the end of the road she was walking on and within minutes she was standing in front of the right house.

It had a brick wall along the front dividing the small overgrown garden from the footpath and road. Once through the gate, she headed up the short path to the black front door. The house was detached from its neighbours with bay windows on either side of the door. The brass door knocker needed a good polish she noticed as she knocked, and then she panicked wondering if she should have gone around to the back of the house. Of course, she should have! What had she been thinking?

When the door opened, a gentleman in a dark grey suit stood there. 'Miss Brodie?' His brown eyes registered surprise.

'Yes. I'm Miss Brodie.' Was he the butler? He was expecting her, wasn't he?

'Excellent. Punctual. Good. I'm Stephen Sheridan.'

She frowned in confusion. Stephen Sheridan was the name on the advertisement in the newspaper and who answered her letter.

He stepped back so she could enter into the hallway which had the staircase running straight up and a walkway down the side of it.

Her gaze noted immediately the sense of mustiness and slight neglect. The floor tiles of green and black diamond shapes were dull, the patterned staircase carpet worn.

'Come this way.' He led her into a front room to the left.

Olivia waited just inside the door until he indicated for her to sit on the green velvet sofa. Again, she wondered if he was the butler, but surely a butler wouldn't interview in the front room or sit on the furniture?

'Your references, Miss Brodie?' he asked, sitting down opposite her in a leather armchair.

She gave them over and looked around the room while he read them, but she was drawn back to him. He was difficult to age, with a liberal amount of grey woven into his black hair. She guessed about forty years old. He wore reading glass which he took off as he passed the references back to her. Mr Sheridan wasn't the kind of man who had the striking good looks and powerful aura of men like Captain Middleton, but there was something arresting in his features that made her want to look at him.

'So, Miss Brodie, why did you leave Hawthorn Manor?'

'The Broadbents sold up and have moved to Paris. The new owners didn't want the indoor staff.'

'How unfortunate for you. I must tell you that the position is for a housemaid, not just a parlourmaid. You will be the only employee I have.'

'I understand, sir.' Her mind spun in different directions. So, he was the master! No other staff? His voice held a slight European accent, but it was so faint she couldn't detect from where.

'And it's not a live-in position. You will arrive by seven o'clock each morning and leave by six o'clock each night, except Sundays. I will not need you on Sundays. On Saturdays, you may leave at one o'clock in the afternoon.'

'That suits me well, sir.' She thought that generous of him. Every Sunday off? She hid her smile.

'You'll not be needed at night,' his voice became tight. 'I don't entertain, therefore you have no reason to be here at night.'

'Very good, sir.' She thought it an odd thing for him to say, but didn't question it.

'The wage reflects the shortened hours. Twenty-five pounds a year. I will pay you weekly. Is that acceptable?'

'It is, sir.' She'd have liked more in her wage, considering she'd have the whole house to care for, but the trade-off was she'd have more hours to herself, something she'd never had in her life. Working five and a half days a week was an enormous difference to being at the beck and call of everyone at the manor every day, all day and night.

'I require the utmost propriety in everything, Miss Brodie.

Honesty, integrity and punctuality are important to me. I saw in your references that Mrs Hewlett wrote you have all these qualities.' He watched her intently.

'I do, sir. Mrs Hewlett would stand for nothing less.'

He nodded thoughtfully. 'Your uniform?'

'I have my uniform from Hawthorn Manor, if that suits you, sir? A striped cleaning dress for the morning and a black afternoon dress with a white apron.'

'Yes, that would work here. although I do not receive many visitors in the afternoon or at any time at all, really. I will, of course, give you an allowance for uniform once yours has become too worn or stained. Shall I show you the house?' He stood. 'A woman washes and irons my clothes and the bedding. You have no concerns regarding that. She, Mrs Oakes, collects the basket each week and returns it the week after.'

'Yes, sir.' She followed him across the hallway to the other front room which was dominated by a grand black piano. Sheet music lay strewn across the top of it and over the seat, as well as numerous flat surfaces, including two small tables, a winged-back chair and sheets of music were even on the floor.

'This is the main room I use, Miss Brodie. Please do not touch anything in here.'

She nodded slightly, so far this room needed the most of her skills.

In the two back rooms, one was a dining room, and the other room was a large storage room leading into a spacious kitchen and scullery.

'I do not have a cook, Miss Brodie. I eat out most of the time or manage to make myself tea and toast.'

She hid her astonishment at this. No wonder he was so lean. Tea and toast for a grown man?

Upstairs were four bedrooms. Two were used for storage, one bedroom was his and the other looked as though it once belonged to a woman.

'Do you live alone, sir?'

'I do. That room belonged to my mother. She died twelve months ago.' He closed the bedroom door.

'My condolences, sir.'

'Thank you.' He led the way back downstairs. 'My mother took care of the house and the maids, but once she died, I found it impossible to deal with the two maids and I asked them to leave. In my naivety, I assumed I could manage quite well by myself.' He gave a self-conscious smile, which transformed his serious face into something rather good-looking. 'I failed. The house is becoming cloaked in a covering of dust, I've no idea where things are. I forget to order coal or pay for the gas or organise for the chimney sweep to come. The garden is overgrown, and the windows have a film of something on them and I can barely see out of them, cobwebs are in the rooms I don't use and well, the list is endless...'

'Not endless, sir.' She grinned. 'I could have it sorted for you in a couple of weeks.'

'That pleases me greatly, Miss Brodie. When can you start?'

'Tomorrow?'

His shoulders dropped slightly, and a brightness entered his brown eyes. 'Perfect.'

She left the house in better spirits than she had in many weeks. She had a job, finally. Mr Sheridan seemed a nice man, if a little odd, living alone in that house like a hermit with no visitors and no staff.

She couldn't wipe the smile off her face as she walked back towards the lodging house. Now she had a position, she could afford to buy something for Lachie for his birthday. She went into a men's clothing shop and gazed about the shelves until she found a thick pair of woollen socks and a woollen vest for when the cooler weather began. The purchases depleted some of her store of coins but now both she and Lachie were working, she could spare it.

At the lodging house, Olivia helped Mrs Marsden set a table for them in the front room, the cake in pride of place in the centre and the presents beside it.

'How long should I let him sleep for?' she asked the older woman, glancing at the clock as they walked back into the kitchen.

'Give him a bit longer. He can have something to eat before he leaves. I've made a nice beef stew to line his stomach for the long night ahead.' Mrs Marsden lifted the lid of the pot, and the delicious aroma filled the room.

'Now I have this position with Mr Sheridan, I'm hoping Lachie can find something better than the pit. I had hoped he could work with me, but I'm not sure there's enough for him to do there. Mr Sheridan doesn't keep a horse and seems to live rather quietly.'

'Lass, let Lachie decide what he wants to do. He's picked the pit for now and you need to respect that. You mothering him won't help him change his mind. He's not a baby.'

'But I've a good job now. He doesn't need to be down that dangerous black hole,' she defended.

'Will you stop going on about it, Liv!' Lachie said from behind.

She spun to face him. 'I got the position, Lachie.'

He rubbed the sleepiness from his eyes. 'I'm pleased, but I'm not going to give up my job. Two wages are better than one.'

Mrs Marsden waved them out of the kitchen. 'Go and sit down, the pair of you. I'll bring out the food. Don't argue on Lachie's birthday.'

In the front room, Olivia sat opposite him. 'Did you sleep well?'

'Like the dead.' He eyed the cake. 'That looks good.'

'Here.' She handed him his presents.

'Gifts?' His shocked expression turned to a slim grin. 'I wasn't expecting anything.'

'I know, but I thought a treat wouldn't hurt.'

'These are smashing.' He held up the vest and socks. 'They'll come in handy for winter.' He wrapped them back in the brown paper. 'How was the house?'

'Awful. It's in such a poor area, Lachie. I don't want to live there.'

'But we need a home, Liv.'

'Not that one.'

'I said we'd take it. Why else would I have the keys?'

She glared at him. 'You never told me that! I thought I was only going to view it?'

Lachie shrugged as Mrs Marsden brought out bowls of stew and plates of buttered bread. 'We needed a home.'

'It's a hovel!' she grated through clenched teeth, annoyed with him for agreeing to something without discussing it with her first.

Two other lodgers entered the room and Mrs Marsden fussed over them.

Olivia lowered her voice. 'It's not somewhere we should live, Lachie. We can find somewhere better.'

'It's near the pit.' He took her hand, his eyes begging. 'Please, Liv. Can we at least try living there and see how we go? We can't keep staying here, sharing a room, and with all our stuff under a tarp in the yard.'

He had a point, of course he did, but she didn't want to live in such a place as Woodcock's Square, or any of the filthy tenement yards lurking at the end of alleyways or hidden behind public houses.

'I know you're used to living in a lovely place such as the manor but that's not our life now,' Lachie said after eating some of the stew. 'I'm a miner and you're a housemaid in town. We can't afford a nice place.'

It seemed as if overnight her baby brother had become a man. 'When did you grow up so suddenly and talk sense?'

'The day we buried our father, the day we were robbed, the day our brother left us, and the day I travelled down a black hole scared out of my wits,' he said unhappily.

Her heart broke at his words. She wanted to make him happy. 'Very well. We'll take the house, but only for a short time,' she told him. 'I will find us somewhere better to live.'

'I'll move our stuff over there tomorrow after I finish my shift in the morning.' He dunked his bread into the rich stew.

'I start work in the morning for Mr Sheridan and we need beds and furniture.'

Mrs Marsden came over to them with a pot of tea. 'Don't worry, lass. I'll help Lachie get a few things delivered. It's been grand having you here. I'll be sorry to see you go.'

Olivia sighed, that would make two of them.

CHAPTER 11

Not wanting to knock on the front door of Mr Sheridan's house, Olivia walked around to the back. She noted a large area of grass, several trees and an outbuilding which looked to once have been a stable and carriage barn.

The back door was locked, and she tutted. She'd have to knock and wake Mr Sheridan, which wasn't a great start to the day.

Abruptly the door opened. Mr Sheridan stood there, dressed in a dark blue suit but his face had a sleepy expression as though he'd recently woken. 'Miss Brodie. I realised I'd not given you a key.'

'No, sir.' She smiled and stepped into the scullery and through to the kitchen.

He wiped a hand over his damp black hair. 'Forgive me, I'm not a morning person, Miss Brodie. I work late and sleep late.'

'I'll remember that, sir.' She had no idea what work he did. As a gentleman, *working* held many different titles that was nothing close to actual work.

She took off her hat, gloves and cloak and placed them in the scullery. The kitchen needed a good clean, but she didn't know as yet where everything was.

'I was about to make some tea...' Mr Sheridan shook the kettle and put it on the hob before turning the gas on.

'Let me do it, sir.'

'Everything you'll need is in the storeroom.' He motioned to the small room leading off the kitchen. 'There's a larder in the scullery and an ice box, but I don't know when the ice man comes. I've not had any ice since Mother passed.' He sounded embarrassed at the failure. 'I used the snow in winter to keep the milk cold.'

'I'm sure I'll soon find my way around, sir.'

'Good, yes.' He rubbed his hands together, his manner awkward. 'Right. I'll leave you to get acquainted with everything.' He stepped out of the room, and she let out a breath.

In the larder she found empty marble slabs on the shelves, except one on which a covered milk jug stood and a knob of butter in a dish. She checked the milk was still useable and returned to the kitchen. Opening dresser cupboards and drawers, she found teacups and saucers, other crockery and cutlery. In the storeroom next to the kitchen, she was thankful to find a tin of tea leaves and a pot of sugar.

She found a tray and arranged the tea things on it and mashed the tea in a white porcelain teapot with a country scene painted on it. Carrying the tray, she found Mr Sheridan in the front room on the right, the piano room, as she was to call it.

'Thank you, Miss Brodie.' He stood by the window using the morning sunlight to read some notes on a piece of paper. 'You made yourself a cup as well?'

'No, sir. I'll have some later, I'd like to get started.'

'Right, of course...' He gazed about the room. 'It's in a state this house, isn't it?'

'Nothing that can't be put into order, sir.'

'The girls before you weren't very good at many things, except annoying me. They weren't discreet, telling anyone who'd listen about my private life.' He walked to the piano. 'They didn't listen to me. So, please, Miss Brodie, listen.'

'Of course, sir.'

'I have few rules, but one of them is I do not, for any reason, ever wish to find a stranger in my home. Should someone come to the door, you are to ask for their name, close the door and come and tell me. I will decide whether they are to be let in. Do you understand? I have few friends, Miss Brodie, therefore no one should enter this house unless I personally invite them in.'

'Yes, sir.' Again, she thought him a little strange.

'You are to never talk about me to your own family and friends. I am a very private person.'

She nodded. 'Very good, sir.'

'Thank you. Close the door behind you, please. I don't wish to be disturbed.'

'Breakfast, sir?'

'I don't often eat breakfast, Miss Brodie.'

'Yes, sir.' In the hallway, she took a deep breath. He was an odd fish, but what did she care? He'd employed her to clean his home, and that's what she'd do.

She started in the kitchen. She washed the window and took down the lace curtain to soak it in a bucket of soapy water. While the curtain soaked, she wiped down all the surfaces, continually rinsing her cloths as the muck and grime of months of cooking, smoking fires and neglect had gone untouched. Had the former maids done any work?

She gave the central table a good scrub and then cleaned all the larder shelves and the cold marble slabs. With the sun shining she hung the curtain out on the line that stretched across the grass, before tackling the outside of the kitchen window.

Returning to the kitchen, she smiled at the light streaming in.

Suddenly, the notes of the piano echoed down the hallway. She stood and listened for a moment. The music was soft, tender.

Mr Sheridan played beautifully. Abruptly the music stopped. A second later she heard odd notes being played and then silence. The sequence was repeated, then a few minutes of playing. She found she liked to work with the music in the background.

After a refreshing cup of tea, she sorted out the dresser cupboards, familiarising herself with its contents. The fine bone china dinner service, the recipe books, stationery, old invoices for butchers and grocers and she sorted through drawers full of items like a ball of string, matches, scissors, a pot of glue, pins, pencils, a notepad and many other useful items.

A trip down to the cellar showed her that it too was in a sorry state of neglect. Coal had spilled across the slate floor, old vegetables lay forgotten and rotten in sacks and barrels, half-eaten by mice.

The hours went by in a haze of steaming water and faltering music.

A little gold carriage clock on the mantel above the gas range chimed four o'clock, and she wondered where the day had gone. Fetching the curtain back inside and pleased to find it dry, she stood on a stool and threaded it back along the rod to hang it in place.

'Gracious, Miss Brodie, do be careful.' Mr Sheridan came into the kitchen, dressed for outdoors and wearing a hat. 'Do you need my help?'

'No, sir, thank you. It's all done.'

'You're taller than most women, so I imagine that can be beneficial to you for such tasks as that?' He carried a wad of envelopes.

'Indeed, sir.' She smiled, stepping down off the stool.

'I'm about to go out to run some errands and then I'll have something to eat somewhere. No doubt you'll be gone by the time I return.' He gazed about the spotless kitchen, all shiny and smelling fresh. 'You've transformed this room.'

'I'm not finished, there's the floor to mop yet. I'll do it before I leave.'

'Take these keys to lock up.' He placed a ring of two keys on the table. 'Front door and back door.'

'Thank you, sir.'

'I'll see you tomorrow.' He nodded and went back into the hallway.

When she heard the front door close, Olivia sat down at the table. Her feet ached from being on them for hours. Her stomach grumbled for she'd not eaten all day and there was no food in the house. She'd have to bring something to eat with her as Mr Sheridan had no clue of her needs.

By five o'clock the floors in the kitchen and scullery were washed and she spent the next hour tidying away the cleaning items she'd used throughout the day and making sure the kitchen was in the best condition for when Mr Sheridan came in later. She set out a tea tray on the table with everything at his disposal, all he needed to do was boil the kettle should he wish to make a cup of tea in the evening.

Going through to the front door she locked it with the key and then paused at the state of the piano room. If possible, it looked even more cluttered and messy than this morning. What did he do in there all day? She itched to sort it, but knew it wasn't Mr Sheridan's wish and so she walked back down to the kitchen. Tomorrow, she'd start organising the storeroom.

Outside on the road, the setting sun cast long shadows. She didn't hurry to Woodcock's Square. She was in no rush to start living in that awful house. Lachie would have left for his shift at the pit by now and she wasn't eager to spend the evening and night alone in a strange place.

She passed two men loitering on the corner, they watched her go by with narrowed eyes. She quickened her step when they began to follow her. Luckily, a couple were walking ahead of her, and she hurried along to walk a few spaces behind them. When she looked over her shoulder for the men, they were gone.

Not knowing enough about which backstreets to take, she followed Mrs Marsden's map and walked up to Eastmoor Road which would take her Stanley Road, from there she knew Norton Road and then Woodcock's Square. One day she'd not need the map, she was sure.

Her feet were throbbing by the time she reached the square. In the dim light of dusk, she walked across the cobbles to number seven. Some children still played outside but mostly the inhabitants had gone indoors.

'Here, Olivia,' Sadie called, coming out of her door at number five. 'Your brother left me the keys for you.' She gave Olivia the keys.

'Oh, yes. I never thought of that. Thank you.' Olivia unlocked her door and let it swing open.

'He's a nice lad, your brother. He was here with a cart of all your stuff. He was talking to my Gerry, and they took your beds and drawers upstairs.'

'Beds? Drawers?' She gasped. 'Where did he get those from?'

'A furniture shop on Northgate, apparently.'

'We don't have money for that!' Shocked, Olivia wished Lachie was here to explain it all.

'Your brother got it on tick.'

'Tick?' she repeated then it dawned 'On credit?'

'Aye.'

Shock turned to anger. Now they were in debt to a furniture shop!

'Your Lachie and my Gerry left together for their shift at the pit. I said I'd wait for you to come and give you the keys. Though no one in this square would have stolen anything. I've kept an eye on it for you.'

'We don't have much to steal.' She peeked into the room. The grubbiness of the front room made her shiver. Mould on the ceiling, murky-coloured walls and a filthy floor. It was the last thing she needed to see after cleaning all day.

'You'll get used to it,' Sadie encouraged. 'You'll make it nice.'

'How is that even possible?' Olivia murmured. She glanced back at Sadie. 'Thanks again. Goodnight.'

'Night. If you need anything, just knock.'

Olivia closed the door and leant against it. Lachie had piled their things in the corner. In the kitchen she saw he'd pulled out the kettle and placed it on the gas hob with a box of matches. Did they even have gas? She turned the knob and found they did have gas. She could have hot water to wash if nothing else. The empty kitchen was depressing, so she went back into the front room and found a note on the top of the crates and also the invoice from the furniture shop stating the amount of each repayment.

Dear Liv,

Sorry I didn't get a chance to sort things out. I slept late and then went into town to get beds for us. Don't be mad that it's on credit, we needed beds. Mrs Marsden gave us a hamper of food to start us off.

See you in the morning,
Lachie.
The neighbours are nice.

She sighed at his note. He was excited to be here. Why she didn't know. It was nothing like the lovely cottage they were brought up in.

Noticing the basket, she opened it to find tea leaves, sugar, bread, butter, plum jam and the rest of Lachie's cake.

Starving, Olivia carried the basket into the kitchen and made tea, before opening some of the other crates. She was so glad they brought a good deal of things from their cottage. She had her mam's dinner service, plain white porcelain, but also the brown earthenware teapot, cutlery, pots and pans, cloths, scrubbing brushes, soap, a tin bucket and candles with the iron candlesticks their father made for their mam.

Eating a jam sandwich and sipping her black tea, she leant against the sink, for they didn't have a table or chairs, and gazed around the kitchen. The walls and floor needed a good scrub, more so than Mr Sheridan's did, and it could use a new coat of paint. No curtains hung at the little window overlooking the bleak backyard. The whole house lacked any form of comfort or niceties. It would take money and work to make this hovel a liveable and comfortable home.

After having a wash using the rest of the hot water, she packed away the food into a large tin, knowing that mice would devour it if she didn't, and climbed the stairs.

In each bedroom was a single iron bed, mattress and a set of wooden drawers, all basic and unadorned. Lachie had placed bedding at the end of each bed, sheets and blankets from their cottage. She gently touched the quilted blanket on her bed, the one made of knitted squares in shades of pink and green that her mam had made her when she was a child. Lachie had one similar in blue and Stu's was in shades of red and orange.

Sitting on the bed, a wave of sadness and longing came over her like a tide. She missed her mam, her father, even Stu, but most of all she missed her former life. Happiness for her had been the manor, the staff, visiting her family, cleaning the cottage, listening to Father's stories of his clients, or sewing up a hole in Lachie's trousers. She missed the routine of the manor, gossiping with Flora, admiring the beautiful pieces of furniture after she'd polished them. She missed Mrs Hewlett's guidance, Mr Skinner's quiet authority and Mrs Digby's wonderful food.

All of it was gone, and along with it was Captain Middleton, the man who'd crept into her heart, her mind, and who she'd never see again.

Tears fell as she made Lachie's bed and then her own. She

changed into her nightgown and turn off the light. She cried for her family, for her situation as she lay in the cold unfamiliar bed.

As she drifted to sleep, she wondered what Captain Middleton was doing at that moment. Remembering his smile gave her the only comfort she had.

* * *

In Belfast, Spencer sat at his desk reading correspondence from his grandmama. The tiny office in his barracks could barely fit a desk and chair, but it afforded him some privacy. He'd been excited to see a letter waiting for him, hoping it was from Mrs Bean with news about Olivia, but as soon as he saw the French postmark he knew it was from his grandmama.

Weeks ago, he'd written to Mrs Bean, hoping she'd heard news of Olivia, but no reply had returned. He was becoming frustrated at not hearing anything and worried that as time went on Olivia would forget about him and meet someone else. A woman as beautiful as her wouldn't stay single for long once out in the world. He was concerned how she was faring away from the safety of the manor and alone with only her younger brother in a strange town.

He moved his arm to place his gran's letter in a drawer and the ache from his wound reminded him again of how close to death he'd been when two nights ago he'd been shot at. He never expected to be in serious danger in the streets of Belfast, yes there was unrest, but he hadn't considered it a threat to his life. He'd been foolish to think so.

The door opened and Alfred Dunbar walked in, a fellow captain. 'Evening, Spencer.'

'Alfred. I didn't know you were back from Dublin?'

'Just arrived.'

'How was it?' Spencer stood and shook his hand.

'No picnic, but then I've heard neither has it been a barrel of laughs here?' He raised his eyebrows at Spencer. 'Got nicked, did you?'

He shrugged, not wanting to make a big deal about the shooting. 'A mere scratch.'

'That's not what I heard.' Alfred sat on the edge of the desk and Spencer regained his seat.

'A flesh wound. Nothing but a bandage required.' Spencer grinned, tapping his upper arm where the bullet had scraped his muscle.

'And a tale to be told, apparently?' Alfred laughed. 'You faced an angry horde and lived.'

'Hardly a horde,' he joked. 'Five men, drunk and looking for a fight.'

'They had guns,' Alfred said becoming serious. 'And they used them. They weren't as drunk as you say they were. I've read the report. It was a coordinated attack.'

'I was in the wrong place at the wrong time.' He was tired of talking about it. He'd made his report and spoken to his commanding officers many times about the incident two nights ago. The five men he faced had been drinking, but they'd also purposely followed him as he walked along a darkened street. Fear and training had given him courage to face them, to try and talk them out of using their guns, or taking him hostage, but afterwards as he sat in a hospital bed receiving six stitches, he'd held his head in his hands and wondered if it was all worth it.

'The Ulster Volunteer Force have created some tension I gather?' Albert said, speaking of the tense situation of the UVF landing guns and ammunition in Larne in April, arms provided by Germany.

'It's a powder keg ready for a match,' Spencer replied.

'Can the police handle it, do you think?'

'I hope they can, and we can stay out of it.' He had no wish to face the local population of men, women and children in a stand-off. Innocent people usually got killed when that happened. He'd seen it in South Africa and in India.

The door opened again and their commanding officer, Todridge, stood in the doorway. 'Gentlemen.'

'Sir.' Both Spencer and Alfred stood and saluted.

'Middleton. Dunbar.' Todridge pulled out a sheet of paper from his jacket pocket.

'Sir.' Spencer stood to attention.

'The regiment is wanted in England.' He gave them the papers.

Spencer read the official orders. 'We've only been in Ireland for two weeks.'

'I'm only following orders the same as you, Middleton. We're to be in England by Sunday. See that it happens. All the details are in the orders.'

'Yes, sir.'

Once Todridge had left, Alfred pocketed the letter. 'You don't seem too pleased?'

'I am, of course.' Spencer forced lightness to his voice. 'But something seems odd about this, don't you think?'

'You think trouble is brewing elsewhere.'

'Has to be.'

'Europe or one of the colonies?'

'My money is on Europe.' Spencer sighed deeply.

Alfred peered at him. 'I've known you a long time, Spence. You've not been the same since we left England. What's wrong?' Alfred opened a drawer in the cabinet and brought out a bottle of Scotch and two glasses. 'Has the bloom fallen off the army rose?'

'Something like that.'

'Soldiering has been your life. What's changed?'

'Me, I suppose.' He accepted the glass and sipped at the whiskey, embracing the burn at the back of his throat.

'Talk to me,' Alfred encouraged. 'Did that skirmish two nights ago shake you up?'

'Naturally, it did. I was close to having a coffin made for me.'

He thought again of how he'd managed to escape that wet and dark street with five men braying for his blood as they chased him.

'You've outrun bullets before.'

'True.'

'What happened in England before you left? I know you've lost your manor but has something else happened?'

'I met someone,' he blurted out, not meaning to mention it.

Alfred grinned. 'Now we're getting to the root of the problem.'

'But she's disappeared from my life. I lost her.'

'Dead?' Alfred stared in shock.

'No, she was a member of staff at the manor. She lost her position and moved away before I had a chance to ask her to write to me.'

'I see…' Alfred said thoughtfully. 'A love lost.'

'I don't know how to find her when I don't even know where she is.'

'Difficult, yes, but not impossible.'

Spencer swallowed another mouthful of the fiery drink. 'Any suggestions?'

'Do you have any idea where she might be?'

'Maybe in Wakefield, Huddersfield, Leeds, who knows where she has found work.'

'A needle in a haystack situation.' Alfred nodded. 'Put a notice in some of the newspapers?'

'And say what? I'm looking for a parlourmaid called Olivia Brodie?'

'It's a start.'

'Do you know the kind of irrational people who will reply saying they are Olivia?'

Alfred tapped his chin. 'I get your point.'

'You've been a great help.' Spencer grinned with a shake of his head.

'By Sunday you'll be back in England, which is better than being in Ireland. You might find the time to get away and visit some of those places.'

'How will that help? Shall I roam the streets shouting her name?' he mocked.

'Well, with that negative attitude you're not going to get far, are you?' Alfred poured them another drink. 'Is this girl worth such misery?'

Spencer thought of Olivia's smile, the way she laughed at her brothers, the love in her eyes for her father and the intense way she'd looked at him. 'Yes. She's worth it.'

'Then hire a private inquiry agent. My aunt used one in her divorce last year. Caused a colossal scandal in our family. My mother refused to talk to my aunt because of it, but my aunt didn't care. The agent found out that my aunt's husband had a mistress in Brighton and two children. It took the agent five months to get all the evidence my aunt needed. Cost a small fortune as well.'

'It sounds so underhanded…' Spence murmured, deep in thought.

'The alternative is an advertisement in the newspapers and crazy women writing to you pretending to be your girl.' Alfred laughed. 'It's the price we pay for love.'

'How would you know? You don't have a girl.'

'I pay in other ways, if you get my meaning.'

Spencer laughed. 'I do get your meaning and the stink of perfume when you return from visiting the brothel.'

They both laughed and Spencer felt slightly better of heart. Soon, he'd be back in England and closer to Olivia, wherever she was.

CHAPTER 12

After working a Saturday half day at Mr Sheridan's house, Olivia locked the back door and walked around to the front. Mr Sheridan had gone out, and she'd left him cold cuts of meat for his supper. Mr Sheridan had given her wages for the first week she'd done, telling her he'd pay her every Saturday. So far, he seemed impressed with her work.

This morning, she had cleaned and organised the front room while Mr Sheridan spent most of the time writing letters, and he wrote a great deal, or playing the piano in the other room. Music filled the house most days, and she'd enjoyed listening to it. Mr Sheridan was an excellent player. She'd taken a tea tray into him at noon, not wanting to disturb him, but he'd simply given her a nod and continued to play. At one clock he came out of the room and gave her the wages owed and told her he'd see her on Monday morning.

Walking along Eastmoor Road, she noticed the same two men sitting on a garden wall as they often did. She assumed they lived around here. Yet, when they fell into step behind, her hackles rose. She walked quicker, but so did they. Heart beating fast, she half ran, half walked, fear inching up her spine.

'We don't want to scare you, lass,' one of the men called.

Stifling a scream, Olivia burst into a sprint. Terror squeezed her lungs as she ran as fast as she could to the corner shop, where she slammed in through the door, startling the customer and proprietor.

'Ye Gods!' A woman sagged against the counter. 'You nearly gave me a stroke, so you did!'

'I'm sorry.' Olivia peeked out of the large window, hiding behind a display. The men were gone as far as she could see.

'What was that all about?' The shopkeeper came to Olivia's side.

'Two men were chasing after me.'

'What in the world!' The shopkeeper flung open his door and stared up and down the street. 'I can't see anyone now, lass.' He peered at her. 'You've been in here before. You're new around here, aren't you?'

'Yes, sir.'

'It's Mr Whittaker, lass. Come and sit down for a bit.'

'Thank you.' She gladly sat on a wooden chair he provided.

The woman gathered her groceries. 'What is happening to society when a young lass can't walk down a perfectly normal street, I ask you?'

'I'm sorry to cause trouble,' Olivia said as Mr Whittaker brought her a glass of water.

'It's no trouble at all, lass.'

'We need the constables patrolling more often if our streets aren't safe in broad daylight,' the woman scoffed angrily. 'I fear walking home, Mr Whittaker, I really do.'

'You live two doors away, Mrs Upwood. I'm sure you'll be fine.' He walked out with her despite his words, before returning to Olivia. 'I can walk you home, lass, if you want?'

'I'm sure I'll be fine, now.' She sipped her water, her hands shaking holding the glass.

'Where do you live?'

'Woodcock's Square.'

'Well, Stanley Road is busy so you'll be safe. Stay close to people until you reach home.'

She handed him the glass. 'You've been very kind, Mr Whittaker.'

'Do you need anything while you're here?'

She nodded, forcing her scattered wits to think of the shopping she needed.

Twenty minutes later, she turned into Woodcock's Square, carrying the food she'd bought at Whittaker's shop.

'Olivia!' one of the children playing on the cobbles called out to her. 'Want to skip with me?'

'No, sorry. I'm tired after being at work,' she told the little girl, who held a piece of old rope. She understood the girl belonged to the Muldoon family at number ten. She'd met Mr Muldoon briefly yesterday morning on her way to work as he was going to his job at the printers.

She'd been living at number seven for a week and hated every moment of it. She hadn't seen Lachie for days as they were like ships passing in the night. On an evening, he'd gone to the pit before she got home, and she'd left in the morning before he got in.

But she'd see him this afternoon when he woke from sleeping and before he left for his shift and tomorrow was Sunday and she had the day off with Lachie, who also had time off. It was weird living in the strange, empty house knowing that Lachie lived there too but she'd not seen him in days.

Stopping at her door, she pulled out her key and inserted it into the lock. Next to her, the door to number eight opened and an older, plump woman came out. Olivia nodded at her in greeting.

'You're the new lass, Lachie's sister,' the woman stated with a friendly smile, her hair in rag curlers and wearing a large apron over her dress.

'I am.'

'I've been trying to see you and say welcome. But you're as slippery as an eel, impossible to catch. You're hardly home. Sadie and Winnie tell me you're nice enough though. Lachie says you work on College Grove Road.' The woman looked about fifty with a dimpled smile. 'I'm Tess, Tess Hobson. Me husband is Larry. He and my lads work at Park Hill with your brother, and Sadie's Gerry.'

'Pleased to meet you, Mrs Hobson.'

'Nay, lass, call me Tess. There's no formality around here.'

'And I'm Olivia,' she replied graciously.

'Your Lachie isn't here, by the way, he's gone to work early and asked me to tell you.'

Disappointment dropped her shoulders. She'd been hoping to spend some time with him before his shift. She didn't fancy being in the house alone after those two men chased her. 'Why has he gone early?'

'For the money, lass. Why else would he go there? Let me give you a hand.' Tess took one of the string bags from Olivia and followed her inside. 'Hell's teeth, lass, you've got nowt, have you?' Tess stared around the empty front room. 'Not a sofa to sit on.'

'No, not yet. We can't afford one.' She went through to the kitchen and placed the bag on the counter next to the sink, noticing that Lachie had cleared the top of the crates they used as a temporary table and stool.

'You need to do something about that, lass. It's no way to live. No wonder your brother sits outside on a crate most of the time.'

Lachie sits outside? Why isn't he in bed asleep during the day?

Tess placed the bag beside the other one. 'I was talking to your Lachie earlier, or trying to, before he left for the pit. He'd been outside dozing in the sun. He says you're a housemaid.'

'Yes.'

'You've recently lost your father and a position at a big house in the country as well. That must have been tough.'

Olivia nodded, annoyed Lachie had been telling all and sundry about their lives.

'Never mind, you'll soon get used to living here.'

Again, Olivia very much doubted it.

'Your Lachie is quiet though, isn't he? Talking to him was as much fun as pulling teeth.'

Olivia frowned. 'He's usually loud. Always talking and whistling, running and yelling.'

'He was sullen today. Perhaps just tired. It's not easy learning a new trade and the hours are long. Night shift is the worst, so my Larry says.'

Worry filled Olivia. Was Lachie just tired? Or sick? She felt guilty for not seeing him for days, not being able to care for him, or to see for herself how he was coping working down that black hole.

Tess touched a wall. 'You've got damp, but then don't we all? It's not too bad in the warmer months but in winter it's a disgrace. Let Ezra know, he's in number three.'

'I don't know him.' Olivia began unpacking the string bags, placing the food she'd bought on the wooden counter next to the sink. All she could think about was those two men. Why were they waiting for her? What did they want?

Tess inspected the cupboards as she talked. 'Ezra is the square's handyman, and thank the Lord for him, too, for the landlord doesn't care about the upkeep of this square. Ezra will do any odd jobs on the building that you can't do yourself. He's at the pit, too. A lovely man widowed young. He's been on his own for fifteen years. He says no one will replace his wife in his heart so he's better off being alone. You'll meet everyone else in the square before long. There's only ten houses so we're all like one big family, really.'

She had no desire to meet any more people.

'Mam?' a youth called from the front door. 'Mam? You in here?'

'Aye, Colin,' Tess called back. 'I can't escape them for five minutes.'

A lanky lad with dark hair ambled into the kitchen. 'What's for tea?'

'Where's your manners, lad? Say hello to Olivia.'

The boy blushed bright red and mumbled some words.

'Lordy, these kids of mine.' Tess rolled her eyes. 'Get back home. I'll be along in a minute.'

'How many children do you have?' Olivia asked, not knowing why she wanted to know. There seemed to be dozens of children in the square at any given time, day or night.

'Five. Five boys. I've birthed eight but lost three along the way.' Tess lifted one shoulder, but Olivia could see the flash of pain the admission brought her.

'Are they still at home with you?'

'Three are, but Lance the eldest is in the army and Simon is in the navy. No idea why two of my boys wanted to join the forces, it's never happened in my family before, but they both said they weren't going down the pit like their dad.'

At the mention of the army, Olivia thought immediately of Spencer Middleton and a pang of longing filled her. Those brief special days in his company seemed a lifetime ago now.

Tess opened the back door, idly looking out. 'My other three boys have followed their father though and are down the pit. Colin, who you just met, is the youngest, he's sixteen and Jonnie and Jules are eighteen and nineteen. You'll meet them before long.' She closed the door. 'Right, I'd best get back and feed my lot.' Tess rolled her eyes, but Olivia could see she didn't mind at all.

'Thank you for calling in.' Olivia walked with her to the front door.

'Nay, it's what we do here. In and out of each other's houses like one big family. Knock if you need owt, lass.'

Olivia closed the door, securing the lock, and faced the empty room. None of this felt like home or one big family. They were strangers to her and this place nothing but a roof over her head for the time being.

In the kitchen, she made some hot chocolate and toasted some sliced bread. She was too tired to do anything else. Working at Mr Sheridan's was much harder than at Hawthorn Manor. At the manor she only had a certain number of rooms to care for, and they had been diligently looked after for years so there wasn't the intense deep cleaning and organising, unlike Mr Sheridan's unkempt house. Each of his rooms needed attention and hours of work to bring them up to the standard that satisfied her.

She was desperate to have a proper good wash, but they didn't have a tin bath, just the bucket. While the water heated, she leant against the sink and eyed the distasteful room. Would this Ezra person give it all a good paint? How much would it cost? Her wages covered the rent and food, but they'd have to use Lachie's wages for gas and coal and to pay the furniture shop. Could their money stretch to paint the walls or even buy a table?

She saw a pile of filthy clothes covered in coal dust by the back door. She had to do the washing as well, which would mean lighting the fire beneath the copper boiler and heating water in it to soak the clothes. Lachie's filthy workwear needed a good bashing to get most of the coal dust off them and so couldn't be washed with her clothes. She didn't have an iron for her uniform, either.

Overwhelmed, she ran out the back door and buried her face in her hands as the sobs broke from her chest. She missed her old home, her father, the manor and the people there. She missed living in clean rooms, surrounded by beautiful furniture and delicate ornaments and striking paintings. At the manor she didn't have to worry about where her food came from, she simply walked into the dining room and ate whatever Mrs Digby had cooked. At her family's cottage she made simple fare her mam taught her to make, stews and pies, and she did it in a nice kitchen surrounded by her mother's things.

Here she had none of that. This dreadful place was damp, it smelt awful, she had strangers just on the other side of the walls, banging about, there was danger just walking home from her work, not to mention the constant threat of Lachie being injured, of having enough money to pay their bills and eat. It was all too much!

She sobbed harder, distraught, wishing she was back at home.

'Hey, lass.' Tess was suddenly patting her shoulder, the back gate swinging open. 'What's all this then? I heard you crying as I brought in the washing.'

'I can't do it,' she wailed.

'Do what?'

'Be here, live *here!*' She cried harder, wishing her father held her, or Spencer.

'Nay, it's not so bad once you're used to it, love. It'll just take some time, that's all.'

'I hate it!'

'Course you do, lass. It's all new and different. Look, come next door with me and we'll have a cup of tea.' Tess wrapped an arm around Olivia's shoulders and led her out of her tiny yard and into her own.

All the houses were the same layout, and Tess took her into her kitchen and sat her at the table. 'Sit there, lovely, and I'll mash some tea. You, Colin, get out and tell your dad to stay in the front room.'

Embarrassed, Olivia raised her head and saw Colin leaving the table.

'I don't want to disturb you.' Olivia made to rise.

'No, lass, sit down. They've had something to eat and can be out of my way for a bit. They'll be off for their shift shortly.' Tess tidied away an open newspaper from the table.

Olivia gazed around the kitchen, amazed at how different it

was to her own. Tess has a narrow dresser against one wall, filled with plates and cups and bowls. All the walls were painted green and held multiple timber shelves, stacked with books, ornaments, candlesticks, jugs and colourful tins and all sorts of knick-knacks.

A red-and-black patterned rug covered the floor, and the chairs were solid wood. An embroidered cream tablecloth covered the table and on top of that was a small waterproof cover in blue. The range was black-leaded to a shine and held numerous iron pots. The copper in the corner steamed with soaking clothes and on the windowsill was a vase holding wilting wildflowers. The clean window and the pretty lace curtain added to the prettiness of the room. Although cramped, and none of the furniture or crockery matched, the kitchen appeared clean and lived in, cared for, despite hosting a large family.

Tess poured out the tea. 'We ain't got much, lass, no one around here has, but we make do. I might not live in a fancy house, but my kids are happy, and healthy and I'm married to a good man. Sometimes, that's all you need. Everything else… well, that's just icing on a cake, isn't it?'

Shame washed over her. 'You must think of me as a spoilt madam.'

'Never. I just see a lass who's had some shocks lately and is stumbling a bit.' Tess sipped her tea. 'It won't always be like this, you know?'

Her bottom lip quivered. 'I don't see a way of changing it. We've got nothing.'

'Not true, my lovely. You and your brother have each other. You're got good health and seem clever. Both of you have jobs, and that's a smashing bit of good luck. You'll work it out. And now you've got me, I'll help you.' Tess smiled and patted Olivia's hand. 'I think you need a hug more than anything.' Tess pulled her into her arms.

Fresh tears spurted into her eyes, and she held onto Tess, a stranger, like she was a life raft.

'Right, first things first.' Tess sat back on her chair. 'Some advice, whether you take it or leave it.' She grinned. 'Keep your boiler going. Coal is cheap, Lachie can get some sacks of it from the pit top. Have his clothes soaking for a couple of days. They'll never be clean, but it'll help to get most of the muck off. Wash your clothes separately on the other days.' Tess turned to shout out the door. 'Colin!'

A moment later, Colin came in. 'Aye, Mam?'

'Get some of that rope out of the cellar and make a washing line for Olivia, will you? Make two lines.'

'Rightio.' Colin ventured down to the cellar.

'I don't want him to think he has to. I can do it,' Olivia offered, as Colin disappeared out of the back door carrying rope, nails and a hammer.

'He can do it. He's good at things like that and he's nowt to do while he waits to go to work. If I don't keep him busy, he'll only mess about with his mates and get into trouble. Next, you need furniture. You're living in an empty shell, lass, that's dispiriting if nowt else.' Tess held up her hand. 'I know you've not got a lot of money, but in Brook Street, near the market hall, there's an old Irishman, O'Shea, who sells bits and pieces of just about everything. You'll be able to get stuff from him for pennies. So, do you have a few spare shillings?'

She hesitated. 'I got paid today. Seven shillings and six pence.'

'Good. You've put money aside for the rent for next week?'

'I have, yes. Three shillings. I spent another shilling on food.'

Tess nodded wisely. 'Good, lass. Always have your rent money kept to one side of your spending. You can live without a lot of food, but you don't want to live without a roof over your head. Right, let's go shopping.'

'But it's getting late.'

'We've a couple of hours yet before the shops shut.'

Within a few minutes, Olivia had donned her hat and gloves and met Tess out the front.

'Where are you two off to?' Sadie asked, standing at her front door.

'Shopping.' Tess gave Larry a kiss and waved off her husband and sons as they headed for the pit. 'Do you need owt, Sadie?'

'Nah, thanks though. If I'd not just finished my shift, I'd come with you, but I'm dead on my feet. My machine at the mill broke down and I've had to work extra hours to make up my wage.'

'Next time.' Tess smiled. 'Let's go, Olivia lass.'

'Where are we going first?' She was nervous yet oddly excited by the shopping adventure with Tess. After those two men chasing her, this was something to wipe away that dread.

'We'll go to O'Shea's, he's the furniture fella, then we'll visit the market. You've been buying food from shops, haven't you?'

'Yes, Whittaker's Grocers on Eastmoor Road.' She followed Tess through a series of streets she'd never been down before.

'No more, lass. From now on only buy from the market and haggle the price. Buy enough to last several days, store it all down in the cellar in tins. The food is fresher and cheaper at the market and will go further, understand?'

'I think so.'

'That said, use Sanderson's butchers on Stanley Road, they're a good family. Place your order for the week and just pop in on your way home each day to pick up that day's portion of meat. Same with the milkman, Kenny, he's called.'

'I never see these people, Tess. I'm away early and home late.' Olivia realised they were getting close to the centre of town and the noise of the traffic grew louder.

'I'll speak with Kenny then. Open you an account. You'll pay him at the end of each week.'

'Thank you.'

A short time later they were on Brook Street and the activity of the outside market stalls only matched those inside. However,

Tess steered her away from the market and along to a shop that was crammed with every conceivable household goods Olivia could imagine. Chairs hung from rods in the ceiling, sets of drawers were piled in tall towers, cluttered aisles, narrow and long, went from front to back of the building like a rabbit warren.

Olivia stared in awe at the tremendous amount of furniture.

'A table, two chairs to start with,' Tess stated, peering at the chaos.

'How does anyone find anything in here?' Olivia's shoulder brushed against a stack of bedside tables, nearly sending them toppling.

'Patience and good luck,' Tess joked. 'Here we are.' She squeezed herself between two huge wardrobes. 'I spy tables on that other aisle.'

Despite her earlier gloomy mood, Olivia soon was caught up in Tess's enthusiasm. They found a square wooden table, scratched on the legs and on the top.

'Don't worry about scratches. You can polish them out,' Tess advised, then laughed. 'Why am I telling you that? You're a parlourmaid, you'll know all about that.'

Olivia grinned, feeling lighter in spirit. 'Polishing is something I do know well.'

The old man who owned the shop finished talking with another man and came over. Tess started telling him what they needed and pointed out the state of the table. She bargained with him and Olivia sensed both Tess and the old man liked the challenge of the haggle.

'Listen, Mr O'Shea, we aren't here for pianos and fancy four-poster beds,' Tess told him. 'We need practical things, and we've not got a lot of money.'

'Isn't that the story of my life now?' he replied in a strong Irish accent. 'You'll be wanting the moon and the stars for a penny next.'

'Aye, we might,' Tess warned. 'But we'll start with this terrible table and take it off your hands for five pence.'

'Five pence? Are you mad, woman?'

'We want two chairs to go with it.' Tess looked around and pointed. 'Those two are fine.'

'And are you wanting them for free now, is it?' O'Shea tutted.

'Aye, we will if you're offering.' Tess marched on. 'A sofa, Mr O'Shea.'

'Sure, and you'll be the death of me, woman,' he grumbled following her.

Olivia had never seen anything like it. She trailed Tess as her neighbour pointed to certain things, rarely checking with Olivia to see if she actually wanted it or not.

An hour later, Olivia parted with two shillings and eight pence, but she suspected Tess had given him some money as well but couldn't be sure.

'I'll have it all delivered in a couple of hours once I close the shop.' O'Shea waved them away.

Olivia glanced at Tess as they crossed the road and into the indoor market. 'I've four pence left.' Her stomach swooped that her wage had been spent in one day.

'Aye, don't worry, lass. Lachie will have been paid yesterday, won't he? The pit pays wages on Fridays.'

Olivia didn't know that. She'd not seen Lachie to ask him.

'These are the stalls I use.' Tess gestured to several vegetable stalls as they walked. 'Their quality is better than others.'

Growing tired, Olivia listened and absorbed Tess's information, hoping she'd remember it all.

Finally, they headed home as the sun began to set.

Sadie was sitting on a chair outside her front door chatting to Winnie and a thick-set, dark-haired man as they entered the square. 'You've been gone ages,' Sadie said.

'The poor lass needed a lot.' Tess stopped to chat. 'Ezra, we'll need you when the cart arrives from O'Shea's.'

'Aye, Tess, I can help.' His eyes never left Olivia's face. 'We've not met. Ezra Swan.' He held out his hand.

'Olivia Brodie.' She shook his hand.

'Stop looking at her like you want to eat her, Ezra.' Sadie chuckled. 'She's too pretty for the likes of you.'

'She's too pretty for the likes of anyone around here,' he scoffed in a teasing way.

Uncomfortable, Olivia headed for her own door just as the cart full of furniture arrived.

'Here we are then.' Tess ordered everyone to grab an item from the back of the cart.

Mr Muldoon, coming home from work, stopped to give them a hand and his wife, Jill, joined in.

Soon Olivia's front room was stacked with furniture. A horsehair sofa in faded red damask and with two wobbly legs sat against one wall. An equally faded chair in cracked leather and missing several studs joined it. A worn rug, its pattern totally washed-out, was laid in front of the hearth.

In the kitchen, Ezra and Mr Muldoon placed the table and chairs and used a piece of wood found in the back alley to prop up one of the table legs to stop it shaking on the uneven tiles.

Sadie put the tin bath outside the back door while Mrs Muldoon brought in a wicker washing basket and a tin of wooden pegs. Winnie carried in a small round table that she positioned next to the sofa.

'You need some shelves in here, Olivia,' Ezra said. 'It needs a good paint as well. I can make a start on that tomorrow if you'd like? As long as you're not fussy on the colour?'

'What colours do you have?' she asked.

'Whitewash and whitewash.' He grinned.

'Then whitewash will be fine.' She smiled back. 'Only I can't pay you yet, not until next week when I get paid again.'

'I don't need payment.' His eyes were kind. 'If you and Lachie give me a hand, it's less I have to do, and if you keep supplying me with cups of tea and maybe a beef sandwich during the day, even better.'

'That I can do, Mr Swan.'

'Ezra,' he prompted.

'Ezra,' she agreed.

'Watch out, Olivia, he'd have you in a church and married to him before autumn,' Winnie teased.

Ezra turned away.

Olivia blushed. 'I'm not ready for any of that.' It annoyed her that Winnie was quick to jibe, turning something nice into something awkward.

'Thanks everyone for your help,' Tess announced, shooing them all outside. 'Olivia needs to settle her things about her properly.'

Olivia gazed around at these people, none she knew very well, some she had only just met minutes ago and was amazed at their offering to help her. 'Thank you. I appreciate you all helping me,' she said to each person as they left.

Alone with Tess, Olivia didn't know how to express her gratitude to the dear woman.

'Now then, lass, feeling better?'

'A lot better. Still overwhelmed but in a different way. Your kindness means a lot to me.'

'We're neighbours, lass, for better or worse, like a marriage.' Tess laughed, then grew serious. 'You've got a friend in me for life now. You're not alone. You'll be fine, lass, I know it.' Tess patted her arm as she left.

Olivia desperately wanted to trust in that. She gazed about the front room. Yes, it was still ugly, still not her home, but it could be if she let it. But not in this current state.

In the kitchen she stood, hands on hips, and surveyed the room. What else did she have to do this evening but make a start on the cleaning? She'd start with lighting the boiler and soaking Lachie's clothes.

For now, this place was her future, for Lachie's sake she had to make it comfortable. She had her memories of her former home, of when her family was whole, of the contentment at the manor, but that was in the past.

She'd take it one step at a time, one day at a time, and if the thoughts of a handsome officer kept her company as she worked, she'd allow it. Spencer Middleton was her secret, and it gave her the only comfort she had.

CHAPTER 13

The following morning, Olivia rose early, wanting to have the tin bath ready for Lachie and to make him a nice breakfast when he got home from finishing his shift.

The only advantage in this square was each house had running water into the kitchen. She knew from Tess when they chatted yesterday on the way to the market that some of the tenement yards along Stanley Road were marked for demolition, slum clearance. Tess warned their square would be considered before long, but until then, she wanted the house to be nice for Lachie.

She boiled eggs and fried bacon and sliced the bread loaf while the tea mashed. Setting the table, she glanced around the clean kitchen, pleased with the results of her efforts. Last evening, she'd fought tiredness and scrubbed long into the night, eager to wipe away years of dirt and grime.

When the back door opened, she smiled at her brother, only for the smile to fade. Lachie's shoulders were bowed, he looked down beaten, covered in coal dust, his trousers wet below the knee, his boots caked in sludge. 'Morning. How was your shift?'

Lachie stood on the back doorstep, his eyes white in a black face. 'It's Sunday, isn't it?'

'Yes.'

'I'm not going to church,' he murmured as though even speaking was taking too much energy.

'That's fine. I'll go on my own. I expected you'd want to sleep, anyway.'

'I need to wash.'

Olivia turned back to the show him the bath. 'We have a bath. It's ready for you. Strip off and give me your clothes.'

His haunted gaze lifted to hers. 'I don't think I can.'

She rushed to him. 'I'll help you.'

He flinched as she reached for his jacket. 'I'll do it. You should have put the bath outside.'

'Help me carry it out then.'

Together they shuffled outside with the bath, which was only a quarter full so it could be continually topped up as he washed.

'I've more water heating.'

'Leave it on the step and close the door.' Lachie sighed.

'What's happened?' She knew her brother well and something was wrong.

'It's nowt.'

Not wanting to push him at that moment, she kept quiet and brought out the pan of water and set it on the step. Lachie had pulled off his shirt, and she stared at the bruising on his back. 'Lachie, you're covered in bruises.'

'Go inside, Liv,' he said dully.

She did as he asked, questions burning on her tongue. To keep busy she pulled out the clothes soaking overnight and rinsed them in the sink. Tess said she could go over and borrow her mangle to take out the excess water. Refilling the boiler with fresh water, she then lit the fire underneath it for another wash.

Glancing out of the window she noticed Lachie sitting in the bath, head bowed. He was still filthy. Had he fallen asleep? She went out to him, carrying a towel and fresh clothes she'd prepared for him the night before. 'Let me wash your back.'

'No. I can do it. I'll be in soon.'

She hesitated, but not wanting to annoy him, she returned inside. From the oven she brought out the plates of eggs and bacon where they were keeping warm and poured out two cups of tea.

'I don't want to sleep all day. I want to see the sun,' Lachie told her coming inside, dressed in his old long johns and with water dripping from his blond hair.

'I will wake you in a couple of hours then? When I get back from church? We could go for a walk to the park?'

'I'll see how I feel,' came his non-committal reply as he ate.

'Will you tell me how you got those bruises?'

'They're nowt. I fell at work. It's dark down there, you trip over all the time.'

She ate some of her egg. 'Are you working with the ponies?'

'Not yet.' His sullen expression matched his tone. 'Where did you get the table and chairs from?'

Olivia sipped her tea, watching him. 'I met Tess, from next door, and she took me shopping for some things down by the market.'

'Oh, so it's alright when you buy stuff but not when I do it?' he snapped.

'I paid for these things with my wage. I didn't put them on credit that we have to pay off for months!'

'We needed beds.'

'Second-hand ones not new, like you bought.' She took a breath to calm down. 'If we're going to stay here, we might as well make the place nicer.'

'Where else would we go?' Lachie grunted. 'We've no money to travel somewhere else and no other jobs to go to. We'd be homeless. So, we're stuck here!'

She scowled, not liking his manner. 'Why are you yelling at

me? *You* wanted to come here. It was *you* who was happy to go down the pit. I wanted to stay in the countryside. I only agreed because it was what *you* wanted!'

He pushed his chair back with a jerk. 'I was wrong!'

'Lachie?' she called after him as he stomped upstairs.

His outburst worried her. This wasn't like him, to be argumentative, surly. Hopefully, he was just tired and nothing more and after a sleep he'd be more like his old self.

Determined not to have her Sunday ruined, Olivia tidied the kitchen and then went next door with her basket of wet washing to put it through the mangle.

'You're at it early, lass,' Tess said, coming out with a broom.

'You don't mind?'

'Nay, go for it. I'll do mine later, after church. They say you're not meant to work on Sundays but honestly, who can manage to do nowt on a Sunday? A day of leisure they say. I'd like them to live in this square and tell me what leisure is. Who'll do my cooking and cleaning if I spend the day doing nowt but attending church?'

Olivia grinned. Tess was such a tonic. 'Which church do you attend? I'd like to go.'

'St Faith's, up the road.'

'The one on the corner of Eastmoor and Stanley Roads? I walk by it every day.' She pulled more clothes through the mangle, the water squeezing out.

'Aye, that's the one.' Tess stood on the step. 'I'll knock when I'm ready if you want to go together. Most of us women and children do, it lets the men who've been on night shift get some peace and quiet to sleep.'

'Yes, I'd like to go with you.'

'See you in a bit then, lass.'

Olivia took her basket back to her own back door and pegged out the clothes. The sun was warm already, another lovely May day.

Dressed in her cream and pink flower dress, Olivia was ready when Tess knocked. The square was full of women and children and some men such as Ezra and Mr Muldoon.

Winnie held Martha on her hip and said her Norman was ill and not going. Sadie rolled her eyes at that, but no one commented on the black eye Winnie sported.

From number nine, Olivia met an old widow called Mrs Betts, and was introduced to the families from numbers two, the Menzies, number four, the Riggs and finally number six, the Berry family.

As she walked amongst them all, Olivia knew it would take her some time to remember everyone's names, but they had all welcomed her to the square and chatted freely with her.

'Just watch out for Norris Riggs,' Tess warned her as they took a pew inside the stone church. 'He's a wandering eye and hands. His wife knows and keeps him on a short leash. He's harmless really. Just don't listen to any of his flannel, for he reckons he can charm the birds from the trees, but the only birds falling for him are dead ones.'

Olivia clapped a hand over her mouth to stop a giggle.

Tess leaned in close to whisper. 'The Menzies have only been at the square for twelve months. Mrs Menzies is a bit uptight. Considers herself better than everyone else. She says her husband had a business in Leeds and they had to give it up. Personally, I suspect they are dodging creditors, why else would they be in the square? Her husband is younger than her by a good ten years as well, which is odd, don't you agree?'

The vicar raised his hands and spoke, preventing Olivia from answering.

After the service, she found herself walking back with Sadie and Winnie. Sadie carried Martha, who was whinging, to give Winnie a break.

'She's teething,' Winnie moaned. 'Cried all night.'

'Is that why Norman gave you a good clout? Because you couldn't shut her up?' Sadie asked.

'Aye, it was one reason. But then, he doesn't need a reason, usually, does he?'

'He'd only hit me the once,' Saide stated heatedly. 'Then next time he'd have a pan over his head and a knee to his bollocks.'

Winnie laughed hollowly. 'Says the woman who is adored by her man and never known how frightening it is to be battered by her husband.'

Shocked, Olivia couldn't comprehend what she was hearing.

Winnie looked at her. 'Take that as a lesson, Olivia. Chose a man who adores you, like Sadie did, and not a man who hates you because you got pregnant as I did, and he had to marry you.'

She could only nod, sorry for Winnie. To be tied to a man without love would be horrendous.

Winnie chuckled harshly. 'With Olivia's looks, there will be princes lining up for her hand.' She took Martha from Sadie. 'I'm off to me mam's house. See you later.'

Entering the square, Olivia noticed Lachie sitting out the front on one of the chairs with Colin. 'You didn't sleep long?'

'No. I want to be able to sleep tonight. I'm on day shift tomorrow. Colin woke me. We're going to watch a cricket match.'

'Oh.' Disappointed he didn't want to spend the day with her, she forced a smile. 'That'll be nice.'

Lachie stood and followed her inside, although he still had that nervous look on his face, he seemed lighter in spirit. 'The front room is nice.'

'Ezra is going to start painting it today. I thought we could help him?'

Lachie's eyes widened. 'It's my day off! I'm not spending it painting. I'm off to the cricket.'

'Fine!' She grabbed his arm as he passed to go back outside. 'Did you get paid?'

'Aye.'

'We need to put some of it aside for the bills. My wage is gone.'

His face twisted. 'Bills? I work all week in that bloody death trap and now I can't spend my money as I want?'

Taken aback by his outburst, her temper rose. 'Did you think I wanted to spend all my money on furniture? We both live here, Lachie, and we both need to pay for it that's what happens when you become an adult, you pay your way. You're not a boy anymore under Father's protection living with no responsibilities.'

'Don't I know it!' He pulled his arm out of her grasp. Groping in his pocket, he tugged out some coins and threw them at her. 'Here! Have it.'

She gasped as the coins clattered onto the floor. She looked up to see Ezra in the doorway, holding a paint tin and some brushes. Embarrassed, she turned away and escaped to the kitchen.

A moment later, Ezra stood by her side. 'Do you want me to come back another day?'

'I'm sorry you had to see that. My brother isn't normally so rude and nasty.'

'Lass, don't take it personally,' Ezra said softly, putting down the paint tin and brushes. 'I hear he's had a tough first week down the pit. Some of the men can be cruel, treat newbies like slaves, or ignore them all together. The hewers work hard to get the coal out and the more they get out the better the pay. When a new fella joins a team, a novice, it can be bad for them if the new fella holds up productivity. Understand?'

'Yes, I think so. Lachie has bruises on his back. He said he tripped.'

Ezra shrugged. 'He could have.'

'But he might have been mistreated by some of the men?'

'Not just men, but the other lads. It's like a rite of passage. Do unto others as what's been done unto them, that sort of thing.' He grinned to take the seriousness out of the conversation. 'Listen, nowt can be done about it. When Lachie's been there long enough, and knows the ways of it all, he'll simply become one of the men.' When she didn't look convinced, he patted her back gently. 'You need to stop thinking of your brother as the boy you knew in the country. He's not that person now.'

'No, he isn't.' She wasn't keen on the new Lachie and wanted the old one back. 'He told you about where we used to live?'

'Aye, on our walks to and from the pit. I sense talking about his old home makes him happy.'

'What can I do?'

'Let him deal with it in his own way.' Ezra picked up a brush. 'If you want, I'll have a word with one of the foremen and see if we can get him working with the ponies.'

'Thank you.' That at least was something positive.

'Right, let's get painting, shall we? Stick the kettle on the heat, lass, and we'll have a cuppa while I put down an old sheet and move your sofa.'

The afternoon passed quickly as they painted. Tess visited often, popping in and out, giving them cups of tea and even bowls of vegetable soup she'd made. Ezra spoke a little about his past, saying he'd been down the mine since he was a young lad and that he married aged nineteen and was a widower by age twenty-six. Olivia didn't press him for details. He asked about her past, the countryside where she grew up, the manor where she worked.

Olivia realised that without Ezra and the afternoon painting she'd have been lonely and at a loss with what to do with herself. She needed to think of things to do on Sundays, especially during the summer months.

The warmth of the day dried the paint quickly, and they did two coats of whitewash on the front room and the kitchen, finishing up as the sun started to descend behind the rooftops.

Ezra surveyed the rooms, which were bright and fresh. 'They've come up grand, haven't they?'

Moving the last piece of furniture into place, Olivia agreed. 'It's like a different place.'

'Get some cheap paintings of some country scenes off the market for the walls,' Ezra added. 'That'll make it more homely as well.'

Olivia gazed at the bare walls. 'Or a mirror. We're in need of a large mirror. I only have my hand-held one.'

'It could go over the fireplace. I'll keep an eye out for one.' Ezra packed away his washed brushes.

Olivia gave him a shilling from the coins, Lachie had thrown at her.

'No, lass. That's not necessary. I'll not take it. You did just as much painting as I did.'

'Yes, but with your paint and brushes.'

'That paint is left over from another job I did last summer. It cost me nothing.'

'It doesn't feel right to give you nothing,' she protested.

'And it doesn't feel right taking anything off you.' He laughed. 'Listen, if you ever bake a cake, bring some over to me. I'm partial to a bit of fruit cake, I am.'

Her face fell. 'I've never made a fruit cake in my life.'

Ezra laughed even more. 'Then you can start practising and I'll be your taste tester. How about that?'

'Deal.' She smiled, determined that next Sunday she'd make her first fruit cake. Tess would show her how if she asked.

Alone, she made a simple dinner of boiled potatoes, cabbage and sliced ham. After washing up the pots and the kitchen tidy once more, she took the tin bath upstairs to her room. Thankfully, it managed to fit between the bed and the set of drawers.

It took an age to carry jugs of hot water upstairs until finally she had enough to have a decent bath. The simple joy of washing her whole body at once, of giving her hair a good scrub was wonderful.

Downstairs, dressed in her nightgown and robe, she sat on the sofa admiring the white walls as she towel dried her long hair. Her father's watch sat on the mantelpiece and she checked the time. It was past seven o'clock. Where was Lachie?

She'd fallen asleep on the sofa when the front door banged, jerking her awake.

Lachie swayed into the room, reaching out to touch the wall to steady himself. 'You're still up.'

'I've been waiting for you,' she snapped. He was clearly drunk for the first time in his life. 'Do they play cricket in the dark now, do they?'

His eyes closed, and he swayed again. 'I don't feel good…'

'Get out the back to the lav.' She pulled him out through the kitchen and shoved him outside. 'Don't you dare make a mess, Lachlan Brodie, as I'll not be cleaning it up!'

She stood on the back step, listening to him vomiting in the lav. Anger swirled in her chest at the state he was in.

A few minutes later he came out of the lav, shoulders slumped.

'Get inside,' she said through clenched teeth, not wanting the neighbours to hear.

Lachie sat at the table, head between his hands. 'Can I have some water, please?'

'Get it yourself.' She stood hands on hips. 'How did you even get like this? You're not old enough to get into the pubs.'

'A lad from work got some bottles of beer.'

'How did he manage that?' In spite of her words, she grabbed a cup and filled it under the tap and thrust it at him.

'He pinched them from a crate at the back of the pub.'

'Oh, great! So now you're a thief as well as a drunkard?'

'I didn't steal it.'

'No, but you drank it though, which makes you a receiver of stolen goods, you damn fool.' She wanted to slap him.

He glared up at her through bloodshot eyes. 'I work hard, if I want to have a drink with my mates then I will!'

'You're fifteen, not fifty!'

'You can't tell me what to do. I'm a man now.'

'A man?' She stood over him full of rage. 'Listen to me, if you think you're going to spend all your wages every week on beer, you can think again. No brother of mine is going to waste his life being nothing but a drunk.'

'I'll do what I like! I'm stuck down that hole and—'

'Stop right there!' She held up her hands. '*You* wanted to go down the pit, not me. I said to wait and find a better job. No one is *forcing* you to work there, least of all *me*.'

All of a sudden, he crumpled and looked like her little brother again, instead of the sullen youth who'd walked out earlier that day. 'I'm sorry, Liv.'

Her anger deflated, and she dragged the other chair over to sit beside him. 'Drinking yourself senseless isn't the answer. Mam and Father would be so ashamed of you if you became one of those type of men who drank his wages away every week.'

'I got drunk *once*,' he defended.

'And it can become a slippery slope towards doing it once a week, and then twice a week and then every day. It happens, Lachie.'

'Aye, I see it at the pit. Men turned away because they're drunk. Some get angry, others cry like babies, because they've families to feed and no money.' Lachie wiped his eyes. 'I just wanted to try it, Liv, and see what it's like to be drunk, to have some fun. The other lads were doing it after the cricket match finished.'

'Colin?' She didn't think Tess would stand for one of her lads drinking.

'No, he'd gone by then.'

'If the police had found you, you'd be in serious trouble.'

Lachie stared at the floor. 'I thought it'd be a laugh, and it was, then suddenly my stomach churned and I wanted to come home.'

'Coming home was the right thing to do.'

'I wanted to be one of the lads, not the new boy.'

'I can understand that, but stealing beer, getting so drunk you're sick, isn't the way to do it. Are they nice, these lads?' She remembered what Ezra had told her while they were painting.

'Aye, they're not bad…'

'But some of the pit men aren't nice?'

'I'm just new, slow. I don't know my way around yet.'

'Listen, you don't have to go back. We'll tighten our spending, just pay the rent and food, until you can find another job.'

He stood and shook his head. 'And let everyone think I'm a baby, a little boy hiding behind his sister's skirts? No thanks.' He yawned. 'I'll continue to work there until something better comes along.' Once more sounding older than he was, he walked to the doorway between the front room and the kitchen, and paused. 'Maybe I should have gone with our Stu.'

'You'd have left me alone?'

'I didn't get the chance, did I? Stu left without telling us where he was going or asking if we wanted to go with him. Stu was selfish. He killed our father.'

'Stu didn't know what was going to happen with Father,' she soothed, understanding his pain.

'It doesn't matter. He should never had left us. Stu is the reason our lives have changed. I'll never forgive him.'

'He's our brother.'

'He's dead to me,' Lachie stated coldly.

She shivered at his formal tone. 'Well, I'll write to Mrs Bean tomorrow and give her our new address in case Stu returns to the forge. I should have done it before now but there's been a lot going on. I'd like to think that Stu knows how to find us if he wants to.'

Lachie shrugged. 'I'd go and get my things from Mrs Bean's loft, but I've no use for a fishing rod here, have I?' He looked about the two rooms from the doorway. 'The paint looks good.'

'Ezra was very kind.'

He had no more to say, and with another yawn, he went upstairs, calling out good night to her as he did so.

Olivia locked the doors and banked down the kitchen range fire, her mind whirling at the events of the day. She had to get Lachie away from the pit before drinking with the lads became commonplace because he was unhappy.

CHAPTER 14

Olivia had been working for Mr Sheridan for four weeks and had only seen the two men in the street a few times since that awful day they chased her. They hadn't come close to her again and sometimes they walked the other way when she came out of the house. Still, she was frightened of meeting them again. Several times, she had nearly stayed at Mr Sheridan's house when Lachie was on nights just so she didn't have to walk home alone or sleep in an empty house. But how would she explain her fear to her employer?

However, Mr Sheridan must have sensed something was wrong, and often he would make an excuse to walk some of the way home with her. She was silently grateful that he did. Sometimes, she perceived someone was watching them, and the hairs would rise on the back of her neck. She wondered if Mr Sheridan sensed it also, for there were times when he'd pause and look behind them, a thoughtful expression in his eyes.

Despite the hidden threat of those men, Olivia began to enjoy her walks home in the summer evenings with Mr Sheridan. He spoke of many things; his music, books, plays, but he also asked her about her life. He wanted to know about her past, her family, working at the manor. She found it flattering that he took an interest, wanting to know her thoughts on different subjects.

It wasn't just walking her home that Sheridan did, he also started to come and find her in the house. Usually, when she was in the kitchen cooking him a meal, Sheridan would come and sit at the table, and they'd chat about all sorts of topics.

Olivia became aware the roles were blurring, just as she had with Spencer months ago. Although she liked Mr Sheridan enormously, she didn't feel the heat of desire in his presence as she had with Spencer. Not that Mr Sheridan ever said or acted inappropriately towards her, but she could sense his friendliness, his eagerness to be in her company and she was flattered.

When Mrs Oakes came once a week to collect the basket of dirty washing, she often stopped to share a pot of tea with Olivia. The laundress was older than Olivia, mid-thirties, she thought, and had three small children and an invalid husband, which was why she took in washing.

'It's a beautiful day, Olivia,' Mrs Oakes stated, coming into the kitchen one Monday in June.

'It is, Mrs Oakes, and I've all the windows open to let in the warm breeze and air out the house and dry the floors I've just washed.'

'I would say to blow the cobwebs away, but I know how good of a cleaner you are and there wouldn't be a cobweb anywhere in this house from cellar to attic.' Mrs Oakes grinned.

'There'd better not be!' Olivia poured out tea for them both.

'Is he in?' Mrs Oakes gestured to the front of the house.

'When is Mr Sheridan ever out unless he's visiting his friend, Mr Cook, or going to the post office? He writes a vast number of letters each week.'

'He's a strange one, but nice enough.'

'Yes, very nice.'

'Don't get any ideas, lass,' Mrs Oakes warned. 'The two previous maids working here were soon dismissed when his mother died, when they each thought they could get a ring on their finger from him.'

'Really?' Olivia hadn't known that.

'Oh, aye. Both fought like cats over him, and he never gave either of them a second look, for sure. They used to live-in and one actually entered his bedroom one night for a little visit.'

'No!' Olivia was shocked. It made sense now why Mr Sheridan told her she'd not be living-in.

The older woman laughed. 'Stupid girls. He was grieving his mother, why on earth did they think he'd be wanting to court either of them? They were ugly and as thick as two short planks. Hardly wife material for the likes of Mr Sheridan.'

Olivia had baked a Victoria sponge that morning, enjoying her new baking skills thanks to Ezra tasting her cake offerings, and she cut a slice for Mrs Oakes. 'Mr Sheridan didn't mention why the previous maids had left and I never asked.'

'He must be thanking the fates you are nothing like them. I bet he's appreciating you in every way. You do your work, and you don't bother him. Quiet men like him just want to be left alone.'

Nodding, Olivia didn't mention the long conversations she had with Mr Sheridan. It was no one's business but their own. 'Now the house is in a good shape and clean as a whistle, I've started using my spare time to cook him meals. He's very grateful as it saves him from leaving the house and going out to find a meal somewhere or eating something plain here. The poor man lived on tea and toast.'

'Does he still meet at the music club on Saturday nights at Mr Cook's house?' Mrs Oakes asked.

'I believe so.' It made her giggle that Mrs Oakes knew so much about Mr Sheridan's habits.

'He's played a few concerts with them at the Theatre Royal in town. There's another concert happening soon.'

This surprised Olivia, for Mr Sheridan hadn't mentioned it.

She couldn't picture him playing in front of an audience. 'Concerts?'

'Aye. He's too good for them, obviously, being a classically trained pianist who has been the sole performer at many concerts in Europe in the past.'

'Really?' Again, she was shocked. 'How do you know that?'

'His mother once told one of the ladies who I launder for, and her lady's maid heard it all and she mentioned it to me once.'

'He's a pianist that has played in concerts in Europe?' Olivia was astounded. She thought his playing was just a hobby. Why hadn't he spoken of it to her when they talked?

'You've realised he's not from this country, haven't you?'

Olivia wasn't stupid. 'I hear a faint accent, but he has not told me details about his birth.'

'He played the concerts abroad. I think he was born in Germany, or Austria or Hungary, I'm not sure where. That's where him and his parents are from, one of those countries.'

'His English is very good then.'

'His mother, Ingrid, was well-spoken but there was an accent there, stronger than his. I only met her a few times. She was a sad woman, doted on her son. The father was never mentioned,' Mrs Oakes mused, finishing her cake. 'Well, I'd better be off and get on with my work.' She picked up the loaded basket. 'Thanks for the tea and cake. See you next week. Ta-ra.'

Olivia took the basket of clean washing, all ironed and folded, and went upstairs to put it away in the linen cupboard. Mr Sheridan's clothes she placed on the end of his bed as instructed. She gave the bedroom a glance with a critical eye. Everything was sorted and tidy. She'd made his bed that morning and opened the curtains while he was downstairs eating the breakfast she'd cooked for him. It pleased her that he enjoyed her cooking and that it gave her something different to do besides cleaning.

Going downstairs, she jumped when a knock sounded on the

door. No one ever knocked at this house. Mr Sheridan hadn't had one visitor the whole month she'd been there.

Opening the door, she smiled at the well-dressed man waiting on the step who held a large brown-paper parcel. 'May I help you?'

'Yes, good morning. You must be Olivia?'

Surprised he knew her name, she nodded. 'I am.'

'Stephen told me he'd hired you. Is he in?'

She hesitated, for Mr Sheridan had told her on her first day to never let anyone into the house. 'I will check, sir. Your name?'

'Mr Charles Cook. Stephen is expecting me.'

'Very good, sir. Please, wait there.' She closed the door on him, feeling rude. Normally, a guest would be invited to wait inside the hallway.

She knocked on the piano room door and opened it slightly to pop her head around. 'Forgive me, sir, for interrupting.'

'Someone is at the door?' Mr Sheridan turned on the piano stool to face her. 'I thought I heard a knock. It'll be Charles.'

'Mr Charles Cook, sir.'

Mr Sheridan rose. 'Send him in, please. Will you make us some tea?'

'Of course, sir. Will you be in the parlour?'

'Parlour?' He looked confused for a moment.

'The other front room,' she clarified, aware that he rarely visited that room.

'Ah, yes. The parlour.'

With the two men seated in the parlour on the opposite side of the hallway, Olivia went into the kitchen to make up a tea tray, including slices of her Victoria sponge. She enjoyed serving morning tea like she used to at the manor. She missed serving to guests. This house was too quiet when the piano lay silent. Sometimes, when Mr Sheridan was writing or reading for hours on end, all she heard was the ticking of the clock or only the sounds she made while cleaning. It was a strange sensation to work inside a hushed house where only one other person was present.

Carrying the tray to the parlour, she stood unseen in the hallway to listen to the conversation, making sure she wasn't about to interrupt anything private being said before walking in.

'Stephen, you mustn't worry,' Charles Cook told him. 'Your father will be careful.'

Olivia's eyes widened. Mr Sheridan had a father who was alive? She thought him to be dead.

'The Reichsrat was suspended, Charles. Father has sent no word for weeks. The military are gaining power and Father has spoken out against Karl von Stürgkh.'

The visitor then spoke quietly in another language.

'English, Charles,' Mr Sheridan whispered. 'No one must hear us speak Austrian.'

'You do not trust your servant?'

'Olivia is a genuine person, and I think very well of her, but it's safer for us all if we trust no one.'

Olivia's skin tingled. What was Mr Sheridan concerned about? Why could they not speak Austrian? The tray was heavy in her hands, so she made a small sound in her throat and walked into the parlour. 'Your tea, sir.'

'Thank you.'

Olivia placed the tray on the table. 'Would you like me to pour, sir?'

'Yes, thank you.' Mr Sheridan gave her a tight smile.

Mr Cook eyed the cake. 'That is very appealing.'

'I shall cut you a slice, sir.'

'Excellent.' Mr Cook turned to Stephen. 'The new music? Is it finished?'

'No, not yet. I will play it for you after we've had our refreshments. I want your opinion on it.'

'The concert is next week, Stephen.' Mr Cook grinned. 'You don't have much more time.'

'It has to be perfect.'

'I'm sure it is.' Mr Cook took the plate with the piece of cake from Olivia. 'What do you think to the music? You must hear it every day?'

'I do hear it as I go about my work, sir.' Olivia gave the other plate of sliced cake to Mr Sheridan. 'It sounds beautiful to me.'

'See, Stephen?' Mr Cook slapped his thigh. 'The music will be marvellous. Olivia is like the rest of the audience, they are there to sit and listen and enjoy. None will be classically trained pianists and not there to critique every note.'

'I will know if it is not correct.' Mr Sheridan sipped his tea. 'I will continue to practise and make the piece perfect as I know it should be.'

Olivia left the two men to discuss music and the concert, but her thoughts strayed to the conversation she'd overheard. Mr Sheridan was Austrian. He had a father somewhere who might be in trouble with someone called Karl von Stürgkh? Who was that? She had no way of knowing or asking anyone. It was all very intriguing.

Later, music flowed through the house and Olivia stepped into the parlour to clear away the tray. The brown-paper parcel was left on a chair. It'd been opened, and she saw it was a bundle of newspapers, foreign newspapers. The one on top was titled, *Illustrierte Kronen-Zeitung*. Interested, Olivia flipped through the newspapers, looking at the illustrations, then a name jumped out at her beneath a photograph. Karl von Stürgkh. He looked a formidable man.

The music stopped, and she heard the men chatting as she picked up the tray. They met her in the hallway, where Mr Cook was putting on his hat.

'You were right, Olivia,' Mr Cook said. 'The music is beautiful. We are lucky to have such talent in our midst.'

'Enough, Charles.' Mr Sheridan shook his head, slightly embarrassed.

Mr Cook chuckled. 'You must come to the concert, Olivia. Stephen has spare tickets.'

'I couldn't, but thank you, sir.' She bobbed her head and hurried down the hallway to the kitchen.

She was washing the tea service when Mr Sheridan came into the kitchen.

'Would you like to attend the concert?' he asked.

'People like me don't go to those kinds of concerts, sir,' she said, wiping her hands dry. She wanted to laugh at the suggestion.

'Do you like the music?'

'I do, yes.'

'Then that is exactly why you should go. It's culture, Olivia. Everyone should be exposed to it.'

'Maybe so, but when people are struggling to pay their rent and feed their families, money for concerts are the last thing they think about.'

Mr Sheridan frowned. 'I understand. However, you will have a ticket. You will be my guest. Will you attend?'

Suddenly, she felt seen as more than just a maid. He was asking her to attend his musical concert as his guest. How could she refuse? 'I would like to attend, thank you.'

'Good.' He nodded once and left the kitchen. He returned a few minutes later with two tickets and a concert pamphlet. 'For you and one for your brother should he wish to go.'

'Thank you, sir. That's very kind of you.' She hesitated in taking it. How could she, a housemaid, possibly go to the theatre with high society? It was laughable.

'You've had to put up with me practising every day for weeks. You deserve it.' His smile transformed his face. He became less serious and more handsome. 'I also must tell you that your food is very good. I am enjoying it far more than my paltry efforts.'

'I'm happy to cook for you, sir.'

'Each day you are here?'

'If you wish it, sir,' she agreed.

'I do.' He pulled from his pocket a small leather purse and took out several shillings. 'Money to purchase food.'

She took it. 'I will go to the market and buy some things to make meals for you.'

'Excellent. No more toast and jam for me.' He rubbed his hands together happily. 'Now I must get back to practising.'

When Olivia returned home later that evening, Tess was sitting out the front of her house watching the children playing in the square.

'How was your day, lass?'

'Fine.' She smiled, taking the empty chair beside Tess.

'Sadie was out here with me, but she's gone to heat the water ready for Gerry's bath. The men will be home soon.'

'I should do the same for Lachie.' Olivia didn't feel she had the energy to do it though. She'd walked home from Mr Sheridan's house, stopping along the way to buy fresh pork chops and just wanted to sit for a while. 'Do you know much about Austria, Tess?'

Tess stared at her as though she'd lost her mind. 'Me? Austria?' The older woman started laughing. 'You're jesting, right? I can just manage to write my own name, never mind learn about another country.' She laughed again. 'You are a strange one, lass.'

Olivia grinned, not offended.

'Why do you want to know about Austria? Planning a trip?' Tess joked.

'No. Mr Sheridan comes from there I understand.'

'Does he now?' Tess raised her eyebrows. 'That's something, isn't it? You're working for a foreigner.'

'He's a pianist, did I tell you?'

'Aye, I think you told me that a couple of weeks ago.'

'He's playing a concert at the Theatre Royal next week. I have a ticket to go.'

'That's fancy, lass.' Tess peered at her. 'Why the miserable face?'

'Should I go? I'm a housemaid.'

'Aye, but you've got nowt to be ashamed of. It's honest work. Besides, you've got a ticket.'

'I've nothing to wear though. When Mrs Broadbent ever attended a social event, she wore silk and diamonds.'

Tess thought for a moment. 'Well, funny you should say that...'

Olivia pouted at her in question.

'I can't find you silk or diamonds, lass, but I've a bolt of azure-blue taffeta in the loft that's been begging to be used for something.'

'Why do you have a bolt of blue taffeta in your loft?' Olivia grinned.

"Tis a long story.' Tess was cagey.

'Is it stolen?'

'Aye well, let's not get into any details, but let's just say it cost me nowt when I found it a couple of years ago.'

'You found it?'

Tess shrugged one shoulder innocently. 'It fell off the back of a wagon. The pitmen were striking, and we had no money. Awful times. Anyhow, I found this bolt of material and thought to sell it to one of the haberdashery shops, but word got out about a wagon of bolts going missing and the material became too hot to handle, if you get my meaning, so I stashed it.'

'You could sell it now though?'

'I've four of my family in work, lass. I don't need to sell it. I'd get more enjoyment making a dress for you out of it.'

'You'd make me a dress?'

'Aye. Nowt fancy, mind. It'll be a plain dress. My sewing machine is getting on a bit, like myself, but it does all right.' Tess stood as the men turned into the square. 'I'll get one of my lads to get it down for me and I'll bring it around after supper.'

'Thank you!' Excited, Olivia was smiling as Lachie came towards her, only his downcast look and the slight limp he had made the smile vanish. 'Lachie? Are you hurt?'

'I'm fine.' He marched past her into the house.

She followed him, carrying the pork chops. 'What happened?'

'I tripped. Is my bath ready?'

'No. I'm not long home myself.'

'Long enough to sit out and gossip with Mrs Hobson,' he snapped.

She let it go, knowing he was tired and seemed in pain as he grimaced when he sat at the table. 'I'll get some water boiling for your bath. Go out and take your clothes off.' She lit the range fire she'd set ready that morning before leaving for work and then filled the kettle and three pots they had with water. 'Oh, and I've some news.'

'Has Mrs Bean replied?' he asked from the yard.

'No, she hasn't, not yet.' Olivia thought it odd that their former neighbour hadn't replied to her letter she sent a while ago. 'I've tickets for you and me to attend a music concert at the theatre.'

'You bought tickets for a concert?' he accused. 'After everything you said about watching our spending?'

'No, I didn't buy them so you can calm down. These were given to us by Mr Sheridan. He's playing the piano on the night.' She got the vegetables out of the cupboard and began peeling the potatoes.

'I'm not going.'

'Why?'

'Why would I? I don't want to listen to some boring music.' Lachie sat on the back step in the fading sunshine. The noise of the neighbourhood ebbed and flowed.

She came to the doorstep. 'I'd like you to come with me.'

'When is it?'

'Next Thursday night.'

'I'll be on night shift then.'

'Can you miss a night?'

'Don't talk daft. We can't afford for me to lose my job.' He pulled off his filthy trousers and Olivia gasped at the ugly bruising on his calf.

'What have you done to yourself?'

He turned away. 'I fell.'

'I don't believe you. We've talked about this, Lachie. If you're getting mistreated, then you need to leave.'

'I'll be fine.'

'Can you report these people to the foreman?'

'And get a clip around the ear from him as well? Not bloody likely.'

'Don't swear,' she hissed, hating bad language. 'Someone must be told. You can't go on getting beatings like this.'

'Don't worry about it.'

'Of course, I'm going to worry about it. You need to leave there, Lachie. I mean it.'

'It'll be different soon. I heard I might be with the ponies tomorrow.'

'If you don't, then we'll go around to all the blacksmiths and ask if there are any apprenticeships.'

'I did that when we first arrived in Wakefield. No one would take me on.'

'Then we'll do it again.' She began to fill the bath with warm water.

'I'll be all right once I'm working with the ponies, Liv.' He gave her a grim smile and grabbed the cake of soap from the shelf.

Tess called in while Olivia was tidying the kitchen after they'd finished their meal of pork chops and boiled potatoes and cabbage. Lachie took himself off to bed, leaving the two women alone.

Olivia admired the shimmering taffeta in the shade of deep azure blue.

'I've some old pattern paper here.' Tess held up the thin brown paper. 'I thought if we take your measurements and then cut out the pattern. Are you thinking of a high waist and a straight skirt that's all the fashion?'

Olivia nodded. Miss Valerie Parkinson came to mind and her cutting remarks that night after dinner at the manor. The awful woman had made Olivia feel insignificant. 'I want to look sophisticated. Not like a parlourmaid wearing her mistress's cast-offs.'

Tess chuckled. 'No, we don't want that.'

Abruptly, the enthusiasm left Olivia. 'We can't do this, Tess. Who am I trying to kid? The dress might be beautiful, when it's finished, but I don't have silk slippers, or a fur cape to wear. I've only got my old black coat and my boots.' She'd been a fool to think she could pull it off.

'Enough of that talk. I'll check the market tomorrow, I'm sure I can find a second-hand pair of evening slippers or even some decent shoes and there's bound to be a nice cloak or something.'

'I don't have the money to spend on such things. It's a waste just for one night.'

'Looking good and having a bit of fun is never a waste, lass,' Tess said rationally. 'I've a bit of money saved, you can pay me back when you can.'

'Oh, no, Tess. I can't take your money.'

'You're not taking it, I'm offering. I know you'll pay me back when you can. Besides, I can haggle better than any dockside fishwife I can. So, put the kettle on and make a brew. We've work to do.'

Olivia did as instructed, still not convinced all this was worth doing.

The following morning as she served Mr Sheridan his breakfast in the dining room, she still pondered on whether attending the concert was a wise thing to do. She didn't want to be in debt to Tess for shoes and a fine cape. She needed to save money to get Lachie out of the pit. If she could show him that they had a little pot of money to last them a while, he might quit the pit and take some time to look for a better position elsewhere.

'No smile this morning, Olivia?'

'Sorry, sir. I was thinking of other things.'

He watched her unload the breakfast tray, something he now had each morning in the dining room. 'I am used to your smiles. They brighten my day. May I ask what is troubling you?'

'My brother, Lachie. He is mistreated at the pit and unhappy. It's dangerous work and I want him to find something else.'

'The pit is the coal mine?' Mr Sheridan forked some grilled tomato into his mouth.

'Yes.'

'Then he must leave and come and work here.'

Olivia stared at him, forgetting to pour his coffee. 'Here?'

'Your brother could maintain the garden. I always forget to hire a gardener in the summer and the grass grows long. The iron railing out the front needs a new coat of paint. He could mend things, keep the fires going in winter that sort of thing.'

Happiness and relief flooded her. 'Oh, Mr Sheridan!' At that moment she could have kissed him.

'Now you smile.' He grinned.

'Thanks to you.' What a good and kind gentleman he was. How lucky had she been to find this job?

That evening she was excited to tell Lachie but while she waited for him to finish his shift, she knocked on Tess's door, who was eager to show her the things she'd bought.

'Look at these beauties!' Tess held up a pair of cream leather shoes with small heels and silver buckles.

'Goodness!' Olivia gasped at the lovely shoes that only looked slightly worn. 'How much were they?' She was worried Tess had overspent.

'Four and six.'

'Four shillings and six pence?' Olivia eyes her suspiciously. 'It's a cheap price for such shoes but I can't afford those.'

'They were a bargain from the cobblers on Northgate. Someone left them to be repaired over a year ago and never came back for them. Your size as well. He wanted fifteen shillings for them. I told him the tale of you, a housemaid, going to the concert and he gave in and gave them to me cheaply. The cobbler told me he was sick of looking at them on the shelf.'

'That's nearly half my week's wage on shoes, Tess.'

'Never mind that. I told you, pay me a shilling a month if you want.' Tess opened a canvas bag. 'What do you think to this then?' She held up a long silver satin cape edged with white rabbit fur.

'Oh, that's fabulous...' Olivia gently touched it. The cape was as fine as anything Mrs Broadbent had worn.

'There's a shop in York Street, I remembered seeing it once, they sold all sorts of things,' Tess told her enthusiastically. 'I ventured in to see if they had anything and the woman was hanging up dresses, huge things they were, from half a century ago, and we got talking and she said she'd just bought boxes and boxes of clothes and props from a theatre group who had called it quits and disbanded. I think they basically gave it all to her. Her shop was rammed with boxes of it all. Anyway, I saw this in a trunk and knew instantly it would suit you.'

'How much was it?' Olivia was scared of the answer.

'The woman wanted ten shillings eightpence.'

Olivia wondered if she'd be ill at the expense. 'Tess, it's too much!'

'Now, lass, calm down. Remember, I can haggle better than most. I got it for three shillings, and she threw in a matching silver purse as well for nowt.' Tess beamed proudly, showing off the small purse with the silver chain strap.

Stroking the rabbit fur, Olivia was amazed. 'Three shillings?'

'I told her your story, but I also promised I'd be back to buy some more things if she did me a good price and I'd tell the whole square as well. As I said, she had loads of stuff, and half of it didn't fit in the shop but was piled out the back. The woman needed to get rid of things to make room.' Tess hung the cape on a coat hanger. 'The woman was offering me hats and parasols, fake jewellery, that sort of thing.'

Olivia opened the silver purse. The clasp was a little hard to fasten and some of the beads on the edge were loose, but it would do for one night.

The door opened and the Hobson men walked in, filthy and tired. Olivia greeted them and gave Tess a hug in thanks for her wonderful shopping, before slipping home to see Lachie.

Her brother was washing in the sink and turned as she entered the kitchen. 'Liv, you'll never guess what!'

'What?' She was happy to see him bright-eyed for once.

'I'm with the ponies! They started me this morning with them, and they said I was a natural. I even worked with the Horse Keeper in the underground stables. There are some lovely ponies, Liv. One is called, Chalky, and I met Blackie, Minty and one that was getting some attention from the vet, he's called Toby. The blacksmith is doing some shoeing tomorrow, and the foreman said I can help him. It's my full-time role now working with the ponies. It was so nice to spend time with horses again.'

'That's great news, but I have even better news. Mr Sheridan said you can work for him at the house. So, you can leave the pit.'

Lachie's smile dropped. 'Work at his house?'

'Yes, with me. You'll mend anything that needs fixing and be in the garden, and I thought we could make a vegetable garden. Wouldn't that be something?'

'A gardener?' He screwed up his face. 'I know nowt about gardening.'

'And maintenance around the house, fixing things and whatnot.'

'I've just agreed to work with the ponies.'

'But this is better, Lachie. You'll be a lot safer at Mr Sheridan's than down a pit.'

He appeared conflicted. 'I'm not sure, Liv. I could work my

way up to be a blacksmith like Father. The horse keeper, Dave, he was impressed with my handling of the ponies. He said I had a special touch. Father used to say the same, remember?'

No, she didn't know Father said that to him but then she was at the manor most of the time. She stared at him. 'You want to stay at the pit?'

'Aye, maybe, at least see how I go now I'm with the ponies.'

Olivia turned away to make him some supper, disappointed he hadn't grasped the chance to work somewhere clean and safe. She'd been convinced he'd be pleased to get away from the pit. A fear crept up on her that Lachie would never leave the awful place.

CHAPTER 15

Spencer held on as Parky drove the motor car fast around a long curve in the dirt road. Stones sprayed up behind them and sheep in a nearby field fled in fear. 'Slow down for God's sake or we'll be in that hedge in a minute.'

Parky laughed but slowed the motor marginally. 'Sorry, old pal. I like to experience a bit of speed when away from the towns and pedestrians. Once in the country I tend to see how fast this beauty can go.'

'Right, but kill yourself another time, hey?' Spencer relaxed only slightly as they headed through the countryside south of Wakefield towards Olivia's old hamlet. It was strange to be travelling in this part of Yorkshire again and knowing he wouldn't visit the manor or see his grandparents who were in Paris.

Parky glanced at him. 'You're really keen on this girl, aren't you?'

'Does it bother you if I am?' Spencer retorted sharply.

'Steady on. I'm only asking as a friend.'

'But there's hidden meaning behind it.' Spencer raised his eyebrows at him.

'She's beautiful, I grant you, but she's not of our class, Spence.'

Parky stared ahead at the road. 'There'll be gossip and rejections by certain people within our circle. Not many will want to socialise with a housemaid.'

'What about you?' he challenged. 'Will you still want to spend time with me if I was lucky enough to marry Olivia?'

'You can't get rid of me that easily,' Parky scoffed. 'A cousin of mine married his children's nanny, and remember Foley from school? His older brother, the Foley heir, married a singer in a stage act. It happens. As long as you're happy, and you really want to be with her, then that's all I care about.'

'Thank you. I appreciate that.' Spencer sighed heavily. 'Now I just have to find her.'

Parky slowed the motor car to a halt in front of the blacksmith's forge. A woman was emptying a bucket of water onto the grass outside of Olivia's family cottage, but it wasn't someone Spencer recognised.

Spencer left Parky having a cigar by the car and knocked on Mrs Bean's door. It took some time for someone to answer and when the door opened, a man stood there dishevelled and unshaven.

'Who are you?' the fellow asked.

'I'm Captain Middleton. I'm looking for Mrs Bean.'

'My wife? My wife is dead,' the man's voice wavered. 'I buried her four days ago. She'd been ill for some weeks.'

Sympathy filled Spencer. 'I am very sorry to hear that. You have my condolences.'

'What did you want with my wife?'

'She was going to write to me if she heard from Olivia Brodie.'

'Liv?' The man brightened slightly. 'I needed to write to her, let her know about…' his voice faltered, 'but I burnt her letter by mistake. It was caught up in some newspapers that I threw on the fire… So, I don't have her address anymore. I can't tell her the news…'

Spencer tried to keep his frustration hidden. 'But you have heard from Olivia?'

'Aye. She wrote saying she's got a job, and young Lachie is down the pit.'

'Where? Where is Olivia working?'

'Some fella's place... I can't remember.'

'Do you know the name of the coal mine where Lachie is working?'

The man scratched his head in thought. He stank as though he'd not washed in days and his breath smelt of stale beer. 'No, I don't remember. I've not been sleeping well...'

'Please try and think. I need to find her,' he begged.

'I think she's in Wakefield, or was it Leeds?'

Swearing inwardly, Spencer gave the man his card. 'If Olivia writes to you again, please let me know. My address is on the card.'

'Aye, Captain. I will.'

Walking back to the motor car, he didn't have much confidence in the man writing to him, he could barely look after himself so the chance of him remembering to write to him about Olivia wouldn't be high.

'No luck?' Parky asked, starting the engine.

'Olivia did write to him, but he doesn't have her letter anymore. She has found work and Lachie is down a coal mine somewhere.'

'What are you going to do?' Parky asked, turning the vehicle around.

'I don't know. I'm due back at my barracks tonight, which makes it difficult for me to look for her.'

'Tonight? I thought you had to return to barracks in the morning?'

'I do, but I need to travel on the night train to be there by morning.'

'That's a shame I thought you might come to the theatre with us. Bernard has tickets. Gloria mentioned a party afterwards.'

'Count me out on this one.'

'The army seriously disrupts your social life, my friend.' Parky chuckled.

'I don't have a social life,' Spence tutted.

'Listen, Spence, we'll find this girl, eventually.'

'Will we?' He shook his head. 'I'm starting to doubt it. Even if I did find her, will she still look at me the way she did? It's been weeks since we last spoke. She's been through a lot since then. Why would I matter to her? Maybe I'm making all this up in my head that she felt the same as I did?' That was his biggest fear, that Olivia didn't feel as he did.

'Or she could be pining for you just as much as you are for her?' Parky offered.

Spence blew out a long breath. 'I'm going to have to write to every coal mine in Yorkshire asking if they employ a lad called Lachie Brodie.'

'Don't be absurd,' Parky mocked.

'How else will I find him? At least I know he's in a pit. It's a start.'

Parky gave him a look of misgiving. 'It'll be a waste of time.'

'We'll see.' Spencer watched the countryside pass by the window and wondered how he was to find a list of all the pits in Yorkshire.

* * *

GIVING the kitchen one last look, Olivia untied her apron and hung it on the back of the kitchen door, ready to leave the house. Mr Sheridan had left for the theatre hours ago, full of nervous energy. He'd come to her at midday and said he couldn't possibly eat a thing so not to cook him anything. He'd been edgy all morning after reading the newspaper articles of the assassination of Archduke Franz Ferdinand in Sarajevo that occurred the day before.

Mr Cook had arrived, appearing upset at the news and the two men had closeted themselves in the piano room for an hour talking quietly.

Mr Sheridan had also told her he'd arrange for a hansom to collect her this evening to take her to the theatre. She was to leave the house early and go home to change. His kindness and thoughtfulness made her once more thank the fates for bringing her to his door.

Pleased that the house was tidy, she locked the back door and headed down the short drive to the road. Today, the two men who chased her weeks ago loitered further down the road. Her skin tingled as it always did when she saw them. For the first time in a long time, she didn't have Mr Sheridan accompanying her.

She'd walked a hundred yards or so before she realised the two men were directly behind her. The fine hairs on the back of her neck rose, and she quickened her pace. Another few steps and the two men were either side of her. She faltered, and the men turned to face her.

'Don't be alarmed, Olivia Brodie,' the tallest of the two men spoke. He had a European accent.

Her stomach churned.

'Could we have a few words?' asked the other man with a full beard. 'We only want to talk.'

'About what?'

'Sheridan.'

She frowned, confused. 'What about Mr Sheridan?'

'Do you like working for a foreigner?'

'What does that have to do with you?' she snapped. 'Let me be on my way.'

The man with the beard grabbed her arm. 'We're being friendly. I suggest you be the same,' he warned.

She became frightened, eager to be away from them. 'What do you want?'

'Information. We'll pay you well.'

'Enough money to set yourself up somewhere else,' the tall one told her.

Olivia stood very still. 'Information?'

'Meet us tonight in the yard behind The Black Horn pub on Warrengate. We'll fill you in about our mission and our organisation.'

'Organisation?' she murmured warily.

'You'll get five shillings just for listening to us, and plenty more money if you agree to help us.' The bearded man dropped her arm. 'Tonight. Eight o'clock. You'll be safe, I promise you. We're not the types to hurt a woman.'

Olivia hurried away from them, her chest tight with fear. That they had accosted her in the middle of the afternoon, not worried they'd be seen, bothered her. That they were part of some organisation, scared her, but that they were after information about Mr Sheridan absolutely terrified her.

She ran along the streets until a stitch in her side slowed her down. She kept checking over her shoulder for the two men, but they hadn't followed her. The entrance to Woodcock's Square never looked so welcoming as she hurried across the cobbles, searching her small bag for the house key.

The door opened and Lachie stood there, rubbing the sleep from his eyes. 'I saw you from the window. Why are you home so early?'

'Mr Sheridan let me.' She dashed inside and shut the door, locking it behind her.

'What's up with you?'

'Two men just stopped me in the street.'

Lachie instantly straightened, his eyes alert. 'Did they hurt you?' He strode to the door. 'Are they still out there?'

'No, it happened near Mr Sheridan's house.'

Lachie came and put his hand on her shoulder. 'Are you all right?'

'Yes, yes, I'm fine.' She tried to shrug it off, but her body shook slightly.

Lachie glanced out of the window as though expecting them to be out on the cobbles. 'Did they want money?'

Instinctively, she held back from telling Lachie the truth. She didn't want him involved or to be worried. 'Probably, but I ran away,' she lied.

'Did they follow you?'

'No.' She forced herself to calm down. 'It's fine. I probably overreacted.'

He watched her carefully. 'Do you want some tea? I was about to make myself something to eat before my shift.'

'Tea would be nice. I'll do it.' She needed to do something to take her mind off what had happened.

'Are you still going to the theatre tonight?' Lachie followed her into the kitchen.

'Yes. Tess has gone to a lot of trouble to make my dress for me. Will you bring the bath in for me, please? I want a bath and to wash my hair.' She filled pots with water to heat. 'Boiled eggs, toast and ham hock do for you?' she asked as Lachie carried in the tin bath and took it upstairs for her.

'Aye. Is there any jam?' he called from the staircase.

'I bought strawberry jam yesterday.' She busied herself making his meal, pushing away the images of the two men, their penetrating eyes, their lowly spoken words and their intimidating presence.

Why did they want Mr Sheridan? How could she possibly help them, and why would they think she'd want to? Mr Sheridan had been the kindest of employers to her. She had to tell Mr Sheridan what happened. Those men were always hanging around and now she knew their purpose. Perhaps the police needed to be involved? Was she in real danger?

Her stomach curled in knots, she couldn't eat. Instead, she sipped her tea and listened to Lachie chatter about the ponies, which he'd grown to love. Since working with the ponies, he'd become more of his old self, a little bit of her brother Lachie had returned.

Eventually, she'd heated enough water for the bath and escaped to her room. As she sat in the inches of water and washed her hair, she couldn't relax. She recalled everything the two men said. They knew her name. They knew Mr Sheridan was a foreigner. They were members of an *organisation*. It all seemed like madness.

'Yoohoo, Liv, lass,' Tess called from downstairs.

'I won't be long.' She quickly rinsed her hair and stepped out of the bath. It took her a few minutes to dress in her undergarments and wrap a dressing gown around herself.

A knock sounded on her bedroom door. 'It's me, lass, with the dress.' Tess cracked open the door slightly. 'Are you decent?'

'Yes, come in.'

'Here we are. All done.' Tess held the dress by the hanger. 'Sadie is downstairs, she's not bad with hairstyling and says she'll give it a go on your hair. Shall I send her up?'

'My hair isn't dry yet.' A part of her didn't want to go out tonight.

'Are you all right, lass? You look a bit peaky.'

Olivia sat on her bed, deflated.

'Lass? What is it?'

Haltingly, she told Tess what had happened.

'Nay, lass.' Tess sat beside her on the bed when she'd finished. 'You can't meet those men. Not tonight, not ever.'

'Oh, I'm not.' Olivia shuddered at the thought.

'Good. No money is worth getting mixed up with whatever group they are from.'

'I wouldn't dishonour Mr Sheridan. He's been good to me.'

'He has, but tomorrow I think you should tell him. They had accents?'

'Yes. Not French for I know the sound of French from working at the Broadbents, they had French friends. Those men... their accent was harsher.'

'Whoever they are, you don't want to get messed up with them. Tell Mr Sheridan.' Tess nodded wisely, pushing back tendrils of her grey-streaked hair from her eyes. 'He needs to know. You can't be accosted on the streets like that.'

'What information could they want?'

'Who knows? But in the morning, I'll walk with you to his house so you're not alone.'

'Thank you.' She was lighter in spirit now she'd told Tess.

'Right, let's get this hair dried and get you ready.' Tess grinned, becoming businesslike. 'Forget those men. You've tonight to enjoy.'

For the next hour, Olivia managed to have some fun as Sadie and Tess helped her to get ready.

Sadie towelled and brushed Olivia's long hair until it was dry. 'I've never seen hair this colour before. It's so different.' Sadie admired, rolling the sides up above Olivia's ears and pinning it. 'Looking closely at it, you have light blonde but also white through it. Incredible.'

'I once saw a horse with its mane and tail that colour. Its coat was caramel coloured, stunning it was,' Tess added, giving the cream leather shoes a final polish.

'So, I'm a horse now?' Olivia grinned, passing Sadie another pin.

'I think we should leave the back longer,' Sadie said. 'I'll roll it up but not so tightly as the sides and let it hang more. What do you think?'

'Well, since I can't see it, I'll leave it up to you.' Olivia smiled.

At last Sadie was satisfied and she and Tess helped Olivia into the shimmering blue dress, that Tess had so artfully created. Its simplicity gave it an allure of a fine couture gown of exquisite taste and expense, when in reality, it was neither.

Somehow, Tess had managed to fit the dress to Olivia's slender frame beautifully. No adornments of frills or lace were attached to the dress, so the sleek style stood on its own merits. Wearing the cream leather shoes, the long gloves and with the cape draped over her shoulders, Olivia instantly transformed from a housemaid to a member of the high society she normally served.

'Ye Gods…' Tess murmured, studying Olivia as she collected the silver purse. 'You look like a princess.'

'I'll do then?' Olivia asked nervously. 'I won't show myself up?'

'Not in the slightest,' Sadie said in awe.

A knock sounded on the door and Tess opened it to reveal one of the Muldoon children. 'There's a cab waiting for Olivia,' the boy said. 'It's on the road.'

'Thanks, lad.' Tess turned to Olivia. 'You look as though you should be in one of those fancy motor cars, but a cab will have to do.'

Olivia kissed the older woman's cheek. 'I couldn't have done any of this without you.'

'Get away, lass. Go on, enjoy yourself. I want to hear all about it in the morning.'

Olivia grasped Sadie's hands. 'Thank you.'

'It were nowt!' She grinned. 'Have a lovely time.'

It seemed the whole square had heard that Olivia was going to the theatre, and they'd all come out to see her off as though she was a queen on a state tour.

Embarrassed, she hurried along the cobbles to the cab, which some of the children had surrounded. Ezra on his way home from his shift, opened the cab door for her. 'You look amazing, Olivia.'

'Thank you, Ezra.' She blushed at the interest of her neighbours and was pleased when the horse moved on.

She smoothed down her skirt, grateful for Tess's hard work. For the first time in her life, she looked more than a simply country girl. She wished Captain Middleton could see her now. Would he be impressed? Would he want to take her hand? Her heart ached a little as she thought of him. How was it possible to miss someone so keenly when you'd only spent such a short time with them?

At the corner of Westgate and Drury Lane, the Theatre Royal and Opera House loomed in its red-brick glory. Outside, the road heaved with vehicles, horse-drawn and motor cars. Olivia climbed down and thanked the driver before heading to the entrance. After showing her ticket, she wandered inside the foyer, gazing around at the people dressed in their finery. Thankfully, she didn't look out of place, except for her lack of jewellery. A great many diamonds and gems sparkled on the ladies under the bright lights.

The crowd began to thin as they went through several doors into the theatre. Olivia gave her cape to the cloakroom attendant and received a token in return. At one of the doors, she showed an usher her ticket and was guided to her seat.

She couldn't stop staring at everything, from the vaulted painted ceiling to the plush chairs. The largest set of curtains she'd ever seen covered the stage. The orchestra were tuning their instruments which fascinated her. Just watching people taking their seats was a spectacle. Wealthy people filled the theatre, and she had a small giggle to herself thinking she would be the only housemaid in the entire building. This was classical music in an opera theatre, not a variety performance in a workingman's club.

'Good evening.' A man wearing a black suit and starched white shirt sat beside Olivia. His wife, wearing a green velvet dress heavy with gold lace, sat on his other side and she nodded to her.

'Good evening,' Olivia murmured, hoping the man wouldn't

engage in conversation with her for he'd soon realise he wasn't sitting next to a member of the gentry.

However, the lights dimmed, shrouding the audience in darkness and the curtains opened. The stage lit up, showing a piano. A thrill of excitement fizzled through Olivia.

Abruptly, Mr Sheridan walked out onto the stage wearing a black tailed suit and the audience clapped.

Olivia watched him bow, and she clapped harder as Mr Sheridan took his seat at the piano.

The theatre grew silent, a long pause of nothingness and then the conductor signalled for the orchestra to be ready, and they started at his command. Soft music flowed harmoniously, filling the grand theatre, then Mr Sheridan's fingers touched the keys. She recognised the piece of music, Tchaikovsky's Piano Concerto No 1. Mr Sheridan had told her the name of it as he practised, but it was also written on the programme she'd been given on entering.

Hearing the familiar sound, Olivia relaxed into the chair and let the music flow over her in comforting waves. The surrounding people didn't matter, the grandeur of the theatre faded away and she simply sat and watched Mr Sheridan play his beautiful music.

Mesmerised, Olivia drank in every simple moment of the concert. She was transported, swept away by each piece of music until the end when Mr Sheridan stood and walked to the edge of the stage to wild applause.

He bowed twice and then held up his hands to silence them. 'I would like to thank you all for attending this evening,' he spoke loudly and clearly to the audience. 'I would like to play one more piece for you. I wrote it myself and I hope you enjoy it. It is called "She with the golden hair".'

Olivia sat transfixed as Mr Sheridan returned to his seat and began to play the original piece he'd written over the last couple of weeks. The music that he'd played for Mr Charles Cook when he called, the music she had heard being created, note by note, as she went about her duties.

She with the golden hair.

Something touched her deep inside. The music swelled, capturing the audience, holding them in its grip, but Olivia kept her gaze on the face of the lovely man playing it. The man she had cleaned and cooked for, the foreigner, and she was so proud.

Afterwards, Olivia made her way out into the crowded foyer with the rest of the audience who were chatting about the performance. She reclaimed her cape, tucking the programme into her purse as a keepsake. She noticed Mr Charles Cook talking with a group of people, but didn't want to interrupt him and so headed for the open doors.

'Miss Brodie!' Mr Cook waved to her from across the room and beckoned her.

Olivia sagged, not wanting to be introduced to others and be embarrassed by her lowly status. Relief made her smile as Mr Cook excused himself and came to her.

'My dear, I did not recognise you! You are simply ravishing! Every man in this theatre can't stop looking at you.'

'Nonsense.' The very idea horrified her.

'None would think you were Stephen's maid, would they?' Mr Cook jested. 'Your secret is safe with me, my dear. What did you think of our magnificent Stephen?' he asked, his cheeks flushed. 'Was he not brilliant?'

'He was, very much,' she agreed.

'Every time I organise one of these concerts, Stephen tells me he won't do it. Of course, he changes his mind. How can he not when he knows it'll be such a success?'

'He is very talented.'

'And that piece of music he wrote for you. Magical, wasn't it?'

'Wrote for me?'

'"She with the golden hair."'

The blood drained from her face. 'I don't think it was written for me.'

Mr Cook chuckled. 'Indeed, it was, my dear. I mentioned to Stephen once that he needed a muse and, only days after you started working for him, he told me he'd found his muse.'

Stunned at the revelation, she didn't know how to answer him.

Someone called Mr Cook's name, and he waved to them. 'I must circulate, my dear, but if you wish to see Stephen, he is backstage.'

'Oh no. I wouldn't wish to interrupt him. I'll go home.'

'We are having a little soirée at my home, afterwards, and you are quite welcome to join us.'

'I couldn't.'

'You wouldn't be shunned, my dear. We are liberal-minded, especially my sister, Elena. She is an artist. That should tell you everything you need to know about her.' He laughed uproariously, and she thought him a little drunk.

'Thank you, I appreciate you asking me, but I must get back.'

'Indeed, my dear, as you wish. Good night.' Mr Cook turned away to speak to a man who was extending a hand to shake.

'Olivia?'

She spun at the sound of her name behind her. She stared open-mouthed at Mr Orville Parkinson and he at her. Captain Middleton's friend was here.

'It is you, isn't it? Olivia Brodie?'

She nodded, unable to speak. Her heart leapt to her throat. Her gaze swept the crowded room. Was the captain here?

Mr Parkinson's eyes grew wider. 'God in heaven. You look magnificent.'

'Who is this ravishing lady, Parky?' A thick-set man sidled up to Mr Parkinson, his gaze raking over Olivia.

'It's… It's Olivia,' Mr Parkinson managed to say. 'I can't believe it.'

'The one Spencer is mad about?' The other man frowned. 'The maid? *She's* the *housemaid* you told us about?' He pointed a finger at Olivia. 'What would a *housemaid* be doing here dressed like that?'

Those people closest to them heard him and stared at her.

Humiliation clawed at Olivia.

'Does she side-line as a gentleman's escort as well?' the man sneered with a mocking laugh.

Like water had been thrown over her, Olivia gasped and whirled away. Pushing people aside, desperate to reach the doors, she ignored Mr Parkinson's calls and ran out into the night.

She raised her hand to summon a hansom cab in the crush of vehicles.

'Olivia!'

She moaned, not wanting another embarrassing moment and took a step to cross the road. A motor car sounded its harsh horn at her, and she quickly stepped back.

'Olivia.' Mr Sheridan grabbed her arm and pulled her into his chest. 'Are you all right?'

'I'm fine.' She didn't know if she was feeling overwhelmed from nearly being hit by a motor car or being in Mr Sheridan's arms. She took a hasty step away.

'Charles told me what just happened as I was looking for you.' His kind eyes gazed at her lovely dress before it rested on her face again. 'Even without any adornments, you are still the most beautiful woman in this town.'

Her stomach swooped.

'I know I shouldn't say such words to my employee, but it's the truth. I would like to say more, but now isn't the time or the place.' His tender gaze was full of emotion.

Mr Cook called to him from the entrance.

'I must go, but we'll talk tomorrow.' Mr Sheridan bowed. 'Good night, Olivia.'

'Good night, sir,' she mumbled.

She started walking, needing to leave the swarming street and find some quiet. Too much circled her mind, the whole evening spun in fragments of music, faces and words. Mr Sheridan's glorious playing, being surrounded by such glamour and richness, Mr Parkinson's sudden appearance, his awful friend's cutting remarks and Mr Sheridan's kindness and his amazing admission. She didn't know what to make of any of it.

She raised her hand for a hansom as it passed and it slowed for her. She was grateful to climb aboard and rest against the seat and close her eyes.

CHAPTER 16

Olivia walked quietly beside Tess along the streets. The morning sun was rising, suggesting a warm day. She felt sluggish from lack of sleep due to replaying the evening in her mind and apprehensive of what Mr Sheridan might say this morning about last evening. Why had he told her she was beautiful? It blurred the lines between them. She was his maid. Yet, he'd also written that wonderful music and named it after her, she was sure of that just as Mr Cook was.

'I'll get all my washing done and dry if it stays warm like this,' Tess said as they walked. 'But the sewers will stink to high heaven. They always do in the heat.'

They parted as a man walked between them on his way to work, and a coal wagon trundled to a stop opposite to offload a sack of coal. At the end of the street, a newspaper boy called out his wares, dragging a cart full of newspapers behind him.

'Are you going to tell me what happened last night then?' Tess asked. 'I can tell something did because you've not said a word since we left the square. I thought you'd make my ears ring with all the chatter about it all.'

'The concert was lovely.' Olivia stared at the ground as she walked.

'Just *lovely?* Did it bore you then?'

'No. Mr Sheridan played beautifully.'

'Was it your dress then? Did you look out of place after all?' Tess sounded disappointed that her efforts hadn't paid off.

'The dress looked better than a lot of others there, trust me,' Olivia reassured her. 'It was an honour to wear it.'

'Ah, that's nice to hear. Then why are you so glum? Are you worried about those two men?'

'Partly.'

'Promise me you'll tell Mr Sheridan about them.'

'I will.' She sighed deeply, wondering how much to explain, and how much to keep hidden. 'I met Mr Parkinson.'

Tess frowned. 'Right, well, who is he when he's at home?'

'Captain Middleton's best friend.'

'Who's Captain Middleton?' Tess screwed up her face in confusion.

'The man I admire…'

'Admire? The captain?'

'Yes.'

'As in you've got feelings for this captain?'

'Yes.'

'Ooh, I say, that's something you've kept quiet. You've a man friend.'

'I don't have a man friend and that's why I've not mentioned him before because there's nothing to tell, Tess. He is the Broadbents' grandson, an army officer, a gentleman. Someone I doubt I'll ever meet again.'

'But you feel something for him?'

'I do. I did. Oh, I don't know anymore. We had such a brief time together. Really, they were only limited precious times, at least they were precious for me.'

'And you're not sure he felt something for you?'

'I like to think so.'

'Did he tell you?'

'Not outright, no, but he hinted at it. He looked at me as though I meant something.'

'And not just a roll in the hay?'

Offended, Olivia glared at her. 'I'm not that kind of girl.'

'Aye, I *know* that, but did *he*?'

'Yes, it wasn't like that.'

'It's always like that with men,' Tess scoffed. 'Once they're in your drawers, nothing is the same.'

'Tess!'

'Well, I'm just saying! It's not all fairy tales, lass.'

'So, you think Captain Middleton only wanted my body, not me?' She wouldn't believe it, not for a second.

'Nay, I'm saying nowt like that!' Tess took a few steps. 'We'll talk about that later. Tell me what was so wrong about meeting this captain's friend?'

'Because he was with another friend who announced to all who could hear that I was sidelining as a gentleman's escort, because I was a housemaid at the theatre.'

'Ah, the nasty swine!' Tess declared angrily.

'I just ran out. It was humiliating.'

'And it ruined your night?'

'It did.'

'Is that all?' Tess quizzed her.

'Mr Sheridan came up to me as I was waiting for a cab and said I looked the most beautiful woman there.'

'He never did!' Shocked, Tess grasped Olivia's arm. 'Has he, you know, has he ever made any suggestions towards you being more than just his maid?'

'No, not once.'

'If he does, you get out of there immediately and come home. You don't have to put up with that nonsense. Understand?'

Olivia nodded. 'He isn't like that though.'

'What did I just say about men?' Tess grumbled. 'You're too naïve, lass.'

They turned the corner into College Grove Road, no men loitered so far, just people heading to work or to the shops.

'You've nowt to be humiliated about, lass.' Tess smiled sadly. 'What that nasty gentleman said about you reflects how *his* mind works. He's a stupid entitled man who doesn't consider a young lass can be more than a housemaid. You're a decent lass with a good decent job. That's nowt to be embarrassed about. Honest work for an honest lass.'

'I've always been happy to be a housemaid. Only, since leaving the manor, living in a large town, I see that there is another world out there. I feel out of sorts. I feel I don't have a place now like I did at the manor. What Mr Sheridan said last night… Well, I feel even more out of place. It's like I've been given these glimpses of other choices, other lives I might be able to lead, first with Spencer and now with Mr Sheridan.' These thoughts had plagued her often since moving into Wakefield and seeing how other people live.

'You don't always have to be a maid, lass. A young lovely lass like you can strive for something different.'

'Our Stu has gone, God knows where, and although I'm angry and sad at him for leaving us, I also admire him for his courage. He's trying something new, seizing the opportunity to find adventure. Stu didn't want to be stuck in the same place all his life, doing the same thing every day. I did, at least back then, but now, I don't know. What does that say about me?'

'Lass, it's nice to dream of such things but it's not always possible to do it. Your Stu is a man, adventuring is easier for men to do than us women.' Tess hitched her shopping bag to the other hand. 'Life is much easier for a single lad. They have freedom. Us women don't. Then we fall in love and marry, and life revolves around our husbands and children.'

'And we're trapped.'

'You're only trapped if you let it be a prison. Me and my Larry we don't have much and we've had some hard times, but we weathered the storms because we do love each other. I'd never want to be without him and that's how he feels about me. Aye, it'd be nice to have a lovely home with a garden, spare money to spend on nice things or spending a day at the seaside. But, at the end of the day, all I want is for Larry and my boys to be safe and healthy, to have a roof over their heads and food in their bellies. I suppose I'm a simple woman, but that's fine by me.'

Olivia stopped at the front of Mr Sheridan's house, pleased that the two men who accosted her hadn't been seen. 'And you never wanted more?'

'More what?'

'Life beyond living at the square?'

'Not really. You see, lass, it's all about who you choose to have in your life. You could make a silly mistake like Winnie and be tied forever to a brutal man, or you can ignore marriage altogether and spend your days working for others, living-in, never having a home of your own, or you could wish to travel the world, but never leave Wakefield. The thing is, whatever path you walk down, it's *your* path. You have to be satisfied by your decisions otherwise you become bitter and that's no way to live.'

Olivia smiled fondly. 'You're very wise.'

'No, I've just learned a few things along the way.' Tess grinned. 'Have a good day, lass. I'll send someone from the square to meet you here at six and walk home with you.'

'Oh, I couldn't ask anyone to do that. I'll be fine.'

'If anyone stops you again just run into the nearest house and ask for help, that'll scare them off.'

'I will.' She waved Tess goodbye and walked up the short drive beside the house. She wished Lachie was on day shifts as he could meet her each evening and walk home with her. On payday they could stop and get fish and chips for supper.

Turning into the back garden, Olivia searched in her small

bag for the back-door key. She jumped on seeing the same two men coming out of the shadows of the large tree that grew in the neighbour's garden. A scream froze in her throat.

'We don't want to hurt you,' the bearded man said. 'We just want to talk. We thought you'd meet us last night as agreed.'

'I didn't agree,' she whispered, scared.

'It'll be worthwhile if you cooperate with us,' the other man mentioned. He took from his pocket a leather pouch that jingled. 'You'll be paid handsomely.'

She stared from the money to his face. 'I don't want it. Leave me alone.'

'You were there last night, at the theatre, weren't you?' the bearded man said.

Olivia began to shake. They'd been watching her? 'What do you want from me?'

'Just information about Stefan Schwartz.'

'I don't know who that is.' She was confused.

'Stephen Sheridan is Stefan Schwartz, that's his real name,' he informed her. 'He's been lying to you. Not revealing his true identity to you.'

Her breathing quickened. Was this true? 'Is he wanted by the police?'

'Not in this country, but there are others who'd like to see him back in Austria.'

'Why?'

'That's not your concern.' The bearded man offered the money again. 'All we want is information. He sends a lot of letters. We want them and the ones he receives.'

'I'm not stealing his letters.' She was disgusted by the thought.

'Let us into the house so we can take them. We'll be quiet.'

'No!'

The tall man advanced on her. 'You'll do as we say!'

'Are you going to hurt me?' She trembled.

The bearded man came forward, giving the tall one a stern stare. 'No, miss, not at all. We aren't thugs who beat women.'

Strangely, she sensed he was telling the truth. 'I won't help you. Leave me alone.'

'If you change your mind, you know where to find us. The Black Horn pub.' The bearded man stopped as he passed her. 'Things are happening in Europe, miss, and your Mr Sheridan might know information that might, one day, be important. Remember that.' He thrust the leather pouch into her hand. 'As a token of our possible working relationship.'

Olivia watched them leave and then, with a shaking hand, unlocked the back door.

In the kitchen she leant against the table and took a calming breath. She dropped the pouch onto the table as though it burnt her and glared at it. A moment later she pushed it into her bag and placed her bag under the kitchen sink.

Stephan Sheridan is Stefan Schwartz. That's all she could think about. People in Austria wanted to talk to him. Why? Questions without answers circled her mind as she began her day's tasks.

It was difficult to keep busy all morning, waiting for Mr Sheridan to wake up. She'd never known a man to sleep as late as he did on occasion. She knew most nights he stayed up very late, not going to bed until the early hours of the morning and no doubt last night he had partied long into the night after the concert at Mr Cook's house.

By midday she'd cleaned all the downstairs rooms and still no movement from upstairs. She was rolling out pastry to make a meat and kidney pie, a new skill she was learning, trying to remember everything that Mrs Digby used to do in the manor's kitchen, when she heard a noise at the front door.

Someone was coming in. Alarmed, she wiped her hands on her apron and picked up the carving knife. Had those men come back, or was it someone else after Mr Sheridan?

She inched towards the passageway beside the staircase. Her heart hammered in her chest. The front door opened.

'Olivia?' Mr Sheridan's voice called out.

Relieved, she slumped against the wall as he came towards her, taking off his hat. 'Olivia?' He rushed to her side, his eyes wide as he stared at the knife. 'Are you all right?'

'I thought…' She closed her eyes. 'I thought it was an intruder. That you were sleeping upstairs.'

'No, I stayed at Charles's house.' He gently took the knife from her. 'Why were you so scared that you needed a knife for protection?'

She looked at him fearfully, seeing him in a different light.

Stephan Sheridan is Stefan Schwartz.

'Olivia?'

'There are two men…' She gathered herself, standing straight, organising her thoughts, needing answers.

'Two men?' he asked warily.

'They've been following me.'

'Come and sit down.' He took her elbow and led her into the piano room and gently eased her into a chair by the fireplace. 'Tell me what has happened. Are you in some kind of trouble?'

She could have laughed in his face. 'They aren't after *me*, they want me to tell them about *you*!'

The colour drained from his face. 'They've come after you to get to me?'

'Yes.'

For a long time, he stood staring up at the ceiling. 'My fears are coming true.'

'What do you mean?'

He knelt before her, his face full of sorrow and took her hands. 'I'm so sorry. I would never want you harmed. Tell me everything that's happened.'

So, she did. Telling him about the two foreign men chasing her weeks ago, of them loitering in the streets, of their offer, revealing his true identity to her, the money they gave her, everything.

'You must have been so frightened,' he stated quietly. 'Forgive me. I never thought they would seek to speak to you.'

'It has been frightening, terrifying, actually. I've been too scared to walk home some nights. I was grateful when you sometimes came with me. Did you sense they were about?'

'I wasn't sure, but I walked home with you because I wanted to spend time with you.'

She couldn't let that sink in right now.

'From now on, I will arrange for a hansom cab to take you home every single day.' He squeezed her hands gently. 'I could not live with myself if anything happened to you, especially if I was the cause.' He took her hands in his. 'I'm so sorry, Olivia. You are precious to me, do you realise that?'

Surprised by his touch and his devoted words, she sat struck dumb.

'I have shocked you?' He gave a small smile.

'You care for me?' She found it impossible to accept.

'Very much so. How could I not? You are beautiful. You take such good care of me. You're kind and caring… How could any man not want you for his own?' He waited for her reaction and when none was forthcoming he straightened. 'We can talk more about that later. First, we must address the situation of those men harassing you.'

Focusing on the two men was difficult after his revelation. She took a deep breath to calm her racing thoughts. 'Why do they want information about you?'

'They weren't English?' he asked, pacing the room.

'They spoke with an accent, but then so do you sometimes when you're tired. I can hear it. You and Mr Cook speak in a foreign language. You aren't English, are you? Can you tell me the truth?' She waited for him to answer.

'Yes. I will tell you the truth. You need to understand. I want you to know me better.' His intense look was filled with desperation as though he needed her understanding. 'No, I'm not English. I came to this country when I was sixteen. My mother made me take elocution lessons to rid me of my accent.'

'Why?'

'Because my father demanded it. He sent us here, away from Austria. To be safe.'

'Safe?'

'My father works within the Austrian-Hungarian Reichsrat, their government.' Sheridan ran a hand through his hair and turned away. 'For many years my father has caused conflict within his party, but he is very wealthy and has many supporters as well in and out of the government. However, my father has strong convictions and opinions. Not all agree with him. We used to receive death threats. A failed kidnap attempt on me was the final occurrence for my father to send Mother and I away. He thought England to be safe, and yet close enough for him to visit, though he never did. We sometimes met him in France, but only a few times. Papa was always anxious, believed we were never safe. He stopped sending for us and all contact we had with him was through letters sent to trusted friends. We were never allowed to return to Vienna, our home.'

'Why didn't he leave with you?'

A pained expression crossed his face. 'Papa loved Austria more than Mama and me. He would never leave Austria.'

'And your names were changed when you arrived in England?'

'Yes, so we would blend in with the British people.'

'Yet you performed in concerts, wouldn't that bring attention to yourself?'

'We thought it safe enough as I became a man, and with my name change, we assumed it was worth the risk at times. A pianist concert in Paris, Madrid or Rome, hidden amongst other artists hardly drew attention on me and didn't claim a link to my father. Besides, I needed to earn money to support myself. At times, it was difficult for Papa to send money to us. We knew at any time he could be jailed and his assets seized. Being a pianist is the only thing I'm good at doing and I refused to give up my music, it brought Mama happiness.'

'And these two men who spoke to me? They know the link to your father now?'

'Yes. They have worked out my true identity.' Sheridan tapped his fingers together. 'Lately my father has been drawing even more attention to himself again. His speeches are more outspoken. People don't always agree with him, some consider he is a traitor. He's made enemies. Those two men who spoke to you could be Serbian, but I assume they are working for the Austrian government. Whomever they are, they will not stop.'

'Do they want to kill you?'

'No. I'm more valuable alive as bait, I think.'

'Bait…' She shivered.

'Somehow, those that want my father dead, possibly Austrian-Hungarian officials he speaks out against, have found out where I'm living. They will use me as a pawn.' He rubbed his hands over his face, clearly worried. 'Since the assassination of Archduke Franz Ferdinand, the tensions between Serbia and the Austrian-Hungarian empire are volatile.' He let out a long sigh. 'I received a note yesterday telling me that my father has spoken against retaliation towards the Serbs over the assassination. He was again ridiculed by the Austrian government, threatened even, to keep such opinions to himself. My father isn't a man to do that. He stands up for the things he believes in. Consequently, his life has been put in danger. He has gone into hiding. What would get him out of hiding is someone holding me hostage.'

Olivia watched his jerky movements, something made her question him. 'No note arrived here yesterday.'

'Not here, but it did at Charles's house.'

'Mr Cook's house? How did they know to send a note to you

there?' Then she realised. 'Mr Cook is a part of all this as well, isn't he?'

'I have spoken enough.' He looked around the room, his expression full of concern. 'I shall need to go away. This place is becoming unsafe.'

'Go away?' She stood abruptly, startled. She didn't want him to leave.

'It needs to be done. These people will want me, and they'll use any means to do that, including targeting you it seems. I can't have you involved.' Suddenly, he took her hands. 'Will you come with me?'

'What?' Shocked, she stared at him.

'Yes, come with me, please.' His strained smile reflected the uncertainty in his eyes. 'Forgive me. I have surprised you again.'

'You have... and I can't leave my brother.'

'He may come to. You said you wanted him away from the coal mine. He can come with us.'

'Where?'

'America. Charles and I have spoken of it.'

'America?' she echoed. A spark of excitement lit within her. Another country, another different kind of life. Stu might be in America. Perhaps she could find him? Lachie would be out of the pit. There were always advertisements in the newspapers about emigrating to America, where there was plenty of work. They could start again. She could forget the sadness of losing her parents, her former home, and Spencer...

'You will come?' Mr Sheridan's gaze pierced hers. 'As my wife?'

She blinked. Had she heard him correctly? 'Did you say as your *wife*?'

He grinned, transforming his serious face to a softer version. 'Yes, as my wife.'

'You want to marry me?' She blinked in astonishment. That changed everything.

'I do, very much so. We can be whoever we want to be in America. I can take care of you. I have money, Olivia, plenty. You'll not have to work, I promise you. Do you like me enough to marry me?'

She did like him. But marriage? He was kind and nice. He treated her well. But was it enough reason to marry him? Captain Middleton came to mind and her heart flipped. He was the only man she wanted to marry, but he wasn't here. She would never see him again. This was her chance for adventure. Tess's words came back to her from that morning. *Whatever path you walk down, it's your path.*

Could she choose this path? She stared at him, seeing him as a different person. He was no longer her employer, he was Stephen Sheridan, the man who just asked her to marry him. Then her father's words came to her, what he said by the river. Father had put his arm around her shoulders. *'My sweet girl. I hope one day you find the love like what your mam and me shared. It's rare, I know, but don't settle for anything less, understand?'*

She'd promised him she would, but that's when life had been simpler and before everything shattered around her.

'You doubt my intentions?' Stephen's eyes softened. 'Didn't my music tell you everything that I feel for you?'

'So, you did write that piece of music for me?' It astounded her.

'I agonised over every note to make it perfect, to show you how you have transformed my life.' He had genuine passion in his voice. 'You have filled my heart and mind since the first day you arrived. I tried to fight it, but I am lost.'

'I'm just your housemaid.' She didn't understand where his desire for her came from.

'You've never been just a housemaid, Olivia. You've turned this house into a home for the first time since my mother died and I fell in love with you because of your sweet kindness.'

'You *love* me?' The air seeped out of her lungs.

'I don't expect you to love me in return, not yet, but I judge you have the ability to love well and deeply.'

She took a step back. She did have that ability. Didn't she suffer such feelings about Spencer? Or did she? Was Spencer just a fleeting moment? 'It's a huge decision, Mr Sheridan.'

'Absolutely it is, but my feelings are genuine.' His tone grew gentle. 'You are much more than my housemaid. Since your arrival you have shown me how diligent you are at your work. You're never still, cleaning rooms, sorting the cupboards, tidying up after me, organising trades, cooking for me. No one has done any that for me since my mother died. The previous maids rarely did more than the very basic of the requirements to keep their jobs. Not you. You wanted to make a difference to this house, and you have. I have watched you go about your day, humming, your bright manner lightens my day. What amazes me the most is that you've no idea how beautiful you are. You have an innocence that is charming, but underneath I see a woman emerging who is strong and magnificent. That's why I had to write that piece of music for you. It could tell you better than any words.'

'I don't know, you're doing a grand job as it is,' she blurted out nervously.

He laughed. 'See? This is what you do to me. You make me laugh. You make me want things I never thought I wanted. You have shown me that there is more to life than hiding in this house. I'm so tired of hiding, Olivia. I want to live. I want to love and laugh and be happy. With you as my wife I know I can be that person, and, hopefully, I can make you just as content. Obviously, I don't expect you to love me or admire me as much as I do you, but in time it may come, and until then, we can build a close friendship.'

'It's all so sudden, Mr Sheridan.'

'Call me Stephen, I beg you.' He smiled. 'For you it is sudden, for me I have been dreaming of you for months. I don't wish to hurry you, but I'd like to leave soon, within days. My father is a wanted man. People know I'm here. They will want to get to my father through me and I can't let that happened. You understand?' Sheridan kissed her hands and released her. 'You need to think. I shall begin to pack. We'll talk again this afternoon.'

Alone in the room, her head spun. Marry Mr Sheridan, Stephen, and live in another country? *Could* she do it? *Should* she do it?

Hammering at the front door made her jump. She slipped into the hallway as Sheridan came down the stairs silently with a finger to his lips. The banging was repeated, then came the sound of running feet. Olivia saw a shadow run past the front window and then past the side window. The person was going around to the back door. Oh God!

She stared horrified at Mr Sheridan.

Sheridan edged his way down the rest of the stairs. The knife he'd taken from her still rested on the hallway table. He picked it up silently. 'Stay behind me,' he whispered. 'If anything happens run for the police.'

Her breath seemed suspended in her lungs as he slid past her towards the kitchen.

She inched behind him, fear making her knees tremble.

'Olivia!' someone called from the kitchen. 'Olivia!'

She knew that voice. It was Tess's Colin. In relief, she stumbled down the passageway and into the kitchen. 'Colin?'

'There's been an accident at the pit,' Colin panted, half bending over to catch his breath. 'You'd better come.'

'Why?'

'Because of Lachie.'

'Lachie is on nights, he'll be asleep now. Why am I needed?'

Colin shook his head sadly. 'No, he stayed back. One of the ponies got injured today, and the vet was seeing to it. Lachie didn't want to leave it.'

Ice ran through her veins. 'What are you saying? Lachie's been in an accident?'

'It was a large roof fall. They think it's trapped some men, and your Lachie was underground when it happened.'

She swayed, light-headed. Oh, dear lord, no. Not her Lachie.

Sheridan's arms came around her to steady her. 'Go. You must go.'

'But you're leaving.' She had to go to Lachie, but what of Sheridan?

'I'll continue to pack and likely go to Charles. I'm safe there. You're needed at home. I'll speak to you tomorrow.'

'We need to get back.' Colin headed for the door.

'I'm coming.' She untied her apron and grabbed her bag. She gave Sheridan a lingering look. He smiled and waved her on.

Olivia had trouble keeping up with Colin as they raced through the streets. Eastmoor Road seemed exceptionally long when you couldn't catch your breath. When they turned into Stanley Road, a jam of vehicles and people dominated the scene.

'Words got out,' Colin said, puffing. 'We can cut across the fields.'

Although Queen Elizabeth Road was a dead end, a gap had been created by the miners to cut a path through the fields to the pit. Over the long grass, the pit buildings dominated the skyline, especially the winding wheel at the top of the tower.

A large crowd of people had gathered around the outskirts of the pit top, kept away from getting too close by the officials, but also close enough to hear or see any developments. Colin weaved through the crowed, pulling Olivia by the hand so they wouldn't be separated. Eventually they found Tess standing with Sadie.

'Any news?' Colin asked.

'Nowt as yet,' Tess murmured, taking Olivia's hand. 'They'll get your Lachie out. My Larry has gone back down to help with the rescue. He's trained for that you see.'

Olivia couldn't speak and fought to catch her breath, staring at the bleak buildings and the bleaker expressions on the men's faces who gathered closer to the buildings. A wagon train full of coal stood quietly on the track, ignored for the time being, next to it was a line of motor cars in which important men in suits arrived and quickly huddled together while miners spoke to them with lots of hand gestures.

Sadie, pale and quietly crying, held onto Winnie, who'd joined them after leaving her baby at her mam's house. Sadie's husband Gerry was also underground as a rescuer. 'I told Gerry I didn't want him joining the rescue team. He's in too much danger. He told me he had to join because one day they might be rescuing him. They're his pals…'

'How many do they think are trapped?' Colin asked, sounding older in his concern. 'Has a statement been made?'

'A foreman said he accounted for fourteen men to be in the area where the roof came down. The collapse is close to the main shaft, apparently,' Tess answered.

Olivia stared at the shaft opening, willing Lachie to walk out of it. Every ounce of her being was strained, needing him to be brought out alive.

As the hours passed, the crowd grew silent, the summer sun beating on their heads. Many took to sitting on the grass, some kind people had circled amongst them sharing food and drink, while children played in the long grass so far oblivious to the pain of their elders.

Olivia stood, her arms wrapped about her waist, her eyes watching the scene unfold as miners came and went down the shaft. The important men had disappeared into the two-storey brick building with its tall tower.

As the sun descended, a sense of urgency swept over the crowd. It'd been too long. Rumbles of discontent began to whisper over the small rise where the families waited.

Colin had disappeared a while ago but returned to his mam and the women. 'Things are happening. They'll be bringing up some of the men soon.'

As he spoke three motor car ambulances rumbled over the

rough dirt road and into the yard. Their arrival started people whispering, and a surge forward of their bodies in eagerness to hear or see a loved one. Olivia joined them, not content to wait at the back.

'Go down there, Colin,' Tess instructed, gesturing to where the ambulances had parked. 'See if you can find your dad or brothers. Jonnie and Jules have gone to help but I've not seen them since. Ezra is helping down there as well.'

Across the bleak pit top as the shadows lengthened a murmur rumbled and suddenly it turned into cries and cheers erupting into the evening sky.

Olivia, thanking her height, managed to see over the heads of the shorter women in front of her. She could see men on stretchers being carried to the ambulances.

'What's happening, Olivia?' Sadie cried.

'I see your Gerry, he's carrying a stretcher. Larry too,' she called back over her shoulder, but they weren't the one she ached to see. Where was her little brother?

'Oh, thank God,' Sadie cried hugging Tess.

'Olivia!' Colin waved to her from down the front. 'Dad says it's Lachie.'

'Lachie!' The scream left her before she could stop it. She pushed and barged through the people in her way and rushed to where Colin stood on the edge of the yard.

Larry, a short man with a gentle spirit, came to Olivia, coal dust peppered his clothes and skin. 'Come, lass. They said you can ride in the ambulance with him.'

'How bad is he?' she asked Larry as he led her towards the motor ambulance on shaky legs.

'He's not come around yet, but he's breathing, and that's a good sign.' Larry nodded to one of the drivers. 'This is his sister.'

'Come along, miss, in you get.' The driver helped her up into the back where two stretchers were placed on either side. On the other stretcher a man lay moaning.

She hurried to Lachie, who was covered in black dust and held his hand, relieved to see him but alarmed by his stillness. 'I'm here, Lachie. You're going to be fine. We're going to the hospital, and you'll be better in no time.' She refused to cry, needing to be strong for her darling little brother.

The doors closed, and she knelt beside his stretcher as the ambulance pulled away.

She gazed down with love at his sweet face which was covered with cuts. She still saw the boy in him, even though he was becoming a man. 'You must fight, Lachie,' she whispered. 'I can't be without you.'

CHAPTER 17

*L*eaving a lecture, Spencer saluted to a passing officer before walking out of the doors and onto the parade ground, which was hot in the July heat.

'Captain Middleton, sir.' A junior officer saluted him and then handed him a bundle of letters. 'A telegram, sir. It came this morning, but I was told not to disturb you until meal break. I was told it didn't seem urgent.' The youth cowered as though ready for a tongue-lashing.

'Thank you.' Spencer returned his salute and headed for his quarters. His mind was filled with notes from the lecture, the distressing news that war was imminent, and all leave was cancelled.

But some instinct made him stop and open the telegram.

FOUND HER.
　Wakefield.
　Letter to follow.
　Parky.

. . .

The fine hairs on his arms rose, and he had to read it again. Found her. Olivia. Parky had found Olivia. A tide of sheer joy filled him, quickly followed by a wave of relief that made him stagger as if drunk. He'd never been more thankful for anything in his life. Parky had found Olivia. It wiped out the bad news he'd just been told. Olivia was in Wakefield.

Once the shock receded, he grew frustrated at not being able to take any leave. How could he patiently wait for Parky's letter to arrive after all these weeks of worrying where she was and how she was faring? Again, the familiar fear lingered regarding how she would feel about him now. Had she forgotten him? He didn't think she would have, no matter how much time apart. He had confidence in the feelings they shared. He hoped to God he hadn't been mistaken, and all this longing was for nothing.

The timing, of course, was terrible. He cursed the European countries braying for blood from one another. He knew he was needed, experienced officers and soldiers would have to defend Britain, and it was the oath he gave when joining the army all those years ago. Only, since meeting Olivia, he wanted a life beyond the army. He wanted to be her husband, to feel the joy of living beside her every day, of loving her without time restraints.

His thoughts swung between happiness, frustration and hope. The heat burned down on him making him sweat under his uniform. He should eat before he received his next orders, but his stomach churned. If only he could see Olivia, speak to her.

'Captain Middleton!' The junior officer was back.

'Yes?'

'You have a visitor, sir. He's at the gates. Civilians are forbidden to enter the grounds without official invitation.'

'Thank you, er, Jones, isn't it?'

'Yes, sir, Corporal Jones.'

Spencer had no idea who could be wanting him, but thought perhaps his father had travelled from York to see him. He'd written to his father a few days ago, alerting him to the fact that war could happen any day and he should be prepared within his businesses, especially the shipping companies he owned. Britain was an island, and the navy would defend them, but shipping would be impacted if war erupted. No doubt his father wanted more information from him.

He saluted the guards at the gates but couldn't hide his grin as Parky exited his motor car and came towards him.

'I sent that telegram this morning but thought you'd be going out of your mind until my letter arrived.' Parky chuckled, looking dapper in an olive-green suit and trilby hat. 'So, I thought to drive here to tell you in person. Aren't I a good friend to drive for three hours to speak to you?'

'The very best of friends.' Spencer shook his hand gratefully. 'You've seen her?'

'Indeed, I have.' They walked over to a large tree and stood beneath its shade.

'Did you mention me?'

'Sorry, old pal, I didn't get the chance.'

His hope plummeted. 'You didn't speak to her?'

'I did, yes. Briefly. Sadly, Bernard was an absolute heel and scared her off.'

'Tell me what happened.'

'Can you imagine that I saw her at the Theatre Royal in Wakefield? We've been there before, remember?'

'I do, yes. Is Olivia working at the theatre?'

'No, she was in the audience.' Parky whistled low. 'By God, Spence, she looked stunning. The most attractive woman there by a long way, I don't doubt it.'

Spencer smiled, remembering her gorgeous face, her willowy shape, the amazing pale blonde hair. She'd been in his dreams since the first moment he met her at her father's forge.

Parky pulled out a silver cigarette case from his inner jacket pocket and offered one to Spencer who shook his head. He fished a box of matches out of his trouser pocket. 'When I first saw her,

I thought I was imagining her. Why she was dressed all fancy and appearing like a lady, I don't know. I would have spoken to her more but as I said Bernard offended her, basically called her out for being a gentleman's mistress.'

Shocked, Spencer's gut twisted. 'Is that what she has become?'

'Well, I thought so as well, but I did some investigating.' Parky lit his cigarette. 'Turns out she's a housemaid for the pianist who the concert was for. Stephen Sheridan.'

'She's his mistress?' Every part of him wanted to reject the thought.

'Not that I can find out, no. Just his housemaid. I spoke to a man, Charles Cook, he organised the whole concert, but I saw him talking to Olivia before I reached her in the foyer. I found his name on the pamphlet and spoke to him before leaving. He wasn't very forthcoming with information, but he told me Olivia was simply this Sheridan fellow's housemaid, nothing more.'

Relief coursed through him. 'She's just his housemaid,' he repeated. 'Did you visit his house?'

'No, not yet. Charles Cook refused to give me Sheridan's address. I'll have to get some people onto it, but first I wanted to tell you that I've seen Olivia. She looked well, wonderfully well, and before I did anything else, I wanted to make sure you still wanted me to contact her.'

'Absolutely. I've not changed my mind. I'd go to Wakefield myself if I could, but all leave has been cancelled.' Frustration rose again. How could he see her?

'Why has your leave been cancelled?'

Spencer blew out a long breath. 'War will happen and sooner than we are prepared for.'

'Well, you go and do all your soldiering stuff,' Parky said, waving dismissively towards the gates, 'and I'll go back to Wakefield and find this Sheridan fellow's house, and speak to Olivia.'

Spencer gripped Parky's sleeve. 'Tell her I wish to write to her and that I think of her.'

Parky grinned and tapped Spencer's hand on his arm. 'Don't worry. I'll sing your praises and tell her how *broken* you are at not being with her.'

'Don't be an arse,' Spencer scoffed.

Laughing, Parky walked back to his motor car. 'I'll keep you informed, Captain.'

'I appreciate it,' Spencer said seriously, trying not to get his hopes up.

'You can name your first son after me,' Parky joked and with a wave climbed into the motor car and started the engine.

Spencer turned to walk back to the gates, not eager to re-enter the army world just yet. His mind raced ahead with what he'd write in a letter to Olivia. He had to make every word perfect.

Suddenly, he stopped and spun back to Parky, waving his arms to stop him from driving off. He ran towards the motor car. 'Parky!'

Winding down the window, Parky leaned out. 'What is it?'

'Stay there. I'm coming with you.'

'How? Your leave has been cancelled.'

'I'll call in some favours. I need to go to Wakefield. Today. Wait here, I'll be right back.' Spencer sprinted for the gates, hoping his senior officer would relent and give him a pass, even if it was only for twenty-four hours.

* * *

Sitting next to Lachie's bedside in one of the stark male wards of Clayton Hospital, Olivia prayed for him to wake up. It'd been a long night and day since they'd brought him up from underground and into the ambulance. During the night, she waited an age in the waiting room until finally they'd brought her to his bedside.

A severe-looking doctor had told her that Lachie had broken his tibia on his right leg, his right clavicle, and three ribs on his right side. However, it was his head injury that caused them concern. It would be a time of waiting and watching.

So, Olivia sat and waited and watched Lachie for hours, drinking the tea the nurses brought her, and refusing to leave his side.

His bed was one of eight in the ward, four on each side of the cold long room. A nurse occupied a desk near the door and at times she'd rise and see to one of the male patients.

As the second night wore on, Olivia dozed fitfully on the chair, springing awake whenever her head dropped. General noises woke her fully as sunlight filtered through the tall narrow window. Olivia leaned over Lachie's still form, relieved to see his chest gently rising and falling. He was still with her.

'He's made it through another night,' the nurse said from the end of the bed. 'That's encouraging.'

'Yes, it is.' Olivia nodded.

'I'll fetch you a cup of tea before I leave. My shift has finished, and there will be another nurse at the desk for the day shift. The doctor will be doing his rounds in a couple of hours.' The nurse gave her a small smile and left her alone again.

Olivia stood and stretched her limbs all the while watching Lachie for any change. On first arrival the nurses had washed him, but he still had coal dust around his eyes like stage makeup. She desperately wanted him to open his blue eyes.

'Here you are.' The nurse placed the teacup and saucer on the small table beside the bed. 'There is a Mrs Hobson waiting to see you. I can bring her in if you want? I don't think matron will mind seeing how serious your brother is.'

'Thank you.' The tears that Olivia hadn't been able to shed

during the long hours rolled down her cheeks as Tess came down the ward and enveloped her in a tight embrace.

'Nay, lass, you look exhausted. How's he doing?' Tess whispered.

'He's got a broken leg, ribs and clavicle.'

'Heck, want's one of those?'

'His collarbone.'

'Ah. Poor lad.'

'He's not woken up yet. The doctor told me that he has a brain injury, which is why he's not woken.'

A frown of worry crossed Tess's face. 'Right, well, we'll deal with that when we know more.'

A new nurse appeared at the end of the bed. 'Miss Brodie, you have another visitor, but I can't allow him in. Even two by the bed is one too many,' she scolded.

'Him?' Olivia glanced at Tess. 'A man?'

'It might be someone from the pit. Official inspectors have been asking all the miners questions. Go out to whoever it is, lass.' Tess gestured to the doorway. 'I'll sit with Lachie for a bit. Get some fresh air.'

'I don't know...' She stared at Lachie's face, not wanting to leave him.

'I'll come and get you if he wakes. You need a break,' Tess encouraged. 'Go.'

Striding out of the ward, Olivia didn't want to waste too much time away from Lachie. In the waiting room, she found not a mine official but Mr Sheridan pacing.

When he saw her approach, he came straight to her. 'I couldn't wait any longer to see you.'

'I'm sorry, you must have been concerned. I haven't left the hospital.'

'Nonsense, none of it is your fault. When I knocked on your door, one of your neighbours told me that your brother was alive but ill in hospital. I had to come and see you.'

247

'I thought you might have already left Wakefield.' It had been one of the things she considered as she waited for Lachie to wake. She wouldn't have blamed Mr Sheridan if he'd gone, leaving her behind. But if Lachie didn't survive, she'd be totally alone, and that had been a frightening notion.

'Shall we go outside?' Mr Sheridan took her elbow and steered her out of the building to some trees close to the entrance. 'Can I get you anything?'

Fresh air and the morning sun on her face revived her somewhat. 'No, nothing, thank you.' She gripped his hand. 'You mustn't stay in Wakefield.'

'I won't leave without you.'

'And I can't leave Lachie.'

'I understand.' Sheridan rubbed his forehead. 'Charles told me a man has been asking about me, he even mentioned you. He wanted to know where I lived. Charles didn't tell him, obviously, but that another person is asking after me gives me more reason to suspect they will use me as a pawn against my father. I can't have you in any danger.'

'Have you heard any news about your father?'

'No, the normal lines of communication have gone quiet. Charles is trying to make contact with people we can trust in Austria but apparently it is chaos over there. The Austrians and Serbs both have reason to find my father. He knows too much and is too vocal. War is bound to happen, with Germany's backing, and my father is against it. Many people will consider him to be a traitor. I don't know where my father is hiding, but that won't stop those who wish him harm from trying to take me.'

'And you must leave and find somewhere safe,' she said sadly.

'If I leave without you, we might not ever find each other again. The world is too large, Olivia. I've been separated from my family before, I know the consequences.' He touched her cheek softly. 'I will stay in Wakefield and wait for you.'

'They know where you live.'

'I will lodge with Charles and stay inside the house.'

'Why is Charles so safe?'

'He has powerful friends in many places. He will be able to get me out of the country, get *us* out of the country when the time is right.'

'But I don't know how long Lachie will be in hospital for, or how long his recovery will be. He hasn't woken up yet. It might be months before he is well enough to travel, and even then, he might refuse to go.'

'He may surprise you?' Sheridan raised his eyebrows hopefully. 'Either way, I will not leave without you. When Lachie is well, I will speak with him, convince him of the opportunities that await him in America. His brother has done it, so surely, he must be interested in travelling to America as well?'

'It'll definitely be America then?'

Sheridan nodded. 'Charles has friends in Boston who are willing to help us. Charles is also thinking of emigrating. America is the future for people like him and me, us.'

'Then go to America now, where you'll be safe. I won't be the reason for you to stay. I have enough to worry about without being responsible for your kidnap.'

He looked wounded. 'You don't wish to come? You've decided not to marry me?'

'With everything that is happening with Lachie, I've not been able to decide about anything clearly...'

'I promise to make you happy, Olivia. Do you believe me?'

'I do.' And she did. His honesty, his earnest manner to please her, and the tender gaze in his eyes told her his feelings.

A man walked past, and Sheridan turned to hide his face. Olivia hated to see him under such strain. 'Please, Stephen, go to America as soon as you can.'

'Not without you.' He cupped her cheek. 'I'll be safe with Charles. Send word to me on Lachie's progress when you can.'

Frustrated, she shook her head. 'Will you not listen to me and go?'

'I'll wait another week and see how things are.'

'Stephen, please...'

A motor car backfired, and they both jumped.

Impulsively, she reached up and kissed his cheek. 'Go now. Quickly.'

'My dear Olivia, my muse.' He kissed her soundly on the lips twice, pulling her tight against him, before abruptly letting her go.

He waved to her at the gates, and she raised her hand in reply. Head down, pulling the collar of his coat high and the brim of his hat low, Stephen Sheridan walked away.

Too tired to absorb all the emotions which swept through her, she returned to Lachie's bedside and sat on the chair next to Tess.

'Who was it? Someone from the pit?' Tess murmured.

'No, it was Mr Sheridan.'

'What does he want?'

Olivia struggled to speak as emotion clogging her throat. How could she explain it? She barely knew how to understand it all herself.

'Nay, what's wrong, lass?'

'He's in trouble. I can't tell you all the details, but he needs to leave the country.'

'Oh, that's a shame. You've lost your job then?' Tess patted her hand.

She wished it was only that simple. 'On the day of the pit accident, he asked me to go with him.'

Tess reared back, eyes wide. 'Never!'

'He wants to marry me.'

Tess's eyes widened even further. '*Marry him?* What did you say?'

'That I would consider it.'

'And have you considered it?'

'It makes sense to marry him and go with him to America. Lachie can come as well once he's recovered.'

'Gracious Lord. That's a commitment and no mistake. America?' Tess shook her head in wonder. 'So far away. What if Lachie doesn't want to go?'

Olivia gazed down at her sleeping brother. 'He will, I'll make sure of it. He's not going back down that pit, not ever again.' She was adamant about that if nothing else.

'And what of your captain?'

Her shoulders sagged at the thought of Spencer. Her heart ached for a man she barely knew. 'There is no captain for me, Tess. I was a silly girl to contemplate otherwise.'

'But this Sheridan fellow *is* the right man for you?'

'He's offering me a new life, for me and for Lachie.'

'You didn't answer my question, lass.'

'Mr Sheridan is kind and generous and caring. He'll take care of Lachie and me.'

Tess gave her a wise look. 'Marriage is for a long time, lass. Tied to each other for years until one of you dies. Is that what you want with Sheridan?'

Olivia looked away, not knowing how to explain her thoughts. 'Mr Sheridan cares for me.'

'Aye, maybe he does, but that still doesn't answer my question, lass.'

'I have to go with him, Tess. I, we, need to start a new life.'

'Why? What's wrong with here?'

'Nothing, but my brother Stu might be in America. I can try and search for him, put ads in newspapers when I get there.'

Tess snorted. 'Good luck with that. Your brother could be anywhere by now.'

Lachie murmured.

Alarmed, Olivia jerked to her feet and took his hand. 'Lachie?' she cried happily. 'Love, it's me.'

He murmured again, his eyes blinking.

She wiped away the tears of joy as he opened his eyes. 'You're in the hospital. How do you feel?'

'My head hurts. I hurt everywhere.' He winced in pain.

'Do you know who I am?'

'Aye, my silly sister.'

She snorted with mock anger. 'They said you might wake up and not know anything. Obviously not. I'll go and find the doctor. They can give you something for the pain. Lie still.'

'Liv?'

She swung back around to him. 'Yes?'

'Will I die?'

Her heart somersaulted, and she took his hand. 'No, darling. You're going to be fine.'

'Liv?'

'Yes?'

'I don't want to go to America.'

She froze, her chest tightening. He'd heard her talking with Tess. 'We'll discuss it later, when you're better.'

'You can marry Sheridan and leave,' he murmured faintly, 'but I'm staying here.'

She turned away to fetch the nurse, fighting the frustration building at his stubbornness, but also deeply grateful that Lachie was awake, which was all that mattered at that moment. She'd deal with the rest later.

CHAPTER 18

Giving the house a final inspection, Olivia was satisfied the place was as clean as she could make it. She'd scrubbed for two days, every room, every floor, every surface, doing everything she could to make it sterile for Lachie's homecoming.

Despite it being the beginning of August, she'd lit fires to keep any possible dampness away. She'd washed bedding and clothes, dried and ironed them, and yesterday she'd started cooking Lachie's favourite food in readiness for his return home from the hospital.

That morning, Larry, Colin and even Ezra had gone to the hospital to collect Lachie and bring him home in an ambulance provided by the mine company.

It pained her that Lachie had withdrawn from her since waking up. For three days, he'd hardly spoken to her when she visited, refusing to discuss his thoughts on any matter, not even when she showed him the newspaper's front page with the headlines that Great Britain had declared war on Germany.

She told him that when the news of the war broke, everyone in the square had cheered. Olivia hadn't cheered though. Her heart had twisted in dread of Spencer going to war, and the fear of Mr Sheridan becoming an enemy. Today's newspaper had compounded that fear as it was announced all foreign nationals had to resister with the police. Had Mr Sheridan registered? He already had a target on his back. How alarmed he'd be, hiding at Mr Cook's house, knowing that now the British police would know about him as well.

A knock came at the door and thinking it was the men with Lachie she rushed to open it. A postman stood holding out a letter for her. 'Thank you.'

Tearing open the envelope she read the note.

OLIVIA, *dearest.*

Do not go to my house for any reason. It has been ransacked. Men tried to enter Charles's home last night, possibly to take me, but his guards chased them away.

We must leave Wakefield today. Charles has secured us a passage on a ship leaving Liverpool in two days' time. We must be on that ship. You and Lachie should meet me at Holt's Gentleman's Tailors on Northgate, a safe place, at eleven tonight. Go around to the back of the shop and I'll be waiting there. We will be taken to Liverpool by carriage.

Your loving, Stephen.

A SENSE of panic overwhelmed her. Leave tonight? She glanced around the front room, not knowing what to do. To pack and say goodbye to everyone today? How would Lachie cope on a long voyage after leaving the hospital? She was yet to convince him it was the right thing to do. When she'd broached the subject with him again in the hospital, he'd refused to discuss it, stating he would not leave England.

How was she to persuade him?

On hearing Larry and Ezra's voices, she stuffed the note into her apron pocket and opened the door to greet Lachie, who was pushed in a wheelchair by the ambulance driver.

'He wouldn't let us carry him.' Ezra grinned, nudging Lachie playfully.

'Come in.' She smiled at them, but kept her gaze on Lachie, who didn't meet her eyes.

Larry and Ezra got Lachie comfortable on the sofa and Olivia placed a cushion on a stool under his broken leg and another cushion under his arm in the sling.

'What can I get you?' she asked.

'I'm fine.' Lachie glanced away, focusing on getting comfortable.

'Are you in a lot of pain?'

'Not much.' Lachie turned his attention away from her and the sting of rejection hurt Olivia.

Their relationship had never soured like this before, and she hated the coolness between them. They had to talk, but soon many of the neighbours were piling into the house, eager to give Lachie their good wishes.

Tess made pots of tea while Olivia handed out slices of sponge cake. Noise echoed off the walls, but Lachie enjoyed the attention.

Finally, as the afternoon wore on, Olivia managed to get a few of the neighbours to leave. Lachie had grown pale with tiredness, and she didn't want him to overdo it. The doctor has insisted on plenty of rest.

She also had to discuss the note with him.

'Tess, Lachie needs to rest,' Olivia whispered. 'He should sleep before the doctor calls later to check on him.'

'Aye, course he needs some rest.' Tess clapped her hands. 'Right, you lot, out. The patient needs some peace and quiet.' She ushered everyone out and gave a nod to Olivia as she closed the door behind her.

'They didn't have to leave,' Lachie said from the sofa, but he appeared pale and tired.

'You don't want to overdo it.'

'I'm fine. The doctor said so, or I wouldn't have been allowed home.'

'You shouldn't be home, you should still be in hospital.'

'I've been in bed for a week, I can rest here the same as in hospital,' he replied curtly.

She collected empty teacups and plates. 'What do you want to eat?'

'Nowt at the minute. I've had some tea and cake.' He gave her a sideways glance. 'When are you marrying Sheridan then?'

Sighing, she sat on the chair opposite him. 'I want to speak to you about that. Mr Sheridan has tickets for us to sail on a ship from Liverpool in two days. He wants to leave tonight.'

He became even paler. 'You're leaving tonight?'

'No, you're not well enough to go now. We can travel on to join him later.'

'I ain't going to America at all, Liv. I told you.'

'We can have a better life over there. There are more opportunities for us both.'

'You go then. I'm staying here.'

Annoyed, she clenched her fists. 'Stop acting like a baby and discuss this with me like an adult.'

'There's nowt to discuss.' His eyes narrowed angrily. 'I ain't going.'

'So, you want to be a miner all your life, do you? Work down a black hole waiting for the next roof to cave in? Is that what you want?'

'You carry on like it happens every day,' he scoffed. 'I've got a job and a house. I don't need anything else. I especially don't need you mothering me. You're not my mam!'

Stung by his harsh words, the tears welled. 'I'm not trying to be our mam. But I love you. Caring for you as your older sister is what I want to do.'

'As long as I do as I'm told,' he snapped. 'Just go, Liv. Leave me like everyone else has done.'

His words shocked her. Her chest tightened at the forlorn expression on his face. 'I would never leave you.'

He waved his hand dismissively at her. 'You've a chance to be married and live a different life. I'm not going to be the reason for you to stay and be miserable like you have been since you left the manor. You hate it here, I'm fully aware of that. If it'd been up to you, we'd have stayed in the country, and you'd be at some big house.'

'My place is with you wherever that might be.'

'It doesn't have to be anymore. I've lived without you most of my life. I can do it again. And I've got Tess next door if I need owt doing that I can't do.'

Although crushed, she wouldn't let him see it. 'I've told you, I'm not leaving you. You either come with me or we don't go.'

'Do whatever you like.' He shrugged, but she could tell he was struggling with his emotions.

She knelt beside the sofa and took his hand. 'I won't marry Mr Sheridan. My place is with you.'

He picked at a thread on his woollen vest. 'I'm not a child.'

'No, but you're my baby brother. Walking away from you is never an option.'

'You'll blame me for not going.'

'No, it's my decision. My place is here, with you.' She believed that.

His thin shoulders sagged slightly, and he nodded.

'But—'

'Here we go!' he scoffed.

'*But* if we are to stay here, then you aren't returning to the pit. I'll give up my chance of a new life, but you must be prepared to meet me halfway on this. You don't return to the pit.'

He stared at her. 'Then what work will I do?'

'Anything else, Lachie, I mean it,' she told him sharply. 'I will never spend another moment waiting on the pit top for news of you, not knowing if you were alive or dead, or buried never to be seen again. I won't go through that again. It was the most awful time, waiting, hoping, praying. You're all I have. So, I'm begging you. Please, don't go back down the mine.'

'If I don't work at the pit, and you don't go with Mr Sheridan, then we're both out of work.'

'I'll find a position elsewhere, so will you when you're better. I'm sure everyone in the square will keep an ear out for jobs going.'

He picked at a loose thread on his vest. 'Everyone looks out for each other here. They'll help us.'

'Yes, they are good people,' she acknowledged.

'We'll be all right, Liv.'

'You still haven't promised me,' she reminded him.

'I promise not to go back down the pit.'

'Thank you.' Sighing in relief, Olivia stood and kissed the top of his head. 'I need to go and tell Mr Sheridan that we're not going with him. Why don't you have a sleep while I'm gone? The doctor will call later.'

'Aye, all right then.'

She grabbed her coat, for the day was overcast, pinned on her hat and picked up her gloves and bag. 'I won't be long.'

'Liv?'

'Yes?'

'I'm sorry about Sheridan and everything…'

'Don't worry about it. Now have a nap. I'll bring home some pork pies for supper.' She closed the door and took a deep breath. She might not be heading off to a new country but at least Lachie wasn't going back to that dangerous place.

As she walked into town, her mind was temporarily blank. She couldn't think of the words she needed to say to Stephen, she couldn't think of anything except that she was going to disappoint him and change his plans, his hopes for a future with her. He'd be so unhappy she wasn't going with him.

The recognition that she no longer had a job would be something she'd concern herself about later. She'd look through the newspapers for vacant positions tonight. Luckily, she still had that money those two men had thrust at her and she'd hidden in her bag. That money would tide them over for a couple of weeks until she got another job.

Mr Cook's house was located on St John's North. A neat short street of Georgian houses. A maid was scrubbing a doorstep and Olivia stopped to ask her which house was Mr Cook's residence. The maid pointed to the end house on the left.

Olivia noticed the three men near the front door. Mr Cook's guards, perhaps? One approached her and asked her what business did she have at the house.

'I wish to speak to Mr Cook, please. Tell him it's Olivia Brodie. He knows who I am.'

Within minutes of the man going inside, Stephen came dashing out of the house. 'Olivia?'

'Sir,' one of the men gestured for him to return inside. The other two circled him and Olivia.

Stephen waved him away and took her hand. 'What are you doing here? Didn't you receive my note?'

'I did, yes.' On the doorstep she halted. 'I need to speak with you.'

The light died from his eyes. 'You're not coming, are you?'

'No. I can't leave Lachie, and he won't come. Even if he was fully recovered, he still wouldn't go. My brother is fifteen, and he needs me. I'm really sorry.'

'Lachie doesn't need to be apprehensive about leaving England. He'll have a good life with us, I'll make sure of it.'

'Nothing will convince him to leave England, and I can't go without him.'

'What a good sister you are to put him first,' he said, but the despondency was clear in his voice.

'He's all I've got left.' She glanced over her shoulder at the guards. 'Please, go to Liverpool, Stephen. Get away from here before you're taken. I feel bad enough that you've stayed an extra week waiting for me. You must go now.'

'I'd wait longer if I believed you'd be coming with me.'

'There's no point. Nothing will change.'

'Are you sure?'

'Completely. Forget about me.'

'That will be difficult...'

'Have you heard from your father?'

'No.' His eyes dulled. 'I may never hear from him again. War will change many things, Olivia.'

'What will happen to your house?'

'Charles will sell it for me. The funds will help me in America.'

She took a step back. There was no more to say. 'Thank you for everything, Mr Sheridan.'

Before he had a chance to reply, a motor car pulled up in front of the house. The guards shielded Stephen, their hands going to the pistols they carried under their coats.

Alarmed, Stephen pulled Olivia behind him to shield her.

'Olivia!'

Hearing her name, she moved from behind Stephen to see who called her. An army officer climbed out of the motor car and her world tilted on its axis.

No, it couldn't be...

But it was.

'Spencer!' Her feet had a will of their own and she was running towards him. In pure joy she flung herself at him from yards away. Spencer caught her deftly, holding her so tight she couldn't breathe.

'Oh, my darling,' he whispered in her ear. 'At last... At last!'

She held onto him like someone drowning, crying with

happiness, relief and all the emotions that had been dammed up since she left the manor.

'I'll never let you go again,' Spencer murmured against her hair.

She leaned back to gaze into his eyes, still hardly believing he was holding her. 'How did you find me?'

'Parky saw you at the theatre.'

'Olivia?' Stephen's voice filtered through her tears, and she realised they had an audience.

Spencer didn't let her go, but they both turned to Stephen who came towards them.

'Olivia?' Stephen asked again in confusion.

'Forgive me, Mr Sheridan.' She dropped her arms from Spencer.

'Who is this man?'

'Captain Spencer Middleton.' She introduced the two men to each other.

'I've been looking for Olivia for months,' Spencer explained. 'We were parted, and I didn't know where she'd gone.'

Stephen frowned, one hand started to reach for her then dropped away. 'You never mentioned this man, Olivia.'

'I didn't know if I would ever see Spencer again.' Embarrassed, she moved closer to Stephen to explain. 'I thought he was lost in my past.'

Stephen's puzzled expression altered. 'But now he is here in the present.'

'Yes...'

Stephen nodded thoughtfully. 'And you've never once gazed at me in the way you gaze at him now.'

Guilt coloured her cheeks. He was right. The love that filled her heart for Spencer could never be matched. 'I do care for you.'

'I believe you, but a man cannot be second choice, do you understand, dear Olivia?'

'Yes...'

'You want to be with this officer?'

She glanced back at Spencer, still adjusting to him being there, smiling at her with such tenderness in his eyes. 'I do, Mr Sheridan. I'm sorry.'

Stephen lifted his chin and coughed slightly. 'Then I wish you every happiness.'

She kissed his cheek. 'As I do you. I hope America is everything you need it to be. Good luck.'

For a moment his eyes closed before he stiffened his shoulders and turned on his heel and went back inside.

'Walk with me.' Spencer took her hand, and they walked around the corner of the street away from them all. 'Am I too late?'

'Too late?'

'That other fellow. Are you and he engaged?'

She shook her head. 'No. Mr Sheridan had asked me to marry him, and I was going to only because I thought I'd never see you again. Mr Sheridan offered us a new life in America, but Lachie refused to go.'

'Are you certain you don't want him?' Spencer's tone was low, anxious.

'All I've ever wanted was you,' she admitted. 'Even when I knew I shouldn't.'

'I feel exactly the same.' His handsome face lit up. 'Didn't you think to leave word for me at the manor?'

'Everything happened at once. It was awful and chaotic, and my father died. I didn't know if you would be returning... They said you'd gone to Ireland...'

'Oh, my poor love. You must have been at your wit's end. You should have written to my regiment,' he said gently.

'And say what? We had planned nothing. *You* had promised nothing.'

'You're right, of course, you are. I handled things badly. I should have said more to you, but I was uncertain myself until it was too late.'

'We shared a few precious moments. How was I to know exactly how you felt? I was a maid in your grandparents' house. Maids don't expect to be courted by one of the family.' She shrugged, unable to explain her feelings.

'I did come back for you, but you had left the cottage. I visited Mrs Bean's house, and she said you'd gone to live in one of the towns. I've been searching, driving myself mad.'

His efforts to find her proved how much he wanted her, and her heart swooped in response. 'I should have written to Mrs Bean sooner than I did and let her know where I was. I meant to…'

'She has died, did you know?' Spence said softly.

'No!' Appalled and deeply saddened, Olivia hung her head. 'How tragic. Mrs Bean was my last link to my mam. I've known her all my life.' She remembered the kind neighbour, and the tears rose. She'd have to break the news to Lachie.

'Spence!' Parky pulled the motor car to a stop beside them and leaned out of the window. 'You must be getting back to barracks, or you'll be court-martialled for desertion. Your time is nearly up and we've the drive back to make.'

Spencer swore. He squeezed Olivia's hands in concern. 'There's no time to talk now.'

'You're leaving again?' No, she wouldn't accept it. They'd only just found each other. 'Right now?'

'I must. The war… I'm to be shipped out soon.'

'But we need to talk. There's so much to discuss.' She wanted to be brave, but the idea of not seeing him again for who knows how long shattered her.

'Listen to me. Only a war would separate me from you, nothing else. If I could stay with you, I would.' He pulled her into his arms tightly and kissed her. 'Write to me. Letters are all we've got until I return.'

She leaned back a little to stare at him. 'You will return to me?'

Spencer lightly placed his lips on hers. 'I promise.'

From his jacket pocket he brought out a small card with his details on it and gave it to her. 'Write to me, yes?'

'Yes.'

He turned to Parky. 'Give me your card. I want Olivia to have that as well.' He smiled at her. 'Write to Parky should you find yourself needing help, or anything.'

She took both cards and placed them in her bag.

'I have to go.' Spencer looked desperate. 'I really don't want to leave you. Where are you living? We can drop you off there?'

'Number seven, Woodcock's Square. But I can walk. You'd best get back to your barracks.'

He gathered her close one more time. 'Don't ever leave that address. I'll come to you as soon as I can.'

'They say the war will be over before Christmas?'

Spencer shook his head. 'Wars are never over that quickly, trust me.'

'Then, we'll have to just write to each other until it does. I'll wait for you.'

He gave a slow sensual smile that turned her insides to jelly. 'I want you to write to me your every thought, every desire you have, all that you do in your day, everything. Your letters will keep me sane and give me hope for a future after this madness is over.' He paused. 'Olivia, I have little to give you, should you want me at the end of all this. The manor is gone.'

'We can make a life together. We don't need a manor to do it. Just stay safe.' Impulsively, she kissed him, wanting to feel the pressure of his lips on hers. How could she let him go?

'I'll do my best, sweet girl.' He kissed her soundly before pulling something out of the pocket of his coat. 'I kept this for you.'

Surprised, she unwrapped the paper to reveal the little bird figurine that had been in his grandmother's cabinet when they made the inventory. 'The squinting bird.' Ridiculously happy to see it again, she held it to her chest.

'I have the tiger as well. One day we shall reunite them. So, keep it with you. Think of me every time you look at it.'

'I will.' She smiled and wrapped the bird up and popped it into her bag.

'Sadly, I have to go.' He cupped her cheek and kissed her one more time. 'It's not goodbye, Olivia. I'll see you soon.' Reluctantly, he stepped away and climbed into the car.

A black motor car passed her, and Stephen stared at her through the window. She raised her hand to him and he did the same in reply. Two men she cared for were going off to face individual dangers and she prayed they'd both survive the ordeal.

'I'll write to you tonight. Seven Woodcock's Square.' Spencer leaned out to give one final wave, and she waved back, her heart breaking.

Whether she liked it or not, the square that she had once hated and been so eager to leave would be her home now until the end of the war and Spencer returned...

FOLLOW Olivia's journey in the sequel, *Where the Poppies Dance*.

AFTERWORD

Dear Reader,

Thank you for stepping into the world of this story—a world shaped by family bonds, quiet courage, and the enduring strength of the human heart.

Writing a saga is never just about one person; it's about a tapestry of lives stitched together through love, loss, sacrifice, and hope. These characters—flawed, brave, and fiercely loyal—came to me with their own tale to tell. I only hope you've enjoyed reading about them as much as I did creating them.

I've used Wakefield, Yorkshire as my setting for this book as I have done in some of my previous books. Wakefield is where my direct ancestors come from on both sides for over a hundred years and more. I like to create characters who walked down the same streets my ancestors did.

I've featured Park Hill Pit as it was a colliery where some of my male ancestors worked and although there were recorded accidents, the incident in which Lachie was hurt is fictional.

Researching my family tree, I found in one of the censuses that Woodcock's Square was where my great-great grandparents, William and Elizabeth Brear lived for a time with five of their children in number 7, which had only two rooms for seven people - it's crazy to think of it, really. I was generous with Olivia and Lachie and gave them a two-up and two-down dwelling!

All the Brear males in that household worked underground in the coal mines. My great-great granny Elizabeth had ten children, seven grew into adults. I can only imagine how hard her life was living and raising children in poverty. Woodcock's Square no longer exists. Like a lot of the poor areas of Wakefield, many 'yards' and slums areas were demolished in the 1930s.

As mentioned at the end of the book, Olivia's journey continues in a sequel, *Where the Poppies Dance*, with a planned release for 2026.

Thank you for reading, for caring, and for your support. When I receive lovely messages from readers it always makes me smile and feel grateful.

Warmest regards,
AnneMarie Brear
2025

ABOUT THE AUTHOR

Author of over thirty-five novels, AnneMarie Brear has crafted sweeping historical fiction with atmosphere, emotion, and drama aplenty that will surely satisfy any fan of the genre. AnneMarie was born in a small town in N.S.W. Australia, to English parents from Yorkshire, and is the youngest of five children. From an early age she loved reading, working her way through the Enid Blyton stories, before moving onto Catherine Cookson's novels as a teenager.

Living in England during the 1980s and more recently, Anne-Marie developed a love of history from visiting grand old English houses and this grew into a fascination with what may have happened behind their walls over their long existence. Her enjoyment of visiting old country estates and castles when travelling and, her interest in genealogy and researching her family tree, has been put to good use, providing backgrounds and names for her historical novels which are mainly set in Yorkshire or Australia between Victorian times and WWII.

A long and winding road to publication led to her first novel being published in 2006.

She has now published over thirty-five historical family saga novels, becoming an Amazon UK best seller and with her novel, The Slum Angel, winning a gold medal at the USA Reader's Favourite International Awards. Two of her books have been nominated for the Romance Writer's Australia Ruby Award and the USA In'dtale Magazine Rone award and recently she has been nominated twice as a finalist for the UK RNA RONA Awards.

AnneMarie lives in the Southern Highlands of N.S.W. Australia
http://www.annemariebrear.com

Printed in Dunstable, United Kingdom